WHO WE WERE BEFORE

WHO WE WERE BEFORE

Leah Mercer

Text copyright © 2016 Leah Mercer
All rights reserved.

Published by Lake Union Publishing, Seattle

www.apub.com

Amazon, the Amazon logo, and Lake Union Publishing are trademarks of Amazon.com, Inc., or its affiliates.

ISBN-13: 9781503938151
ISBN-10: 1503938158

Cover design by Lisa Horton

Printed in the United States of America

For my father

1
ZOE, SATURDAY, 12 P.M.

People always say a child's death is the worst thing a parent can suffer, but that's not true. The worst thing is knowing your child died because of you.

One second. Less than a second, even. That's all it took for Milo to slip from my fingers, and then he was gone. Forever.

No one said I was to blame, of course. No one except for my husband, as we faced each other over my son's unmoving body. So much easier to think of Milo as still, rather than dead. Even now, I can't get my head around that word.

Why weren't you watching him? Why didn't you stop him? How could you let this happen? Three sentences that hammer my brain each time my heart beats, along with the look on Edward's face – a look I'll never, ever forget. To describe it as hatred is like saying scalding water is tepid. In that moment, he could have easily killed me, if only it would bring his son back. I was the enemy, someone who'd taken away what he loved the most.

But I didn't need Edward to tell me I was to blame. He was right. I should have grasped harder, run faster, lunged quicker. In the two years since Milo died, countless people have pressed my arm, touched my hand, and said there was nothing I could have done. But there was. There was.

I turn from the train window and gaze at my husband, trying to feel something, *anything*, as I trace his familiar silhouette. Long black eyelashes Milo inherited – midwives always commented they were wasted on a boy – along with an aquiline nose and dimpled chin. Edward's apologised for those words countless times, saying he didn't mean them; it was just the shock. Of course he knows it wasn't my fault. It could have happened with him, too.

But it didn't happen with him. It happened with *me*, and that has hung between us ever since: a concrete barrier frosted with jagged glass. No matter how many times he tries to hug me, or comfort me, or even just talk, I'm already ripped to shreds. I can't bear any more.

Two days together in Paris, and then we can go home – back to our quiet, four-bedroom house in an idyllic village both of us now hate, and where neither of us spends any time . . . not that he knows what I do with my days. We wouldn't even be on this trip if my parents hadn't sprung it on us, saying wouldn't it be nice to have a romantic getaway? If they knew the last time we had sex (I can barely remember), they'd realise just how laughable a weekend of romance is.

The tannoy comes on, announcing we're about to pull into the Gare du Nord. Edward stops fiddling with his phone and raises his head. 'Almost there.'

God, he sounds as excited as me. I nod, shifting my gaze to the couple across the aisle. They look about mid-twenties, still young enough to believe nothing can go wrong. I wonder what they think of Edward and me? We haven't touched this whole ride; we've hardly spoken. I bet they're telling each other they'll never be this way: a stale married couple who'd rather be anywhere else than with each other. *How sad*, they're saying. *How do you get like that, anyway?*

I can tell them: lose your son. Have a huge, gaping hole in your life, a kick in the stomach each morning you wake up, and a pain that leaves you struggling to breathe. That's how you get like that. Like us.

The brakes squeal as we pull into the station, and Edward stands to get our case. I can barely recall what I threw in there. It doesn't matter what I wear, anyway. Edward rarely looks at me – I mean, *really* looks. I could show up one morning in a clown suit and he'd carry on crunching his burned toast as usual, then kiss me quickly on the cheek and dash out to get the 7.07 a.m. commuter train to work. That kiss makes me feel worse than no kiss: dry lips, eyes already on the door, heart already gone from our home. Just like it has been for two years.

'Zoe? Come on.' Edward's voice is tinged with impatience, and I jerk towards him, blinking to clear my thoughts. I spend a lot of time inside my head. I like it there, blanketed from the world. It pisses off Edward, though. That much I notice.

I follow my husband down the platform, the tannoy bleating out muffled announcements in French. The misty air is cold and clammy, and I cross my arms to keep warm. Edward turns to make sure I'm behind him, then swings back, striding along with our case clicking across the tiles. There was a time when he'd give me his jacket, or put his arm around me, gently slapping my hands against his to warm up my perma-blue fingers. Now, he doesn't even walk beside me.

He reaches the main concourse and stops, grabbing his phone from his pocket as he waits for me to catch up. That bloody phone! He and his mobile have more of a relationship than we do, not that it would take much.

'I need to find a cashpoint and get some euros,' he says, still tapping away. 'Why don't you have a mooch around, and I'll ring you when I'm done?'

'Leave the case here, then,' I say, but he's already gone, cutting through the crowd and heading in the direction of a cash icon. I wonder why he's so anxious to hit the cashpoint on his own, but I'm not complaining. As soon as Edward disappears, so does the heavy tension pressing on my chest whenever we're together. I almost feel like I can breathe again. He probably feels the same way – or does he? I can't begin to read him any more.

I wander around the station, turning aimlessly in this direction and that. As far as train stations go, the Gare du Nord is rather grim. It doesn't even try to pretend it's a mall – not like St Pancras, with the world's longest champagne bar and myriad of shops. I can almost picture this place doing a Gallic shrug while blowing smoke across the Channel.

I glance at my watch, eyebrows rising as I notice Edward's been gone twenty minutes already. I should be used now to time slipping by, the hours moving on a conveyor belt past my foggy gaze, but sometimes it still catches me unawares. What's taking him so long? I have to say, I'm a little surprised he's waited until now to get euros. He's like a Boy Scout: always prepared. Even a trip to the supermarket requires a half-hour preparation and endless lists, whereas I usually just wing it. Funny, I can't remember the last time I was actually in a supermarket. There's no need. Edward's never home for supper, and I'm lucky if I can choke down a sandwich from the corner shop on my way home.

Twenty-five minutes now. Maybe I'll give him a ring. My hand slips into my bag in an automatic gesture, patting the sides for my mobile. Where the hell is that thing? This bag is like a black hole. Sighing, I swing it off my shoulder and crouch down on the grimy station floor, rooting through old receipts and random tissues to catch a glimpse of its silver case. Frustration rising, I dump out the contents then sift through them, staring in disbelief. It's not there. And . . . My gut clenches. Neither is my brown leather wallet.

Shit.

I scoop up my stuff and throw it in the bag, rising on shaky legs. Did I forget them at home? I shake my head, my mind's eye clearly seeing me slide both items into my handbag. I did pack them; I know I did. So where are they? I spin left and right, as if the answer lurks somewhere around me, then drop to my knees and examine the floor in case I dropped them.

Nothing.

I stand up slowly, my head buzzing. Somewhere, in my wanders around the station, I must have been pickpocketed. What a great start to our romantic rendezvous! At least cancelling my cards will give me something to focus on in the hotel room. I'm already dreading the silence between us in such a close space.

My eyes widen as a thought enters my head. Without a mobile to arrange meeting up again, I'd better run to catch Edward at the cashpoint. I head in the direction he went half an hour earlier, my legs churning as I dodge suitcases and travellers. Finally, after what feels like a marathon, I reach the cash machine. There's a long queue, but Edward's not in it.

I lean against the wall, wiping my sweaty top lip as my breath tears at my lungs. Okay, *think*. If he's not here and he couldn't reach me on the mobile, he must have gone back to where he left me. That's what I would do, but then, I'm not him – that's never been clearer than in the past little while. Our differences have become magnified, mountains we can't traverse.

I retrace my steps to the busy concourse, but there's no sign of my husband. Frantically, I scan the moving crowd, hoping to catch a glimpse. People flow past my eyes in waves, and after a while, they blur.

I slide down the wall onto the grungy floor. Edward's not here. Or if he is, I can't find him. What the hell am I going to do now? He has our case, not to mention the folder with all our accommodation information – I can't for the life of me remember the name of our hotel. Even if I'd been paying attention, it's unlikely I'd remember, anyway. French is not my strong suit.

So, here I am. Alone, in a foreign place, with no clue where I'm going.

Not much different from my life at home.

2
EDWARD, SATURDAY, 12.15 P.M.

I race through the crowd, my jaw unclenching more and more the further away I am from her. I don't need euros – I have a fat wad in my pocket that I got out yesterday after work. I just want to get away for a few minutes to ring Fiona, to hear a friendly voice before spending the next two days with my wife, who barely even notices I'm in the room.

It's obvious she doesn't want to be here any more than I do – the way she pressed her lips together when she opened her parents' gift was a dead giveaway. It's a new expression for her, but one I've come to hate over the past couple of years. *Just say something*, I want to scream. Just tell me how much you hate me, how much you hate this, how awful life is. *Something*. Something that will end this terrible silence between us, one way or the other. But she never does.

Making up an excuse to get away from her probably wasn't even necessary. Today, as always, Zoe has that vacant, I'm-not-here expression on her face. I could have had phone sex on the train and she wouldn't notice. I feel my groin tighten at the thought. Even phone sex would be more than I'm getting now.

I shake my head and walk faster, trying to dodge the thoughts flying through my brain. I miss her. I miss how she used to do big donkey-style guffaws that made me laugh, how her eyes used to crinkle as she smiled, how she used to curl up against me, her cold feet pressing on my calves.

I didn't just lose my son, I lost my wife.

I knew it would take us time to move on from Milo's death, and that it would be a difficult period to get through. After all, isn't that what everyone says: *time is the best healer?* I can't count how many people told us that in the first few weeks, and I stupidly believed them. Now, I want to laugh in their faces. Time? Time has done nothing but solidify the silence between us, to freeze-frame every horrifying moment in technicolour. When it comes to death, nothing can numb the avalanche of grief, loss . . . *anger*. An avalanche that will bury you if you don't keep moving.

I wish I could take back the first words I said to Zoe, there in the hospital room. I wish I had put my arms around her and held on to her. But I didn't – I couldn't. I was so disbelieving, so incredibly *not* wanting this battered boy to be our son. It was like, if only I could figure out how this happened, I could go back and make things better, change the end result.

I tried to explain that to my wife, but Zoe just checked out, closed up shop. On me, on anything to do with Milo, on her life. I made all the funeral arrangements, I chose the gravestone and the inscription, I packed up his room, thinking that shutting away all his things might help her – although I couldn't have been more wrong. A muscle in my jaw jumps. Does she think that was easy for me: having to comb through each and every belonging of his short life? With every tear of the packing tape, I felt like my gut was tearing, too. My chest tightens when I picture that small pine coffin, dressing Milo in his beloved Spider Man outfit, placing the worn blue blankie into his fist . . .

I swipe a hand across my face, leaning back against the wall beside the cashpoint. Almost two years, for God's sake, and sometimes I still walk into his room expecting to see him looking up at me with that cheeky grin. He would have been four this month – hell on wheels, I'm sure, sliding down banisters and jumping on the sofa. If I close my eyes, I can hear his laughter now.

God! *This* is why I'm barely home. I can't stand the emptiness. Not just in the house, but in my wife. I know she blames herself. I'd blame myself, too, if I were in her shoes. But there's no point going down that road, is there? It's not going to change things – not going to make it better. Two years on and we need to live again. *I* need to live again, and if she doesn't want to, well . . .

Get a grip, I tell myself, conscious of the queue's curious eyes. I dig in my pocket for my mobile. I just need to talk to Fiona. Whenever I feel like this – like the avalanche will engulf me – she always calms me down. I wish I could say that about Zoe, I really do, but there it is. No one can say I haven't tried. And actually, trying makes me feel even worse. It's like banging my head into a brick wall over and over, feeling the crunch of pain with every impact.

'Hey, honey.' Fiona's warm tone comes on the line, and already I feel better. 'Everything okay? How's Paris?'

'I wouldn't know, actually. I'm still at the station. Just wanted to give you a quick call and say thanks for the drinks last night.' Fiona and I both work at a computer software company outside London – me as a software engineer, and Fiona in marketing. I've been there for years, and although I scaled back my hours when Milo was born, lately I'm there from seven in the morning until nine at night. You can lose yourself in coding; it makes sense in a way my life doesn't.

We've always been friends, but ever since Milo's accident, we've become . . . I'm not sure what, exactly. She knows about my son's death – she organised the huge bouquet of sympathy flowers from my work, someone told me – but she doesn't look at me with eyes full of pity, offer meaningless hugs, ask how I'm doing . . . or how

Zoe and I are doing. With her, I'm the same Edward I've always been, and I can laugh and joke without feeling awkward. She reminds me a bit of what Zoe used to be, actually: always laughing, full of energy, up for any adventure. Fiona and I haven't kissed, we barely even touch. But the more time we spend together, the more I want to.

'It's my pleasure.' Fiona's voice sounds sleepy, and in an instant, my brain flashes to an image of her wrapped up in crumpled bedclothes, stretching out one long, white-as-snow leg. My groin tightens again at the thought of being there with her, and I push away the image before I really give this queue something to stare at. Forty-one years old, and I've become an erection machine.

We chat for a bit about her weekend plans, the workweek ahead and a thousand other inconsequential things that make me catch my breath, feel back in control of my thoughts. Finally, I look at my watch, noticing we've been talking for almost twenty minutes.

'I'd better go find Zoe.' Not that she'll care I've been gone for so long. I'd wager she's staring off into space, just where I left her. Tension filters through me again as Fiona says goodbye, and I hang up. I dial Zoe's number to see where she's got to, listening absentmindedly as the phone clicks through to voicemail. I let out an impatient puff – has she forgotten to turn the bloody thing on again? My wife has never been the best at answering her mobile. Before we had Milo, she'd even forget to bring the phone with her half the time, defeating the meaning of the word 'mobile'. Lately, I'm lucky if she answers maybe ten per cent of the calls I make. Not that I call her much any more.

I ring again, but once more I only get voicemail. Now my impatience is turning to red-hot irritation, the kind that's like heartburn, spreading through your chest and gripping your throat.

Pushing off the wall, I hurry through the crowd and over to where she was standing, but she's not there. I ring again – still no answer. God! She knew I'd be calling. How hard can it be to make sure your phone is on? I stride up and down the station, craning my neck for a glimpse of her dark ringlets threaded with grey (I didn't even know she *had* grey hair until she stopped dying it after Milo. Actually, I didn't even know she dyed it). I peek into the few shops and cafés, stride back to the cashpoint in case she went to find me, ring her phone another ten times . . . nothing.

I head to the exit and look out, scanning the taxi queue in case she decided to grab us a cab, but there's no sign of her. I glance at my watch. It's almost an hour since I went to get cash, and if she were still here, surely we'd have found each other? It's a busy station but not huge – not like St Pancras – and there aren't many places to go. I walk up and down the concourse a dozen more times, annoyance growing with each step. Perhaps she's gone off to the hotel? If she didn't feel like waiting, the least she could do was call.

I suppose I would be more anxious, but Zoe's pulled a few disappearing acts before. For some time after Milo's death, I'd leave work early and head home to take her out for supper, but she was never there. I'd ring her mobile for hours, waiting as the house got darker, worry swirling inside when she didn't answer. When the front door finally opened, she'd just say she'd been with Kate, didn't hear the phone ring, and now she was going to bed.

And then there was that one night, a few months after the accident, she didn't come home at all. I didn't sleep, ringing up her friends, her parents, even the police – who made me feel like an idiot, calling with a wife 'probably out on the razz, mate'. Zoe crept through the door around ten the next morning, her face pale and closed. As usual, she blanked all my questions, steadfastly ignoring me as she padded up to bed, disappearing under the covers. I still don't know where she was.

Well, I'm not hanging around. I've wasted enough time in the past two years worrying about her, and right now, I'm done. I ring again, this time leaving a voicemail that I'm going to the hotel so I guess I'll see her there. I don't even try to hide the frustration in my voice.

'Hotel Le Marais,' I say to the taxi driver, ignoring his smirk at my mangled pronunciation. I lean back on the seat and close my eyes as the driver pulls away, counting down the hours until this trip is finished.

3
ZOE, SATURDAY, 1 P.M.

I should be worried. I'm alone in a foreign city, with no money, no mobile and no idea where I'm going. But as I set out through the door of the Gare du Nord and stare at the cars whizzing by, I don't feel scared. Instead, I feel free, as if by shedding all identification and ties to my former life, I can be an empty shell – empty in a *good* way, a skeleton wandering around with just skin and bones and no emotion.

I guess that's what I try to do back home. I lie in bed each morning, pretending I'm asleep as Edward bangs around downstairs, the scent of his morning espresso tainting the air. My eyes still pop open right at six, the exact moment Milo would wake up and waddle into our bedroom, legs still encased in his sleep sack. It's as if my internal clock is set permanently to 'mother', even if I'm not one any more.

I take a deep breath as grief slices through my heart, my eyes scanning the streets for a café. I could really do with a drink right now, a small glass of wine or three. I'm hardly an alcoholic, but I do have more than the paltry recommended intake. Just enough to blur the world for a while, to let my pain slide out of focus.

I know drinking that much isn't great – isn't me – but I don't want to be me. I can't stand our house, can't stand the village with its cloyingly cute cobbled streets clogged with mothers and babies, can't stand the way people's eyes slide away from me, as if tragedy is catching. Or, even worse, those who are attracted to it, ghouls titillated by calamity.

So every day, as soon as the door thuds shut, I watch from the window as Edward disappears down the lane. Then I hop in the shower and pad back to the bedroom where I throw on my daily uniform of jeans and a T-shirt, ignoring all the crazily coloured clothes I've shoved in the back of my closet. The pinks, the neon greens, the strawberry reds . . . They hurt my eyes now, as if I'm staring into the sun. I bypass my favourite perfume, too, unable to bear the blast of memories that come with the scent. I jam my feet into an old pair of flats, throw on my light spring coat, and I'm off. I don't glance in the mirror, because it's like looking into glass at a funfair: my face is the same, but somehow all different, like a Picasso painting with jagged edges and pointy noses.

Then I hurry by the closed door of Milo's empty room – the door where morning sun used to stream through, making the hallway gleam with gold – and past the detritus of Edward's breakfast. Once upon a time, my nagging to tidy up was a part of our morning routine. He'd roll his eyes, but he'd always rinse his plate and glass then place them neatly in the dishwasher, saying he wouldn't want to mess up my 'pristine office environment' – a real joke, given the kitchen table was always half-covered with invoices, project pitches and mock-ups. Fed up with the corporate nine-to-five, I started freelancing as a web designer just before Milo was born, and it's safe to say I'm not the world's most organised businesswoman. Not that there's much to organise any more. I can't concentrate on trivial details like shades of magenta or finding the right stock photo for an estate agent's website. My clients have drifted away, and that's fine.

It's funny. Before Milo came along, I worried how I'd keep my business ticking over while tending a newborn. Turns out it wasn't that difficult – or maybe I just stopped caring so much about work; web design was never my creative calling. And when you stare into the slumbering face of a tiny creature so new to the world, it's amazing how everything else fades. Either way, my life was the perfect balance. I could stay home with my baby, with just enough work to keep my tired brain ticking and feel like something other than a human milk machine. Everyone said how lucky I was.

Lately, Edward's started urging me to take on work again. *Something to keep me busy*, he says, but what he really means is something to get me back on track, to distract me from what happened. But I can't go back to a job that once balanced my perfect life, because there's nothing left to balance. Just the memory of sitting at the table with my computer while Milo cooed in his basket makes my throat close up, my body thrum with guilt. I wasted precious minutes on a job I didn't even love . . . minutes I could have spent with my child.

Anyway, after ignoring Edward's breakfast mess, I slam the front door. I keep my head low as I hurry down the lane towards the train station, then push through the barrier and onto the platform. Sometimes, I stand here for ages as the fast trains whoosh by, the diesel air slapping my face as the windows flash past like blinking eyes. Then my legs propel me forward and onto a waiting train, into an empty seat where I stare out as villages, rivers and trees fill my eyes. When the train pulls in to London, I follow the trail of other commuters out, out, out through the bowels of the station and onto the busy concourse. This is my favourite place, where people push and twist around me; where no one knows who I am. I'm just a slightly dazed (*very* dazed, if you listen to Edward) woman in her mid-thirties, rushing off somewhere, like thousands of others.

Out on the street, I turn this way and that, my feet inevitably leading me to a pub. It's not that I'm desperate to drink, but where else can you sit for hours whatever the weather without someone moving you on? Inside, they're almost the same: the musty smell of old beer and dust, padded benches and wooden chairs, light slanting in through dirty panes. I take a seat in the corner, wait until noon (because you can't start drinking before noon; that would really make you an alcoholic), then order my first glass. No one cares who I am. No one knows where I live. And no one knows what's happened to me.

Just like here in Paris, I think, pivoting once more before realising that, café or not, I have no money. My mouth is dry and I feel a little faint, and although I should try to find a way out of this predicament, my legs start moving, carrying me down a street. The mist has cleared and the sky above is bright, light glaring off the white buildings. People push past me speaking quickly in French, and the chaos of the traffic washes over me in a wave of numbing, comforting white noise.

I want to stay lost forever.

4

ZOE, JUNE 2008

'I'm sorry, but you'll need to make those a few sizes larger.'

A male voice cuts across the *click click click* of my knitting needles, and I shield my eyes against the bright sun as my gaze travels upwards. Baggy jeans with a hole in one knee, a boring checked shirt, dark hair and insanely long lashes I'd kill for. At least he doesn't look crazy, homeless or drunk, which is usually what you get when strangers speak to you in London. Plus, he's cute.

I lower my needles. 'A few sizes larger? Why?'

He plops down on the bench beside me, and I notice he smells damn good, too – a mix of vanilla and spice, just right.

'Well, I have rather large feet.'

He stretches out a leg, and even though it's such a rubbish pick-up line, I can't help smiling. His cheeks are tinged with pink, as if he's embarrassed himself, but he meets my eyes with a grin.

'You mean you'd actually wear these?' I shove my half-finished creation his way. Bright-pink yarn edged with green probably wouldn't be his first choice of socks. I wrinkle my nose. Truthfully, it wouldn't be mine, either. I'm not the world's best knitter by far – my repertoire extends to socks and scarves – but the repetitive motion is so soothing, and I love looking at a pile of yarn and transforming it into something else, even if that something is full of dropped stitches and unravelling seams.

'If I agree to wear those,' the bloke says, tilting his head to the side, 'will you let me take you out to dinner?' His cheeks are even redder now, but his gaze is steady.

I laugh, trying to imagine him in bright-pink socks. 'It'll take me a bit to finish them.'

'How long?'

I shrug. 'A week, maybe.'

'Okay, then.' He nods with a determined expression. 'I'll meet you here next week, same time, same place. Bring the socks, and I'll buy you dinner.'

I stare up at him, trying to decide if he's worth the risk of a potentially painful blind date. Either way, it might be worth the dinner just to see him wear these socks. I like the forthright way he strolled up and asked me out – I even like the way he blushed. Confidence without arrogance, and a willingness to push his boundaries: so far, so good. Anyway, it's not like I have hundreds of viable men to choose from. I keep waiting for men to improve with age, but thirty-something blokes my age are just as bad. Okay, so he's an absolute stranger and we've only just met, but we'll be right here in broad daylight on the South Bank, and he's hardly going to jump me over dinner.

'Why not?' I say, trying to sound casual, but feeling nervous excitement at the thought of an evening together.

'Brilliant.' His face lights up, and I can't help smiling, too. 'My name's Edward, by the way.'

'Zoe.' I extend my hand, praying he doesn't have a limp, sweaty grip that's an instant turn-off. But his fingers curl warmly around mine with just the right amount of pressure, and now *my* cheeks colour as a tingly feeling starts up in my tummy.

'See you here next week, then. And don't forget the socks!' And with that, he strides off before I can even ask for his phone number.

5

EDWARD, SATURDAY, 1.30 P.M.

The taxi turns onto a narrow, dead-end street, and through an arch at the end, I can see a grassy square – the Place des Vosges, I reckon. I wonder if Zoe is there now, stretched out on the grass, arms flung out as she soaks up the sun. A true sun worshipper, she used to drive me crazy with her insistence to lie outside and bask, the way cats constantly flop on sunny patches. I picture the way her skin would turn the colour of almonds, and my mind flips to a memory of tracing my finger down the inside of one leg . . .

I shift, forcing my mind away from that image. These days, I'd be lucky to even get near a bare leg. Frigid doesn't come close to describing my wife. It's more like— shit, I don't know. What's colder than frigid? About a year ago, I casually mentioned we could start trying again for another baby, something to revive our home, to fill it with laughter . . . and, just maybe, bring us back together. But apart from going off sex, Zoe's also gone off the notion of family. She wouldn't even discuss the possibility with me, even if – despite all our attempts – it is just that: a possibility. Guilt sweeps through me once more that I couldn't give her another child, back in the days when we longed to add to our family, when we were on the same page. Maybe if I had, we wouldn't be in this place right now.

I pay the driver and tug our small case out of the back seat, then duck inside the narrow entrance to the hotel. The reception is small and dark, dust hanging in the air and the ceiling pressing down as if the building is enforcing on you just how old it is. I should have been expecting something like this: Zoe's parents pride themselves on finding 'authentic' hotels, steering clear from bland chain hotels in favour of quirky, the kind of thing *The Guardian* would describe as a 'hidden gem'. Fingers crossed our room at least has an en suite.

'Edward Morgan, checking in,' I say to the woman behind the desk. 'My wife might be here already?' I slide the mobile from my back pocket – still no messages, apart from a smiley face from Fiona and a reminder to have a drink for her. I can't help grinning in return.

The woman rifles through an antiquated filing system. Clearly they've never heard of computers here, along with dusting. 'Ah yes, monsieur. No, your wife has not been here.'

'Oh.' I raise my eyebrows. If she hasn't come here, where else would she go? And why hasn't she rung? I look at my watch. It's only been a couple of hours since we parted ways at the station. She has her mobile, she has her wallet, and she's a big girl. I'm sure she'll turn up, just like she did those other times. I'll enjoy this time away from her while I can. Perhaps she's trying to do us both a favour, reducing the unbearable time we spend together.

I take the key card from the receptionist and climb the twisting stairs, shaking my head. Sometimes, I can't get my head around the fact that we've become this couple: two people who can hardly stand to be in the same room – so much that one half has actually disappeared.

I fling the suitcase on the bed, then close the door again and head back outside. Zoe can do whatever the hell she wants.

I'm going to have that drink for Fiona.

6
ZOE, JUNE 2008

I'm meeting Edward on the South Bank tonight, and of course it's raining. Not the soft, gentle rain that hangs in the air, making halos in the streetlamps and adding a softness to London, as if you're seeing the city through a filter. No, this is a driving rain out to get you, paired with a biting wind that flips umbrellas inside out with such ferocity the spokes break. The kind of rain that makes you want to crawl under your duvet and knit another pair of socks, not drag your work-weary self to a windy, waterlogged bench on the river.

As I log off my computer at work after yet another crazy day designing websites for clients who haven't a clue, I contemplate blowing off my meeting with Edward. For all I know, he could be the world's biggest twat, a borderline alcoholic who'll get blind drunk, or one of those blokes who take you for dinner and think you owe them a shag.

As if on cue, my mobile bleeps.

All set for tonight?

I think my best friend Kate has more invested in this date than I do. Ever since she got engaged to her 'one and only' (as if that exists), she's been desperate to pair me up, too. I think she feels guilty about moving from our two-bedroom flat to live with Giles (*Giles!*), even though she's agreed to keep paying rent until she finds someone to take her place. So far she hasn't, and that's fine by me. I loved living with her, but I'm also happy with my own space at the end of the day.

Not sure I'll go, I text, leaning back in my chair as my mouth stretches into a yawn. Already I'm fantasising about that turquoise yarn, and after the day I've had – the day I have *every* day – I'm craving making something just for me. When I first went into web design, I had grand visions of creating artistic masterpieces my clients would truly appreciate. In reality, though, it's all about budgets, ease of use and trying to explain that no, you can't use your son's photo on the product page just 'because he's cute'. Still, it's better than lots of jobs out there, and the one time you do get a client who gives you free rein makes it all worthwhile. Plus, I work with a great group of people who can usually be counted on to join me after work for a drink, or hit a random gig if I have a spare ticket.

The shrill ring of my mobile jerks me upright, and I sigh as I spot Kate's name.

'Not going?' she squeals before I can even say hello. 'Are you on drugs? Do you know how hard it is to find a man once you get past thirty? They're either married, about to get divorced with loads of baggage, or bachelors for life. You've had a man – a cute man, based on what you said – practically land in your lap. You *have* to go!'

I roll my eyes. Talk about pressure! But I suppose she's right. I'm in no hurry to settle down, and marriage couldn't be further from my mind, but I do want to be with someone. I've tried online dating for months at a time and got absolutely nowhere, so why not? I smile, remembering the cute way his cheeks turned red and how he hurried off as if he was scared I'd change my mind. Anyway, I don't have his number to cancel, and I hate to think of him sitting on that bench in the rain, waiting for someone who never comes. I glance down at the lurid-pink socks in my handbag, smiling again as I picture them on his feet. His feet *were* quite large, it has to be said, and if that myth has any truth to it . . .

'Okay, okay, I'll go.'

'Good. Make sure to ring me afterwards. I want to hear everything.'

I hang up and stand, glancing at my watch. I'd better get a move on if I don't want to leave him waiting too long. From my office on Warren Street, it'll take about thirty minutes to hop on the Northern Line and make my way to Waterloo, then over to my favourite bench by the river on the South Bank, where we met last week. As it is, I'll already be about ten minutes late. I spritz on some perfume and shut down my computer.

The streets are a combat zone of stabby umbrellas, and by the time I get to the station my feet are wet and my hair is whipped across my face. I approach the entrance only to see the attendant pull down the iron grate that blocks the entrance.

'Sorry, folks!' he bellows. 'This station is closed due to over-crowding. There's a signal failure at Camden Town and no trains are running at the moment.'

Bloody Northern Line!

Rain pelts down on me as I stand in the swarming crowd, trying to decide what to do. Should I try for a bus? I've no idea what buses to catch, or how long it'll take me. I spend the next ten minutes or so trying to find my mobile in my black hole of a handbag, then frantically opening the browser to plan my new journey. Just as I'm about to push back up the stairs, the grate opens and the crowd surges forward. *Phew!*

I leap off the train at Waterloo and dodge the rush-hour commuters towards the exit to the South Bank, splashing through puddles and running down stairs until I'm out on the riverside terrace. It's empty except for a few forlorn souls, and my heart is pounding as

I race towards the bench at the far end of the walk. Given I almost didn't even come, it's funny how much I want to see Edward now. I squint, trying to see if there's a person on the bench, but it's still too far away to make out.

I'm sure he'll be there, I think, breath tearing at my throat as I fly past the National Theatre. Okay, it's pouring rain and I am a little late – a *lot* late – but still. Finally, the bench comes into focus and my heart drops.

It's empty, except for a pigeon pecking away at God knows what. I shoo off the bird and flop down, trying to catch my breath. As the minutes tick by, rain soaks through my trousers and my hair is plastered to my forehead, but I don't care. I stand and pivot in a circle, straining my eyes for someone coming my way. The walkway is deserted.

He's not here. Either I missed him, or he didn't turn up. Whichever, it doesn't really matter. Water trickles down my cheek, but I don't know whether it's a tear or a random raindrop. I let out a laugh, telling myself not to be ridiculous.

How can you feel like you've lost something when you never had it in the first place?

7
EDWARD, SATURDAY, 2 P.M.

Now that I'm sitting outside in the sun, a frothy beer on the table in front of me as the parade of chic Parisian women march by, I'm starting to unwind a bit. I'm on my second pint, and it's taken the edge of the niggling guilt that I should be doing something to find my wife. Is it so bad that I *don't* want to find her? If she were here now, she'd be staring into her glass of wine or gazing blankly down the street. We'd be sitting in silence, just like we did the whole train ride over, and I'd be itching to get away. Away from the permanent reminder of grief and loss that radiates from her with every breath, away from the bleakness of the past two years.

Anyway, I'd bet a hundred pounds when I get back to the hotel, she'll have checked in. I gulp my drink, watching the punters come and go from the tables around me, then take a selfie of me with my beer and send it to Fiona. My phone buzzes straight away and I grin, picking it up.

Looking good! Have another for me. Xxxx

I'm not going to argue with that. I flag down the waiter and order a third, sipping it slowly as the clenched fist of tension inside me relaxes even more. It's been ages since I've drunk this much, but right now, the soporific, numbing effect is doing the trick. Ever since Milo died, I find it hard to sit still longer than a minute. Even at the funeral, Zoe reached out a hand and, without looking at me, pressed on my knee to stop my jiggling leg. That only worked for a minute.

Reluctantly I finish my drink and stand. I can't put it off any longer – I need to go back to the hotel. As I plod down the street back towards our 'gem', I pray the effects of the alcohol will be enough to get me through the rest of the day. What will we do? A sombre dinner, a forced march along the Seine, like two lovebirds whose monogamy has become a death sentence?

'Ah, monsieur.' The receptionist stops me in the entrance, and I turn, sure she's going to say Zoe has checked in. Automatically, my shoulders tighten at the thought of the two of us in that tiny room.

But the receptionist just smiles and says if I need any extra towels, to let her know as the hotel is a member of such-and-such green scheme, *blah blah blah*. I nod and squeeze into the coffin-sized lift, the thread of worry I buried under booze rising up again. It's one thing to disappear back home, and another to take off in a foreign city.

What the hell could Zoe be up to?

It's not like she knows the city. I remember her saying, years ago, when we were discussing honeymoons, that Paris is *such* a cliché and that, if we were going to embrace tradition, we could at least go somewhere more exotic. I'd clamped my lips closed; Paris would have been my suggestion. It didn't matter in the end. With her morning sickness, we ended up in Dorset.

Maybe she ditched Paris all together? She could be home right now. But why would she even bother coming, if she felt so strongly about it? Can she not bear my company so much that she needs to reverse direction to get away from me? Despite myself, I feel a pang of hurt and rejection at the thought. I shake my head, thinking that's what we've both been doing for the past two years: reversing directions from each other, like two magnets that once attracted, now flipped upside down, repelling.

I try Zoe's mobile one more time, but once again, it goes straight through to voicemail. Sinking down on the too-soft bed, I tap my foot on the rug, trying not to inhale the resulting cloud of dust. What to do now? I'm not keen to wait around the poky hotel room in case Zoe reappears, but I need to do something to make sure she's okay.

I bet Kate knows where she is. Those two used to drive me and Giles crazy whenever we all went out together, giggling and whispering over God knows what. They've always been close, and Kate was such an enormous help when Zoe got pregnant – against all expectation. I definitely owe her.

I pull up her contact and hit 'call', then stretch out my legs on the bed and stare up at the ceiling fan slowly pushing the air.

'Edward!' Kate sounds surprised to hear from me, and I can't blame her. I've been so busy working that I can't recall the last time we spoke. Kate's always been more Zoe's friend than mine, and our usual interactions – over lengthy lunches with Giles burning steak on the BBQ as the kids go wild in the garden – came to an abrupt halt with Milo's death. I can hear the clamour of children now in the background, and a mixture of longing and sadness burns in my chest. I wanted that so badly, to fill the bedrooms of our house and to fill our hearts. If only . . . I shake my head. Where to start?

'Hi, Kate. Sorry it's been so long since we chatted. We really should meet up soon.' I grimace, thinking how much I don't want to do that. Giles has given up his job to write novels, constantly bleating on about complex and boring plot lines. 'Anyway, just wondering if you've heard from Zoe today?'

The line is silent for a few seconds, and I wonder if we've been cut off. 'Kate? Hello?'

'I'm still here,' Kate says slowly. 'Um . . . no. No, I haven't heard from Zoe today. I don't think I've heard from her for the past year, actually.'

What? I swing myself up to sitting position, as if that will help my hearing. Has Kate just said she hasn't heard from Zoe for the past *year?* On the rare occasions our conversation progresses past needing loo roll, sometimes Zoe tells me – in a slurred voice, her eyes unfocused – she's been out with Kate, who now lives in a neighbouring village. It's obvious the two of them have a drink together (quite a bit of drink, if Zoe's old level of high tolerance is anything to go by), but I never worried. I was happy Zoe was out there, doing something, even if it wasn't with me . . . It gave me hope. At least she wasn't knocking around the house on her own, I thought. *Drinking* on her own.

So much for that.

'Sorry, Kate.' I speak slower and louder, in case the line isn't clear or Kate can't hear me properly over the shrieks in the background. 'Did you just say you haven't heard from her in over a year?'

I hear a door close, and then silence. She must have escaped to another room. 'It's been at least that long,' Kate says. 'Not that I haven't tried. I can't tell you how many times I rang or came to the house. Zoe never called back or answered the door – I'm not even sure she was home.'

I nod, Kate's words flowing over me. If Zoe isn't home, and she isn't with Kate, what does she do all day . . . besides drinking? Where does she go? A sharp pain jabs my gut as I picture her slumped alone, po-faced in an empty pub – a stark contrast to the animated girl who'd drag me clubbing, laughing as we pulled crazy dance moves on the packed floor.

'Is everything okay?' Kate's tone is tinged with concern.

'Fine, fine. Everything is fine.' The words leave my mouth automatically, the same way they have over the past two years. I think I believed that if I said them enough, everything *would* be fine. It had to be. *Time is the best healer,* and all that. I wish.

'Please tell her I miss her,' Kate says. 'God, we've been friends for yonks, and been through loads together. I wish I could help her through this too, you know? I want to be there for her.'

I swallow. 'I know.' And I really do, except I'm not sure I feel that way any more. I did want to be there for her. I *tried* to be. I tried my best to help. But how can you help someone who won't just let you in, but who is also *lying* to you? Anger builds as I realise Zoe hasn't merely been sleepwalking through our marriage these past couple of years; she's been pushing me away, lie by lie.

We say goodbye and I hang up, then stand and open the window, gazing out across the rooftops. *Where are you?* I want to scream, and I know I don't mean just now. Wherever my wife has disappeared to – here, at home – I don't think she's coming back.

8
ZOE, JANUARY 2009

'Happy New Year!'

Kate's voice is shrill in my ear, and I pull away from her sweaty embrace, planting a big fat kiss on her cheek. 'Happy New Year to you, too.'

'This is the year I'm getting married!' She raises her hands in the air in victory, then leans drunkenly against Giles' side. 'Can you believe that this time next year, I'll be a *wife*? Now we have to get you hooked up, Zoe!'

I roll my eyes at her familiar refrain as one of my favourite songs starts pounding through the air.

'Come on!' I grab Kate's hand. 'Let's dance!'

I tug her away from Giles and through the crowd, elbowing my way onto the dance floor. Kate's so smashed she can barely stand upright, so I grab her hands and move her back and forth in a crazed version of swing dancing, grinning as people around us give us funny looks.

I spin her around and we crash into bodies, but we've both drunk so much, we don't feel any impact. Kate tries to spin me, too, but her arm somehow winds around my neck, tilting me to one side. She sways back and forth . . . then topples over in what feels like slow motion. I shriek as she pulls me down with her, feeling the damp of spilled drinks and I don't even *want* to know whatever else seep through my tights. We lay there for a minute, both breaking out in huge guffaws as feet stomp around us and the bright lights from above hurt our eyes.

'Can I help you get up?'

A deep male voice filters down, and my heart stops. For a second – for *just* a second – I think it might be Edward. I've often thought, or more accurately wished, for this since I met him. Then, a hairy arm reaches down and hauls me upwards, and I'm staring into the face of a bloke my height, a man without Edward's long legs or, presumably, big feet.

'Thanks,' I mumble, trying to ignore the disappointment crashing through me as I pull Kate to her feet.

'What's your name?' Kate reaches out to steady herself. 'Ooh, nice arms.' She leans into me. 'This is Zoe. She's single and looking for love!' It sounds bad enough normally, but with Kate's drunken slur, it's even worse.

'Can I buy you a drink?' The man's eyes bore into mine, and I shake my head.

'No, sorry, we have to get going. Thanks.' I hustle Kate off the dance floor and back through the crowd, depositing her into Giles' arms.

'Kate! For God's sake!'

'What? If you're not going to try to find this Edward bloke, then . . .'

I shake my head. Ever since our failed rendezvous, Kate has been constantly at me to go to the South Bank, sit on that bench, and keep doing it until I find my man. And if I'm being truthful, I can't say I haven't done just that . . . every once in a while, when the weather's nice, or when I have time, of course. I've even kept those silly socks in my handbag, just in case.

If only he'd given me his bloody phone number! If only the Tube had been working . . . if only. I'll tell you one thing: if I do manage to find that bloke again, I'm going to get all his contact details, from phone number to Twitter handle. There'll be no place to hide.

I sip my cocktail, trying not to vomit as I watch Giles slobber all over my friend. It's funny that Edward's in my thoughts so much, given we only spoke for five minutes. It sounds so cheesy, but something about us just *worked* – in a way I haven't experienced since my last relationship crashed and burned a few years ago. I've learned not to believe in a one-and-only, but out of all the dates I've had in the past year or so, I have to say that men like Edward – men I'd want to spend more than five minutes with – are thin on the ground.

We might end up hating each other after those five minutes, or he could reveal some hideous deformity. But one thing's for sure: this year, somehow, I'm going to find out.

9

EDWARD, SATURDAY, 3 P.M.

I stare at the mobile, then roll my neck and shoulders in a futile bid to ease the tension inside. I still can't believe Zoe's lied to me for so long, but in an odd way, it makes me feel better. Better about the past, and better about the present. Zoe's not lost; she's been doing what she wants, going where she needs to. Wherever she is, wherever she has been, she definitely doesn't want me to know. And you know what? That's fine by me. I just need to check that she's all right before I can hit the streets and see what Paris has to offer. I'm not going to waste the trip here.

Right, last attempt. If she has gone home – and I can't think what else she'd be doing in a city she doesn't even like – I can ask her parents to see if she's there. If she turned around and went straight back, she could be home right about now. I don't want to worry them, but they know as well as I do how difficult it's become to track Zoe's movements.

Sighing, I hit 'call' again, bracing myself for the inevitable barrage of it's-been-way-too-longs. There was a time Zoe's mother practically lived in our house. Her parents moved into the village a month after we bought our place there, wanting to be closer to their grandson. I know they drove Zoe crazy when she was growing up, always after her to study harder, dress more sensibly and stop wasting time in drama and art clubs. But once Milo appeared, she and her mum seemed to click, as if he was the missing piece of the puzzle. Zoe would actually call for advice: unheard of in her pre-Milo days.

I don't even know if they still talk.

'Hi, Helen, it's Edward. Listen, can you pop round to the house and see if Zoe's there?'

I hear a sharp intake of breath. 'Zoe? Isn't she with you? Jack and I were so pleased when she agreed to go along with you. We thought she might take a bit more convincing.'

I nod, wondering for the first time why she *did* decide to come. Why did I, for that matter? 'Well, she was with me, but we got separated at the station when we arrived. Her mobile's going straight to voicemail, and I just thought, well, if maybe all this was too much for her she may have headed home.' Or something like that.

'Oh.' Zoe's mum sounds disappointed, and I realise how much she must have been counting on this trip to jump-start her daughter. If only it were that simple. 'Hold on, then. I'll get Jack to run down and check.'

I hang up, picturing Zoe's spritely, white-bearded father pulling on his wellies, heading out into the fresh spring air, and hurrying the short distance between our house and theirs. In the first few days after Milo died, that short distance was a blessing. The two of them were constantly there, filling the house with food and sound, unlike my parents who wanted 'to give us some space'. Now that Milo's gone, the presence of my in-laws so nearby seems superfluous, a reminder of what's missing. I guess that's why we both avoid them.

My phone rings, and I pick up. 'Is she there?'

'Well, Jack didn't actually see her,' Helen says. 'But he did hear music, and the lights upstairs were on, too. Zoe didn't answer the doorbell, but then, that's hardly unusual.' Her voice is tight.

I let out my breath. 'Okay, thanks.' So Zoe *did* do a runner, I think as I click off. Well, at least I know she's safe. My jaw clenches, and I get to my feet. Shit, could she not even tell me she was leaving? What kind of person gets on an intercontinental train, then takes off back home without even a phone call?

My wife, I guess. My wife.

Before the familiar cocktail of anger and despair hit, I pick up my phone again and dial a number.

'Fiona?' I say quickly, trying to hold the feelings at bay. 'Want to come to Paris?'

10
ZOE, SATURDAY, 3 P.M.

The sun slants from the sky as I wander down streets, turning this way and that. I don't even know what time it is, since I always use my mobile. Without anything tying me to my life, I feel like I'm about to float up and away, into the dazzling blue heavens. If only.

People push past me on the pavement, muttering under their breath as they nip my dragging heels. As I catch sight of myself in a shop window, I can only imagine what they're thinking. My salt-and-pepper curls are tangled, my cheeks are hollowed out, and my grey T-shirt hangs like a tent. Clients always exclaimed how young I looked, and whenever we went out, I was sure to get ID'd – much to Edward's embarrassment, since at five years my senior, he always joked he was robbing the cradle. I peer closer, noting the perma-bags under my eyes and the wrinkles etched on my forehead. Now, I suspect people would be surprised how young I actually am.

If I look older than my years, Edward's gone the opposite direction – or he's trying to, anyway. He's never been a hipster, keeping Gap in business with his regular supply of basic shirts and baggy jeans. Lately, though, he's started using gel to get a quiff, his baggy jeans are skinny, and even his normally crinkled work shirts are slim-fitting and crisp. It's like he's trying to shed his old self, to evolve into something new, while I've been rooted to the spot, barely able to brush my hair.

I wonder what he's doing now? I start walking again, turning down a narrow street. That one time I went off the radar, he moved heaven and earth to find me – calling the police, scouring the station, driving our car through the streets . . . At least that's what he told me. A car whooshes by and my head snaps up, almost as if I expect to see him driving by now. Has he informed the hotel staff I'm missing, maybe made some inquiries what to do next? Or have I disappeared too many times for him to really worry?

Paris is different than I expected – at least this part is. I don't spot many tourists, the Eiffel Tower's nowhere to be seen, and I reckon I must be miles from the river. Quirky galleries and shops line the street, the kind I'd have rushed into in a heartbeat way back when. Now, I let myself drift by, their wares passing in a blur.

Up ahead, I spot a gendarme, hand on hips, surveying the street. I stop for a second, my mind whirling. I could talk to him, tell him what happened, and ask for help. He'd lend me a phone, help me find my way back to my husband. But that's not what I want – I want to stay here, in this unknown landscape, where nothing makes sense and I don't need to try: try to block out the past, try to shut my eyes to the dreadful familiar, try to force myself to breathe. If I stop taking in air, well . . . I'm already a skeleton, anyway.

And maybe it's better I stay in this state, that I *don't* find my way back to Edward. He's doing fine; he's moving on, if his new wardrobe is any indication. That, and the fact he's rid the house of anything to do with Milo, cleansing it of any trace of our son.

Pain flares when I remember that morning, barely even two months after the accident, when I hauled myself from bed amidst the noise of ripping packing tape. I stumbled through the door of Milo's room – what used to be his room, anyway – recoiling like I'd had a punch to the gut. The once-cluttered space, packed with toys, books, nappies and baby clothes I hadn't the heart to pass on, was stripped to its bones, a carcass of what it used to be. The mattress stared at me like an accusing eye, the bookshelves screamed their barrenness, and guilt streamed down the bare walls like a waterfall. In the middle of the space knelt my husband, emptying the toy chest into one last cardboard box.

Packing up my son. My soul.

I wanted to scream, to kick the box and let the contents fly out. Instead, I stood there, frozen with hurt and disbelief. How could he do this? How could he consign our child to the past, when he'd only just gone? And how the *hell* could Edward not ask me first? That one action put us firmly in two separate spheres, and we've remained there ever since.

I walk even faster now, moving past the gendarme and away from my husband.

11

EDWARD, JULY 2009

I don't think I can stand the rest of this date, even on the off-chance of the night ending back at mine. Nod nod nod; sip sip sip; nod nod nod. Who knew so many breeds of horses existed? The way this woman's on about them, I'm sure human males are a disappointment.

Julia – or is it Julie? – pauses to shovel in some lettuce, and I take the opportunity to signal for the bill. It's only gone seven and the sun's still high in the sky, but I have to get out of here now. That's the peril of online dating: the girl might look nice on a computer screen, but there's no mute in real life. The more dates I go on, the more I can't forget Zoe, 'South Bank Girl', as my friends have taken to calling her with a roll of the eyes. She's the one I really want, but it's been over a year now since that day we met, and despite my frequent trawls along the river, I've yet to see her again.

I need to forget her, I know. If Zoe really was interested, she would have turned up that rainy evening. I probably scared her off with my pathetic pick-up line. What the hell was I thinking? I usually need a good three or four drinks before approaching women like that. It's definitely not something I should do sober.

I shake my head as Julia drones on, recalling how I sat on the bench in the rain, cold moisture trickling down the back of my neck and wind whipping my face. I was already soaked through to the skin, but that didn't matter. For the first time in ages, I was excited about meeting a woman, even if we'd barely spoken. Zoe's laughing eyes – okay, and bloody fantastic legs – had looped through my mind 24/7, making my routine workweek suddenly seem full of possibility. I'm normally a local pub kind of bloke, but I'd spent hours researching and planning our date: a walk along the river, a drink at the Founder's Arms, then all the way down to Borough Market where we'd have dinner at a new restaurant that just opened. I was even prepared to wear those hideous socks – and given my usual colour palette of black and grey, that's saying something. That's how much I liked what I saw.

After about forty minutes, my fingers turned numb with cold, I was drenched, and I had to accept she just wasn't coming. That's what you get for taking a punt. I dragged my waterlogged self back home, then drowned my sorrows in Heineken.

'Shall we make a move?' I ask now, scraping back my chair as Julia finishes her salad. I'm not even sure why she suggested this place on the South Bank, seeing as how she's only eaten a handful of rabbit food. I usually meet internet dates at the café around the corner from my North London flat, so I can make a quick getaway if they turn out to be like Julia.

At least it's not pouring with rain tonight, I think, holding open the door as we walk out to the terrace. The golden sun flares in my eyes and I slip on my glasses, trying hard to suppress a yawn.

'Which Tube do you need to catch?' I ask to make it clear I won't be accompanying her anywhere else, and vice versa. Her long face gets even longer, and a pang of guilt goes through me. Apart from the horse fixation, she's a nice girl with a good body . . . but she's definitely not for me. Zoe's face flashes into my mind for the countless time, and I sigh, pushing it away.

'I can go from Waterloo,' Julia says, then launches into a long story about her favourite horse growing up. Her voice washes over me and I stare out at the river, gleaming now in the evening light instead of its usual sludgy brown.

No more internet dates, I decide. I've met loads of nice women, but none of them appeal. Maybe it's not the women. Maybe I'm not ready to settle down. Thirties are the new twenties, right? So I still have plenty of time. Look at what happens to all my mates once they're in a relationship: they disappear, emerging with new haircuts, pastel jumpers and a dazed grin. I should enjoy my freedom while I can.

Even as the thoughts run through my mind, though, I know that I *do* want to settle down. I'm thirty-five now, and I want to find my future wife and start building a life together. If Zoe had turned up a year ago – and if she turned out to be who I thought she might be – I'd happily be wearing a pastel jumper right now. Christ, I was going to wear pink socks!

I wave Julia off just outside the station, then wander back to the river, wondering what to do. It's still early, the weather is perfect, and I don't feel like heading home to my stuffy flat. Ever since I moved into London proper, the walkway by the Thames has become my spiritual home, as lame as that may sound. I can wander on my own for hours there, just watching the water.

I'll have a drink at the Founder's Arms and combine my two favourite pleasures: the river and beer. I pick up pace, already anticipating the frothy bubbles slipping down my throat. As I near Zoe's bench, I can't help casting my eyes towards it, the same way I have countless other times this past year. It's normally occupied, but that person is never Zoe. There's no reason to think that this time, it'll be any different. And even if it was her, she's probably long forgotten me.

Still, I have to check. As usual, someone is sitting there, and it does look like a woman – hardly something to shout about, since the chance is 50:50. I squint, only just making out the back and forth movement of what looks like knitting needles, and my heart jumps. How many people knit? And on that particular bench?

The same dark hair, lovely curvy legs and pixie-like face come into view, and before I get any closer, I duck behind a tree. I've no idea what to say to her! Shit, I hope she hasn't seen me. First the lame pick-up line, and now she's going to think I'm stalking her. You'd think after all this time, I'd have come up with an opening gambit, but my brain is blank.

She makes a move as if to gather her things, and I jerk out from behind the thick trunk. Even if she does reject me, I'm not going to miss out on talking to her again. Striding towards her, I can hear my pulse whooshing in my ears. I wish I'd had more of that wine at dinner.

'Still have those socks?' The words fly from my mouth and I mutter a curse under my breath as my cheeks heat up. I stop in front of the bench, jamming my hands in my pockets in a way that I hope looks casual, and not as if I have a misshapen dick.

Her head flies up and her coffee-brown eyes meet mine, the eyes that have been haunting me since I first met her. They widen in what I hope is recognition, then crinkle at the corners as she smiles. 'You!' The word bursts from her in a laugh. 'I didn't think I'd ever see you again.'

'Did you *want* to?' I make the question sound like a joke, but I'm serious. After all, she never did come that night.

She nods. 'Yeah, of course I did. And I'm so sorry I never made it to see you, like we arranged. There was a problem with the Tube, and I guess by the time I got here, you were gone. I didn't have your mobile to let you know.'

Relief rushes through me and I lower myself down beside her on the bench, trying to keep my eyes from the rise of her breasts underneath the tight white shirt. So she *did* come, I think, breathing in the soft scent of her perfume. I knew I should have waited longer. If I hadn't been approaching hypothermia, I would have.

A warm glow builds in my stomach, like I've downed a shot of whisky, and I turn to face her. 'So, do you?'

'Do I what?' she asks, her brow furrowing in a cute way.

'Do you still have those socks?' I grin as she rummages around in her handbag, thinking that there's no way she still has them in there, but hoping, too, that she does. That means she's been thinking about me as much as I have about her.

She holds them up triumphantly, and my smile gets bigger. God, those things are hideous. 'I knew something good would come from never cleaning out this bag. I *do* still have them.' She tilts her head. 'And are you going to make good on your promise?'

'Well, that depends.' I pause, my gut churning. 'Are you going to go out with me tonight?'

'Of course,' she says. 'I've been waiting a year.'

I'm grinning so hard my cheeks hurt, but I can't help it. I take the socks from her, jimmy off my shoes and black socks, then pull on the pink knitted ones. They barely come to the back of my heel, they're itchy as hell, and I look ridiculous, but I don't care.

If I could, I'd stay here in this spot, with her, forever.

12
EDWARD, SATURDAY, 3.30 P.M.

As soon as I hang up from my call to Fiona, guilt prickles. Yes, my wife has abandoned me here without so much as a word, but I *am* married . . . if that still means something. I glance down at my ring, remembering just how much it used to mean, back when I believed that bond could carry us through anything.

Am I ready to sleep with Fiona? Because I'm sure that's what she's expecting. You don't invite a woman to Paris without sex on the agenda, and if we're sharing a room, then it's a given. There's so much I like about her: the way she focuses in on me whenever we're together, as if I'm the only thing in her world. The easy way we talk and laugh, with no hidden meanings or added layers. How she's a blank slate, reflecting only the *good* things in me . . . the way I want to see myself once again. Not to mention her fantastic body; the woman has an arse Beyoncé would die for. I shift in my chair, getting horny just thinking of it.

Although we've never crossed the line from friends to something more, I know we've both thought about it. Last night, when we went for a drink after work (or, more accurately, several drinks), I leaned in to kiss her goodbye on the cheek. She turned her head, and my lips brushed hers – just briefly, but enough to feel the air spark between us. Having sex with Fiona is just what I need right now, but sleeping with someone else really does put the final stake in my marriage: the point of no return. Is that what I want?

Aw, fuck it! My fist slams down on the dingy duvet cover. I'm tired of sitting here, tired of thinking of my wife. The silence of the hotel room presses on me, and I get to my feet again. I have a few hours to kill before Fiona arrives, and now that the alcohol is wearing off, that familiar restless feeling is making my legs twitch. My body throbs with fatigue from the long workweek and the late nights, but my feet carry me back to the lift and out to the street again.

I shield my eyes from the late-afternoon sun and pivot, not sure where to go. Down the street past the rows of cafés, or under the arch and into the square? It's the first time in ages I haven't had something to do, work to go to or people to meet. The glint of a fountain draws me towards the square, and I walk under the archway and sink onto the grass. Closing my eyes, I let the sound of the fountain fill my ears. The *sssshhhh* of water against concrete reminds me of the Thames lapping the walkway, and that same blissful calm washes over me. It feels so good to sit, to be still for once, and to let the water numb my thoughts.

I missed the river when we moved from London. It brought me and Zoe together, a benevolent matchmaker: our watery Cupid. Our new village was beautiful – stuffed full of 'olde worlde' charm, yummy mummies and their equally adorable offspring, complete with doting dads, but there was no river or lake . . . not even a fish pond. But by then, we didn't need the river. We had Milo to hold us together.

My jaw tightens and I get to my feet again, striding across the square. It was a mistake to stop. I don't know where I'm going, but I have to keep moving.

13
ZOE, SEPTEMBER 2009

'So are you in *loooovvvve*?' Kate grins at me then swigs her ice water. 'I knew it had to happen sometime. First comes love, then comes marriage, then comes . . .' She raises an eyebrow. 'It's great that he's a bit older than you, too. He won't waste your time.'

I shake my head. 'We've only been together for two months, Kate. Give it a rest.'

I have to say, though, this summer *has* been magical, like a montage of those fairy-tale romances you see in Hollywood films – not that I believe in fairy-tale romance, not any more. Relationships are a risk, and not every ending is happy. I learned that the hard way.

Still, the setting is perfect for falling in love, and the stunning weather's helped: day after day of scorching sun as London bakes in a rare heatwave. Come five o'clock, the whole city floods into cafés and pubs, making the place seem like a carnival. Edward meets me at my work and we head down to the South Bank, wandering among the other couples before claiming our bench. I knit while he relaxes, staring out at the river or sometimes reading.

From the very first night – when I took him to a hole-in-the-wall Mexican restaurant in the bowels of Elephant & Castle, then forced him to swing dance to the jazz band on the corner – things have been so easy, so natural. Our worlds have overlapped just enough to make me feel warm and fuzzy without being submerged. As clichéd as it sounds, I feel even more 'me' with Edward than without him, and I think he feels the same. I hope so, anyway.

But love? Well, I'm not sure – not yet, anyway. And marriage? *Kids*? The thought makes me feel like I'm about to jump off a bridge into the unknown, and I want to curl up in a corner, screw my eyes shut and cover myself with a blanket.

'When it's right, it's right.' Kate leans back in her chair, crossing her slender legs. 'No point hanging around. You're on the wrong side of thirty now, and your biological clock is ticking, my friend.'

Jesus. 'The wrong side of thirty'? I've only just hit the big 3-0, for God's sake. I manage to keep my face neutral as I swig some cheap red wine. With her Christmas wedding looming, Kate's become obsessed with THE FUTURE (the way she says it, it should be in capital letters) and benevolently bestowing words of advice on all the poor singletons around her.

I just laugh. My biological clock might be ticking, but I'm miles from one of those women chomping at the bit to get married and procreate. And besides – although I don't say this to Kate – I'm pretty sure now that I don't believe in marriage. How can you trust yourself and that person enough to pledge for eternity? How can you promise to be with someone *forever*? People change, and what suits you now may not in fifty years' time. Anyway, if you're confident enough in your relationship, why do you need a piece of paper to legalise it, to tie you together?

'Look, Edward isn't that wanker Ollie,' Kate says, and I cringe at the mention of the name. Four years on, he still has that effect.

'Thank God,' I mutter. Actually, Edward couldn't be further from my ex-fiancé, which just goes to show that people want different things at different points in their lives – or that they get smarter. Ollie and I met one alcohol-fuelled night in a bar, and straight away

I wanted to be with him. We liked the same music, loved trying new things, couldn't wait to travel to India. I'd just moved into London to start a new job, and he introduced me to Camden Market, vintage shops, indie music: everything that was funky and unique, just like him. For God's sake, he had a better wardrobe than I did, and I often borrowed his clothes. Even now, I can smell the heady mix of incense and ash.

When he casually mentioned – in the very romantic setting of a sticky-floored post-gig pub – we could get married, I said yes in an instant. I didn't need to think about it: my heart knew what was right, or at least it thought it did. He didn't give me a ring, but that was fine. I was certain he loved me, and that was enough. He was going to be my *husband*! The word made me shiver with excitement. I couldn't wait.

Then Ollie's music promotion business took off, and he started travelling. A lot. I told myself to be patient, that this was just a phase, and soon he'd be back to discuss the finer details of our wedding . . . like setting the date. Then, when he was on a trip to Ibiza, he sent me a text saying he'd decided to stay in Spain – so *hasta la vista*, Zoe (or something to that effect). A text! After almost three years together, he dumped me, his future wife, by *text*.

I felt as if the carpet had been pulled out from under me. The flat, these streets . . . I'd envisioned him, our life, here. I loved him. I *trusted* him. How could I not know this was coming? Had I been that blind, or had Ollie's feelings magically morphed away during one Spanish siesta? I didn't sleep for days, the questions running through my mind like caffeinated hamsters on a wheel. I never found any answers, but after many pep talks from Kate, along with strict instructions to not even *think* about contacting him, I finally moved on. I still sometimes think of Ollie, though, and wonder what he's doing.

That experience changed me. I vowed that the next time I was in a serious relationship, I'd take things day to day, because that's all you can do. You can't control the other person, you can't control emotions, and you can't control the future. Edward and I are happy now, and that's enough for me – and for him, I think, given that our discussion rarely veers beyond what to have for dinner. Anyway, like I said, it *has* only been two months.

Kate and I spend the rest of the meal discussing wedding logistics, important things like champagne or cava, when a wave of fatigue washes over me. I'm just about to ask for the bill when she clears her throat.

'So, I've got something to tell you,' she says, her eyes sparkling. 'I can't wait any longer!'

'What is it? Did you manage to get The Barons to play at the reception, after all?' Trust Kate to wait until now to tell me. I've been trying to track down the up-and-coming band for months, but to no avail.

'I'm pregnant.'

My mouth falls open, and Kate grins at me. 'What? Really?'

She nods. 'Yup. Only about six weeks, so it's still very early.' She shakes her head. 'I'm going to be a mum!'

'Oh my God.' I reach over and take her hand. A wife . . . a mum . . . all in the space of a year. Talk about future! 'Congratulations!' I force a smile, trying to get over the shock of it. I've only just got my head around her getting married, and now this.

'It happened much faster than we thought,' Kate says. 'I mean, we only decided to start trying this summer.'

'What, so it's planned?' I sit back, feeling a little miffed she didn't tell me they were even thinking of having a child. I suppose I should have guessed, given her eagerness to get started on the whole love-marriage-baby conveyor belt, but I can't imagine why you *would* start trying before you're married. I can't think of a worse way to start a new marriage than a screaming infant in the matri-monial bed.

Kate swats my arm. 'Of course it is! We both want a family and we figured, why wait? Anyway, the older you get, the greater the risk of birth defects, and you never know how long it will take.' She gives me a pointed look and I barely refrain from rolling my eyes.

'How are you feeling?' I gaze down at her belly, still flat as a pancake.

'I'm fine – so far, anyway. Giles and I have been reading up on it, and some people get through without morning sickness or anything. Hopefully that'll be me. I've accepted I'll be huge for the wedding, but I don't want to walk down the aisle being sick into a bucket.'

'I'm sure you'll be one of those glowing women with thick, glossy hair and perfect skin,' I say.

'Fingers crossed.' She sips her water. 'Can you knit the baby something? Maybe a little hat? I need something to make this feel real, you know? God, I can't wait to start shopping for outfits.'

'Of course,' I say. 'More than a hat! I'm really good now with cardigans. I'll do a few for your baby. And some booties, too.' God, that sounds weird. *Kate's baby.*

She babbles on about the first trimester, and I nod along, a strange feeling sweeping over me. We're exactly the same age, but we couldn't be in two more different places. Kate's got everything all nailed down: a husband, a baby, a new life as a mother. I'm in a relationship, yes, but we haven't even got to the 'L' word yet.

But that's okay, I tell myself. I like the fact my future's an unwritten book; it means that anything could happen. And if you don't expect anything – don't *want* anything in particular – then you can't be let down.

Perfect.

14
ZOE, SATURDAY, 4 P.M.

I squint against the sun in the sky, my blistered feet stinging with each step. It must be about supper time, and I've been on the street since noon. Back at home, I'd be peeling myself off the pub's sticky banquette, dragging my feet on the way to the train station, mind fuzzy and vision blurred.

Now, even though I haven't had one drink, I feel much the same. My mouth is dry, my body's sticky with dried sweat, and every inch of me longs to sit down. I peer into the darkness of a shop, eyes adjusting just enough to make out comfy chairs in the corners and a long, low sofa I'd love to throw myself on and stretch out. The floor creaks as I step inside and the whoosh of the air conditioner makes goosebumps spring up on my arms.

'Bonjour!' A woman with a steel-grey bob and neat blue cardigan peers at me over the top of her chunky specs.

'Hi,' I mumble, eyes half-closed, not wanting to be jolted from my daze. The cool air is so refreshing, I just want to stand here for a few seconds and let it flow over my hot body.

'Can I help you find something?'

I shake my head. 'No, thanks.' I don't even know what the shop is selling, and I don't care. It's deliciously quiet and dark, a refuge from the cacophony of the street. The floor creaks again as the woman moves away.

Finally I lift my lids, stepping backwards at the sight before me. Trust me to find a store selling knitting supplies; Edward always joked I had a special sonar seeking them out. Despite everything, I guess that's unchanged. Vibrant yarns in every colour are piled high on shelves lining the walls, and before I can stop myself, I've reached out and picked up a royal-blue bundle. I draw it to my nose, breathing in the mix of wool and dye.

Instantly, I'm transported to the past. I'm sitting in a chair, in our old flat. It's the paisley armchair in front of the bay window, the one Edward jokes looks like a cat threw up on it. Sun streams in, bathing my bump in light and warmth. The baby spins and somersaults, and my needles move rhythmically, the blue ball of yarn slowly unravelling as I knit yet another pair of baby booties. That last week before Milo arrived, I was a little obsessed. Edward joked my nesting instinct should have been called knitting instinct. Morning, noon and night, I made pair after pair of booties, as if by keeping busy I could keep my unborn baby safe inside me.

And that was just the start. For Milo's first and second birthdays, I fashioned jumpers so unintentionally hideous, Edward laughed that social services would remove our child for fashion abuse. Milo was wearing his second-birthday jumper the day—

I jerk my mind away. That jumper was the last thing I knitted – I couldn't bear to pick up the needles again once Milo had gone. It was like doing something so familiar, something so *normal*; it meant my life now was real. I don't even know where my needles are. Packed away with the rest of me, I guess.

Now, though, the weight and softness of wool make my fingers itch for that familiar motion. The rhythm of the needles was so comforting and cosy, and I adored creating something so personal for the people I loved. The yarn was connected to my heart, entwining emotions into every row.

An image flashes through my head of those terrible pink socks I made Edward wear (or did he offer?), and a smile twists my lips. He kept them on the whole night, and they must have been so itchy. I'd knitted them from wool, and that July evening was a scorcher. I remember how impressed I was that he didn't care how ridiculous they looked. All he cared about was me.

After the impromptu swing dance, I invited him back to my flat. We drank more wine, and finally he took my hand, tugged me to my feet and tipped up my chin so his eyes could meet mine. I remember leaning in to him, our mouths meeting without any awkward chin-bumping or teeth-scraping. Sex with Edward was so *easy*. I didn't even have to fake an orgasm like I sometimes did the first time, just to get it over with.

The next morning, after he'd left, I found those pink socks balled up under the bed. I wonder where they are now? A shot of sadness goes through me that the laughing couple, so full of happiness and excitement in each other, is gone . . . knocked flat by life.

Or death, in our case.

'Madame? Are you all right?'

I jump as I realise I'm standing stock-still in the middle of the shop, and my cheeks are wet with tears. I lift my head in surprise as I wipe away the liquid with my hand. I've felt so dead, so numb, inside that I couldn't cry, even if I wanted to. I don't know where those tears came from.

I shake my head, placing the yarn back on the shelf. I'm not all right. I'll never be all right again.

'I'm fine,' I say, not wanting to explain. How could I, anyway?

I wipe my face again, then step out on the street and quicken my pace. I need to put some distance between that shop and me – those memories and me. I can't let them catch me like that again.

15
EDWARD, DECEMBER 2009

'Congratulations!' I grin at Kate and Giles, thinking how happy they look on their wedding day. Married, with a baby on the way. A pang of jealousy goes through me. I can't wait for that to be me – married, anyway, even if the baby will never materialise.

Kate leans forward to kiss my cheek. She looks absolutely gorgeous, her small bump rising up beneath the white lacy dress. 'Thanks, Edward. Maybe you guys will be next.' She wags a finger at Zoe and me. 'If you like it, you better put a ring on it!' Her faux Beyoncé makes me laugh, even though I agree wholeheartedly with the sentiment.

Giles cringes and covers his ears. 'Don't give up your day job, my wife. Right, we'd better go say hi to my aunt and uncle.'

They disappear into the crowd, and I smile down at Zoe. I know it's not very charitable to the bride, but as lovely as Kate looks, Zoe's definitely the most beautiful woman here. Her dusky-pink brides- maid dress sets off her dark skin, and her curls are swept up in some intricate hairdo I can't wait to dismantle. I glance at my watch. A few more hours and then I can get her into our room.

'So what do you think?' I give her a playful nudge. '*Are* we going to be next?' The words leave my mouth before I can stop them. I'm not quite sure what's possessed me, except maybe all the champagne I had earlier. Usually, I steer all conversations away from the future, because I know that if I bring it up, I also have to bring up my condition. And things with Zoe are so good right now, I don't want to give her any *hint* of a reason to end it.

Selfish, I know, but these past few months have been incredible, and not just because I've had sex at least once a day. Zoe and I have spent almost every night together, and now I understand the meaning of 'whirlwind romance'. Zoe's the whirlwind: always doing something, always interested in something, always dragging me out to some fringe play in the East End or a new pop-up burger joint in a godforsaken place the Tube doesn't even stop at. Even though I complain, secretly I'm glad we go to these things – although I'd never tell her that. With Zoe, I feel like I'm escaping the box I put myself in, and I like that feeling.

The thing is, I *do* want to get married. Thanks to some complications from when I had mumps as a child, I already know I can't have the 2.4 kids. I've never told anyone, but then, I've never needed to. I never felt someone was 'the one', not like I do with Zoe. I haven't even told my mates, who'd probably think it was cool I wouldn't have to worry about knocking someone up. I never thought much about it, either. It all seemed so theoretical until now – until I found a woman I wanted to spend the rest of my life with.

I may have given up on children, but I'm not going to give up on marriage. I want the vows, the forever commitment. And I want it from Zoe . . . if she still sees a future with me after I tell her I can't have kids. I swallow hard, hoping I won't need to do that tonight. I'm not ready to risk this being over, not yet.

'Let's just enjoy the evening,' Zoe says finally. She smiles but it doesn't reach her eyes, and something twists in my gut. 'Oh, look, they're about to cut the cake!'

I watch her push through the throng, releasing the breath I didn't even realise I was holding. I'm off the hook for tonight, but . . . *does* she see a future with me? Because I can't imagine it with anyone but her. I want us to be next, like Kate said. I want Zoe to want that, too.

'Edward?' Zoe looks back over her shoulder. 'Come on!'

I nod and make my way towards her. *Slow down*, I tell myself. *You've plenty of time to be together. You've the rest of your lives.*

Hopefully, anyway.

16
EDWARD, SATURDAY, 5 P.M.

I'm passing through the archway away from the fountain when my phone buzzes. I hope it's not Zoe, I think, fishing the mobile from my pocket. The last thing I want is to talk to her right now, to hear her feeble excuses for why she took off.

But no, it's Fiona, thank God. 'Hi. Everything okay?' A couple more hours, and she'll be here. I can't wait.

'Actually, no.' Her voice is glum. 'There's some sort of problem with the train – I couldn't understand what the announcement said – and we're stuck on the track for the time being, in the middle of bloody nowhere. They've called an engineer, but they don't know how long it'll be. Apparently all the trains are delayed now.'

'That's awful. Are you all right?'

'Well, I've got champagne, so I'm fine.'

Typically upbeat, I think. I love that about her.

'Hopefully it won't take too long and I'll get there for a late dinner,' she says. 'I'll keep you posted. In the meantime, can you find me something to wear to bed tonight? I packed so fast I forgot my PJs.'

'Okay.' My voice emerges, sounding strangled. Find her something to wear to bed tonight? Is that some sort of manoeuvre to uncover my true intentions? *I* don't even know my true intentions. And what the hell do women wear to bed, anyway? Zoe always slept naked . . . until she started coming to bed fully clothed, right after Milo died.

'Right, better go. I need to save my battery.' Fiona clicks off, and I slide the phone back into my pocket. Well, at least her request has given me something to do, something to focus on, other than the detritus of my life and my runaway wife. Now, where can I buy pyjamas? I fish out the map the hotel gave me, noting an advertisement in the corner for the Galeries Lafayettes. Perfect.

I flag down a taxi and hop in, leaning back on the seat as it wends through the streets. A strange feeling descends as the shopfronts flash by: a feeling like I'm in an alternate life that isn't mine. I'm in the middle of Paris, off to a mall to buy something for a woman who isn't my wife – a woman I'll spend the night with. It's so far from where I thought I'd be this morning that I almost can't grasp it.

But isn't this what I want? A new start? A clean break from the past? A chance at being happy again? Christ, if Zoe can seek solace somewhere besides me – even if it is just a glass of wine down the pub – then *lie* about it for two years, surely I can find some pleasure of my own.

'We are here, monsieur.'

I blink. I hadn't even realised we'd pulled up to an ornate façade, whose windows are slathered with photos of glamorous women. Shoppers rush across busy streets and into the mall in a steady stream, and I step from the car and join them. Not too long ago the thought of shopping was enough to send me into my man cave. But over the past year, shopping has become one of my favourite pastimes . . . besides work. On the evenings when I finish my projects and Fiona's not free, I take myself off to a mall near the office. The blinking lights, the music and the constant buzz of people remind me that life does exist. Although I still can't claim to enjoy shopping itself, I have to agree with Fiona's assessment that my new wardrobe is a million times better than my old one – not that my wife's noticed. For the first time in my life, I'm actually 'on trend', or so the personal shopper told me. Despite all my time in the mall, I wouldn't know a trend if it slapped me in the face.

I push through the revolving door and enter the perfume section, the heady mix of fragrance hitting me between the eyes. To my right, a woman sprays scent in the air, and it hangs like mist before dissipating. Even though I can't see it any longer, the smell washes over me in waves. It's *Flower* by Kenzo, the scent Zoe used to wear right up until – well, I don't know. I rarely get close enough to smell her any more.

My feet stop, as if they're frozen. I breathe in, memories tumbling over me like sharp stones down a slope, each one coated in that fragrance. The day we decided – or, more accurately, *Zoe* decided – we could do forever, after all. Our small but intimate wedding ceremony, where she threw her arms around me and kissed me before the registrar even had a chance to declare us husband and wife. The watch she gave me the next morning as we lay in bed, the one I'd been craving for months. The delivery suite, where Zoe was determined to smell nice despite the sweat and slop of labour, and Milo's sweet face when he first appeared. For the first few hours, he was so scrunched up, we actually did call him Flower, waiting for him to unfurl. A million and one wonderful gifts are wrapped up in that fragrance, their boxes now barren and empty.

But even as the same old loss and pain ricochet through me, another realisation does, too. I was happy, yes, and I loved Zoe with all my heart, but our relationship was never really equal. She was the one calling the shots, making the final decisions: when it came to marriage, babies and even dealing with death. She's the one who's gone off, who's chosen to disappear.

I'm through with running on her time, I think, sliding off the watch I've worn since our first day of marriage. I'm done with catering to her needs and desires. From now on, I'll make my own schedule. I'll make my own *life*.

I step on the escalator. It rises up, carrying me higher and higher, away from the lingering scent.

17
ZOE, FEBRUARY 2010

'I've got something for you. An after-Christmas present.' I roll over onto my tummy and smile up at Edward. 'Something to tide you through the long, dark days of winter. It's always so depressing once the festive season's over and everyone goes back to being a zombie.' A lock of dark hair flops over his forehead, and I reach out to push it back as my heart picks up pace. God, I hope he likes his gift.

'An after-Christmas present?' Edward raises an eyebrow, looking a little nervous. I can't say I blame him. As a joke, I gave him a particularly hideous, itchy Christmas jumper in a garish orange adorned with a deformed-looking elf. Kudos to him, though: he actually wore it to the pub that Christmas night.

I grope under the bed, then pull out a gift-wrapped package. 'Here.' I hand it over then cross my fingers, hoping this will be the magic bullet to make him smile again. Ever since Kate's wedding and that awkward conversation about our future, things have been a little weird between us. We haven't talked about it, but I know my response – or lack of response, really – hurt him, and I've been kicking myself ever since.

Because I *do* love him. I *do* want to be with him. I still don't think marriage is for me, but I know what we have is special, and I want to enjoy it as much as we can, every day. Taking this step forward means it'll hurt more if things don't work out, but for the first time, I'm willing to take that risk.

I hand him the box and he turns it this way, then that, shaking it. 'Open it!' I laugh to cover my nerves.

Edward carefully undoes one corner, and I grab the box. 'We'll be here forever. Just rip the paper!' I grab hold of a corner and tear off a strip, and before I know it, there's a pile of silver wrapping on the bed. 'Sorry, but you're killing me,' I mumble as I hand him the cardboard box.

'Whoa!' Edward shakes his head, then jimmies open a corner – not hard, given my lack of Sellotape skills – and lifts the lid.

'What's this?' He fishes out a key, laying it in the palm of his hand.

My heart feels like it's trying to break out of my chest. 'It's the key to my flat.' My voice is shaky, and I clear my throat. 'I love you.' God, it's been a while since I've said those words. 'And I want to be with you, like, all the time. So I was wondering . . . if you want to move in?'

My fingers grip his as I meet his eyes, and my heart sinks at his tense expression. He doesn't look happy. He looks more like a rabbit trapped in the headlights. *Oh, shit. I knew I shouldn't have done this. I should have waited longer, should have—*

I slip my hand from his grasp and slide the duvet cover over my legs, my movements jerky and stiff. 'Forget it. Just forget I said anything. If you're not ready or whatever, that's fine.'

Edward takes my hand again. 'Zoe, no: that's not it at all. I love you, too, so much. It's just, well, there's something you need to know before we go any further.'

Oh, God, here we go. 'You're really a woman?' I try to smile, but the corners of my mouth wobble.

'Ha. Funny.' Edward squeezes my hand and takes a deep breath. 'I had mumps when I was thirteen.'

'So?' I can feel my brow furrow, and I try to relax it a bit. What the hell does mumps have to do with living together?

'So, one of the complications can be issues with fertility,' he says, like he's just admitted he has bubonic plague. 'I can't get you pregnant. I can't get anyone pregnant, apparently.'

Relief whooshes through me so quickly I feel lightheaded. That was what he needed to tell me? That he can't get me pregnant? I'll take that over other possibilities any day.

'I'm sorry I didn't tell you sooner,' he says, biting his lip, 'but I wasn't sure how serious you were about us. If it's really important to you, I can get some more tests done, see if there's other options, maybe, or—'

I lean forward and kiss him gently on the lips, cutting off his words. '*You're* the main event. The star attraction.' I smile to take that solemn look from his face. 'Children, well . . . I'm not *against* the idea, but I can take them or leave them.'

Edward sits back. 'But what if you do want them, say, two years from now?'

I shrug. 'I dunno. We can deal with that if it happens, I guess. We can see some specialists, like you said, or we could always adopt. There are plenty of kids who need two good parents.' I wince. 'Oh, God: us as parents! Can you imagine?'

Edward laughs. 'You'd have the whole wardrobe knitted before the child was born. Poor thing.'

I clunk him on the head. 'Lucky thing, you mean. You should see what I've knitted for Kate's baby! Anyway, there is a plus side to all this, you know.' Apart from removing any pressure about marriage, and babies, and all that. 'Bye-bye birth control!' I rummage in the drawer by the bed and chuck the packet in the rubbish. 'I hate those pills.'

Edward watches me with a grin. 'I love you, Zoe.' He starts to ease me down on the bed again, but I squirm away.

'What?' he asks, suddenly looking worried again.

'You never answered my question. Will you move in?'

He smiles and moves lower and lower, down my tummy and over my thighs. 'Let me answer you another way.'

18
ZOE, SATURDAY, 5 P.M.

No matter how fast I walk, memories nip at my heels. It's as if by allowing that one foray into a corner of my former life, the door has been cracked open. Tears drip from my eyes, like a tap has been turned on. I'm groping blindly, frantically in the dark to shut it off, but images leak out.

The wedding jumper I knitted Edward, our initials entwined. The revolting non-alcoholic wine we toasted our marriage with. The way he touched my tiny bump as we walked from the registry office, his fingers lightly resting on my taut stomach as if his whole world was inside me.

My lungs heave as I quicken my pace even more, scanning the street for somewhere to hide. Up ahead, I see the stone steps of a church, and I hurry towards it. Churches are a neutral zone for me: a place with no ties. I didn't marry in one, and we didn't hold Milo's funeral there, either. An image of his service on a bright, sunny day in the back garden, where he loved playing, pushes at my mind, demanding entry. I hold it back with all my strength, rushing up the steps and into the silent sanctuary of the church. I can't go there. I *can't*.

I collapse into a pew, legs shaking as my chest burns. I might be skinny, but I'm in the worst shape of my life. Hardly surprising, given my mainly liquid diet. I let the silence and the dark sink into me, willing myself back to a numb place. The cavernous space is huge and filled with tourists peering at everything, but their voices are nothing but a low muffle. Then the crowd parts, letting through a beaming bride and her groom, followed by family and friends. God, I didn't even realise there was a ceremony here! Imagine getting married with dozens of tourists milling around you.

Good luck, I silently mouth to the woman as she passes, not certain if I'm being sarcastic or if I really mean it. I'm not even sure how I feel about marriage right now. In the past two years, any concern for the state of our union has barely crossed my mind. How could I care, given that the most important thing in my life had already been taken away?

Before meeting Edward – seven years ago now, I think? – I was certain marriage wasn't for me. And then, well . . . everything changed. I let myself fall, succumbing to his idyllic, family-friendly version of the future. Despite my tiredness, the foul nappies and the bleeding nipples, I was in love: with my husband, my baby, my life. I suppose that's partly why I've been so shut off from Edward, why I can't bring myself to feel for him again. I risked everything by buying into his vision – and he was wrong. He couldn't have been more wrong, actually.

I twist my wedding band, envisioning the inscription inside, and a memory of us lying in bed the morning after our wedding floats into my head. Edward turned and smiled, then told me to slide off my ring and read the inscription. I raised my eyebrows, thinking it was such a romantic gesture, yet praying to God it wouldn't be something uber-cheesy I'd be stuck with for the rest of my life. The spindly script and crowded letters on my narrow band were practically undecipherable, but after staring for a few minutes, I was able to make them out.

E & Z. Our own happy ending.

'Perfect,' I said, thinking that actually, it was. There was no 'always' or 'forever', two sentiments which, at that time, still made me feel vaguely uncomfortable. And this was a nod to the story we were writing on our own – our journey, our unique version of the fairy tale.

Pain grips my throat when I picture what that fairy tale has become.

I wonder what Edward thinks now. Does he still believe in forever? Does he still *want* forever, even if our happy ending's shattered? The way he's acting lately, he's already bowed out. Has he, or does he still care?

I'm not sure which answer I want.

19
EDWARD, APRIL 2010

'It's a girl! Kate had a girl!'

My eyes fly open at the sound of Zoe's voice, and I reach out from where I'm sitting in the waiting area and grasp her hand. Her cheeks are flushed, her eyes spark with excitement, and even though it's the middle of the night, she's never looked so beautiful. 'Is everyone all right?'

Zoe nods. 'Yes, the baby's absolutely gorgeous, and Kate was amazing. Come on in and say hello.'

'Okay.' I rub my eyes, every cell in my body longing for bed. When Kate asked Zoe to be her birthing partner 'because Giles is useless', I didn't realise my presence offside would be required, too. Still, I was only too happy to drive Zoe here once Kate rang to say she was in labour at the hospital. And once we arrived, Zoe kept telling me 'it wouldn't be long now'. Twelve hours later . . . I don't mind, though. Actually, I've been a little curious, since the odds of having my own child are firmly stacked against me.

Zoe takes my arm and leads me into the room. On the bed, Kate's cradling the tiniest baby I've ever seen, with crinkly pink skin. Both she and Giles are staring at their child as if they can't believe she's here, that this will be theirs forever. Something inside me lurches painfully and I smile to cover it up.

'Congratulations!' I touch Kate on the arm and give Giles what I hope is a manly pat on the back. 'She's beautiful.'

'Isn't she?' Kate grins over, glowing despite the long, hard labour. 'I mean, I haven't a clue what to do with her now, but . . .'

'You'll figure it out,' Zoe says. 'And you can always ring Auntie Zoe to come round when you need a break!' She takes my arm again. 'Right, we'll give you some family time now. Call me when you're home, okay?' She leans down to kiss Kate on the cheek, puts out a finger to stroke the baby's cheek, then propels me from the room.

Family time. Zoe's words ring in my head. Giles and Kate are a family, a neat little unit taking on the world together. Husband, wife and child, bound together by genes and love. After seeing them, I realise now how much I want that, but I know it's not going to happen. It makes me long for the intimacy of marriage all the more.

'Phew.' Zoe sags against me out in the corridor. 'Now *that* was an experience! Did you see how tiny the baby was? I can't believe how small her fingers were.'

'I know.' I wrap my arms around Zoe, stroking her hair.

'And can you believe Kate's a mother? I mean, for God's sake, they've only been married less than a year! It's all happened so fast.'

I nod. Kate and Giles are the first couple we know really well to have a baby. It's like they've crossed an invisible divide from marriage to parenthood. That same feeling tugs at my stomach and I swallow hard. Has this changed Zoe's mind about having a baby? And what will that mean for us?

It's approaching a year now since we met – two months since I moved in – and things between us have never been better. In fact, I don't think they *could* be better. I worried at first about Zoe feeling too crowded, or a little freaked out about taking such a big step. But she's been as loving and happy as ever, and the two of us have transformed her flat into a home for us both. Every photo we put up and piece of furniture we buy together lends a sense of permanency to our relationship, and I hope that someday in the future – the near future – she'll agree to be my wife. I haven't said anything, since I want it to be a surprise, but I've already started looking at rings. I can't wait to see the look on her face when I propose.

'How are you feeling about everything?' I scan her face, my shoulders tense. 'Has this made you change your mind about having kids?'

'Oh, God, no.' She shudders. 'I've never seen someone's stomach contract like that, and I never want to again. It was like something from *The Exorcist*! And no drugs? Shit. And that baby! So cute, but I'd be afraid to break it.' She looks up at me. 'No, I think we're brilliant, just as we are.'

I drop a kiss on her head, breathing in the smell of her favourite perfume. How have I managed to get so lucky? 'Come on,' I say through a yawn, then I take her hand. 'Let's go home.'

20
EDWARD, SATURDAY, 6 P.M.

I'm in a man's version of heaven or hell; I'm not sure which. Bra after lacy bra hangs from rails, along with matching pants. Negligees float on padded hangers, along with some sort of suspender contraptions that look like they'd be better suited to S&M clubs than my bed. Although Zoe did push my boundaries with furry handcuffs, even she never sported lingerie like this.

My brow furrows and I spin slowly in a circle, waiting for divine inspiration . . . Nothing. Fiona said she wanted pyjamas, but I'm hardly going to buy her something long and flannel, am I? Especially now that I've made up my mind: Zoe and I are through. Our marriage is over, and unless I want my life to be over too, I need to move on. Funny how I used to believe that by simply uttering a vow, you'd stick together for all eternity. I hate to admit it, but my wife was right to be suspicious of 'always' and 'forever'. Maybe I should have listened. My heart throbs with a hollow ache, but it's more of a niggling pain – like an old tooth with a cavity – than the sharp kick-in-the-jaw it used to be. I guess you can get used to anything.

'Monsieur? Can I help you?' A woman with her hair pulled back tightly and wearing bright red lipstick approaches, and I take a step back.

'Er, yes, please.' I can feel my face turning red already. 'I'm looking for some nightwear . . . something sexy,' I finish lamely.

'For yourself?'

Oh, Christ. 'No, no,' I say, my cheeks heating up even more. 'For my . . .' I stop myself from automatically saying 'wife', hastily adding 'girlfriend'. It's bizarre to be using that label again, and I'm not even sure that's what Fiona is. I sigh, remembering how proud I was to call Zoe my wife, how I used it every chance I got. I force my thoughts away from that and try to focus on the countless options the saleswoman is shoving under my nose. *I'm not cut out for this,* I think, longing momentarily for the easy familiarity of my life with Zoe.

But that's gone, I remind myself, and it's been gone for a while. There's nothing familiar or even remotely likable about our life together now.

'I'll take that one,' I say, pointing at a dark-blue . . . is it a top or a nightie? I'm not sure, but it doesn't matter. It's sexy as hell, and Fiona will look incredible in it.

'Size?'

'Um, medium, I guess.' She's not as slender as Zoe is now, thank goodness, and a little bit taller. God, I have to stop thinking about my wife. I force my thoughts back to Fiona's phenomenal arse, and Zoe's face disappears from my mind.

I pay an ungodly amount for such a small scrap of fabric, then head back down the escalator, losing myself once again in the cacophony of the massive mall.

21
ZOE, JULY 2010

It's the first anniversary of the day we met – or met again, I should say – and I'm rushing to get to the South Bank on time. My client meeting overran, my computer played up, and I had to dash back to my desk to get my gift. I hope Edward likes it. It's a watch I know he's been craving; I see him pause and look at it every time we walk past the shop. Buying it almost wiped out my meagre savings, but it will be worth it to see his expression when I give it to him. Of course, as tradition dictates, I've also knitted him a hideous pair of socks, in neon green. This time, though, I won't demand that he wear them. He's done more than enough to prove his love, just by being *him*.

As I hurry down the walkway towards our bench, I can't believe it's been a year already, and that we've been living together almost half that time. The days have gone by, from one to the next, with no arguments or angst. It's an easy, natural flow that makes me think that, at this moment, we truly belong together. Okay, so he could tidy up those bloody toast crumbs each morning, and possibly be more adventurous in bed (I'm working on that!).

But on the big stuff, we're in sync, both happy taking things as they come. You can't really do much else, can you? Not if you want to live an emotionally honest life. Edward hasn't brought up marriage since that moment at Kate's wedding, and to be honest, he was so drunk, I don't think he remembers. I'm sure he'd have mentioned it if it was really important – he's not the type to keep things to himself.

I start smiling as I catch sight of Edward on our bench, his long limbs stretched out in front of him, and I force my legs faster. Even though I just saw him this morning before I left for work, I can't wait to throw my arms around him and give him a huge kiss. I never want us to be one of those couples who stop touching.

'Hey!' I throw myself onto his lap, loving how I fit against his body. We shouldn't, really – he's tall and lean while I'm the definition of short and curvy – but somehow, it works.

'Happy anniversary,' he says, leaning down to kiss me on the lips.

'So what are we doing tonight?' I begged him to let me organise the date, but he insisted, saying he had a special plan. Since I'm usually the one spearheading our outings, it's kind of nice to let him take the wheel. Although he never says anything, I know he sometimes finds the shows I drag him to a little baffling. I smother a tiny giggle as I remember his expression last week, when the all-male cast of a gay musical dropped their trousers in sync.

'Well.' His chest expands as he takes a deep breath. He swings me off his lap in one motion and gets to his feet. Slowly, he lowers himself to one knee, and my mouth drops open. Oh, no. *No!* He's not going to propose, is he? I thought . . . I thought . . . I gulp, forcing back the bile building in my throat.

Whatever I thought, I was wrong.

Fear grabs my gut as he draws out a small velvet box. I want to yell, want to shout at him not to do this, not to ruin what we have, but my mouth is dry. All I can hear is my pulse in my ears as he cracks open the top, revealing a diamond nestled in between two entwined bands. It's an absolutely gorgeous ring, one I'd love to wear, but I don't want to wear the sentiment attached to it. I *can't*.

My stomach churns and for a second, I think I'm going to be sick.

'This past year has been the best in my life,' Edward says, his voice shaking. I'm dying to reach out and steady him, to tell him it's okay, but it's not okay. I don't know where we can go from here, but I have a feeling it won't be good.

'And, well, I don't want it to end.' He clears his throat, and I know I have to do something. I have to stop him before he actually asks me to marry him. I don't want those words to get out, and for me to reject them. Because it's not him I'm rejecting, but I'm not entirely sure he'll see it that way. 'I know we haven't talked about this, but—'

'Edward.' My voice emerges as a croak. 'Come sit beside me.' I grab his hand and try to tug him up, but he resists.

'Just wait a second,' he says, trying to free his hand.

'No, really, sit here.' I give another pull, but still he doesn't budge. God, this will descend into farce soon. 'Please.'

My voice must sound desperate, because he gets to his feet then sinks down beside me, defeat written all over his face. I turn towards him, my heart pounding. 'I love you, you know that. Right?'

He nods, his eyes fixed on mine.

'And we're happy together. Amazingly happy. This year has been one of the best of my life, too.'

Edward nods again slowly. 'Exactly. So don't you want that to continue? Forever?' He pushes a curl behind my ear. 'I want to promise you I'll always be there, through thick and thin. I want to do that, Zoe.' He moves the ring towards me again. 'Don't you?'

His gaze holds mine, and silence stretches between us for what feels like ages. I want to be with him, of course I do. But how can you promise forever? You can't; I learned that the hard way, and I can't bear to think of the two of us being strangled, eventually, by impossible vows. Better to stay as we are, in this perfect place, without expectations or ties that bind. We're together because we choose to be, and nothing else. My mouth opens and shuts as I struggle to find a way to convince him, but he turns away.

'I love you, Zoe.' He gazes at the ground, his voice breaking, and my heart nearly breaks along with it. 'But I want that commitment: commitment to the future, to us. I want to call you my wife, and to be your husband. I thought you wanted that too.'

I reach out and touch his cheek, moving his head towards me again. 'I'll commit to us and to where we are now with all of my heart. But as for marriage . . . I'm sorry, but . . . I can't.' My voice drops to a whisper as sadness presses down. Why? Why did he have to do this?

'Do you think . . .' Edward clears his throat. 'Do you think you'll ever want to get married?'

For the first time, I wish I could read the future. I wish I could tell him that yes, eventually, I'll come around. That one day, I will believe in happy endings, soulmates, and all of that. Maybe someday I will – although it doesn't seem too likely. All I know is that right now, I just can't do it. I can't blithely promise forever when I'm blind about the years ahead. I won't do that to Edward. Or myself.

'I don't know.' I wrench the words from my throat.

'Right.' Edward's face is pale and pinched, and he leans forward to put his head in his hands. I hold my breath, my heart galloping. Is he going to walk away from me? Am I going to let him? *Can* I change my mind? Can he?

'I . . . I need to go,' he says finally, meeting my eyes. 'I love you, but I need to go.' He levers himself off the bench and walks slowly away, as if working against an invisible force. Every bit of me longs to call out, to say come back . . . but for what? We've reached an impasse, a barrier neither one of us can lift for the other to crawl through.

I gaze down at the brightly wrapped box, still containing his watch. Then I get to my feet and walk in the other direction as tears stream from my eyes.

22
ZOE, SATURDAY, 6.45 P.M.

The sun is low in the sky when I leave the darkness of the church and make my way down the stone steps. Despite attempting to turn off my brain, the memory reel inside me spins even faster. If I needed a drink an hour ago, now I'm absolutely gagging for one. I can see by the way the cafés are slowly filling up that it must be dinner time, and I know I should somehow find my way to the hotel – or, at least, to reach Edward.

But I don't want to – not to the Edward I know now. Thinking back to that first night and the early days of our marriage has made the gap between where we were and where we are even wider, and a wave of sadness roils through me. I miss the way we used to be: how we laughed without caring how loud we were; how Edward held my hand, his fingers rubbing my wedding band. Is that couple gone for good, or can we somehow find ourselves again? After all, despite our coldness, we are both here in Paris, albeit not together. Not yet.

I sink down in a wicker chair at a café, deliberately looking away in case a waiter tries to catch my eye. I'll just rest my legs for a bit before moving on . . . God, that sun feels nice. I close my eyes and drink in its warmth, laughter from the two women chatting at the next table sliding across my consciousness. Their friendly Liverpool accent stands out from the smooth French surrounding them, and from the way they're giggling and the easy flow of conversation, I can tell they've been mates for years.

One of the women catches my eye and smiles. 'Sorry we're so loud,' she says, as if expecting me to speak English. 'My friend just told me some excellent news!'

'Congratulations,' I respond automatically, envying their huge smiles and the happiness radiating from them. 'Enjoy your celebrations.'

'If you're alone, why don't you join us? The more the merrier, right?'

I pause for a second, unsure whether I'm really up for a conversation with two strangers. But that's the thing: they're strangers. They know nothing about my past, and I don't need to carry the heavy weight of guilt and sorrow on me as a shield. I used to be a real chatterbox, talking to everyone. I might be way out of practice, but right now I miss just *talking* to people.

'Sure, that would be nice. Thanks.' I stand and squeeze between the tables towards theirs, then hold out my hand. 'I'm Zoe.'

'I'm Lucy,' says the woman, pushing back a heavy black fringe, 'and that's Rachel.'

Rachel, a teensy tiny thing with long blonde hair, shakes my hand.

'So what's the big news?' I ask, eyeing the water on the table with envy. God, I'd kill for a glass right now.

'I'm pregnant!' Rachel squeaks out, her hand sliding down to her tummy.

'Which explains the water.' Lucy rolls her eyes towards the dewy carafe on the table. 'I mean, who drags their best friend to Paris for the weekend, then forces them to drink *water*?'

'Oh, that's wonderful,' I say automatically, wondering why – of all the tourists in Paris – I have to find the two celebrating pregnancy. And I can tell just by looking at Rachel she's going to be one of those annoyingly glowing, fresh-faced pregnant women that make it all seem so easy. I was one of the lucky ones whose morning sickness lasted day and night – for practically nine months.

'It really is.' Rachel nods earnestly. 'We've been trying for a while . . . and been through two rounds of IVF. This was our last shot, and it worked! Thank God. I can't imagine our life without children.' She pauses to sip her water, and for the millionth time, I think how ironic it is that perfectly healthy people who should have no trouble getting pregnant can't, while Edward and I somehow managed. 'Do you have kids?'

A sharp pang goes through me. 'No,' I mumble, staring down at the metal table. 'No, I don't have kids.' Words claw at my throat, words that would let loose everything about Milo. For the first time, instead of keeping everything wrapped in layers of gauze, I want to let him out. I want people to know he existed, that he *lived*. But as I look up to meet the expectant eyes of Rachel, I can't force out the words. Because talking about his life also means talking about his death, and I just can't do that.

'Don't mind her,' Lucy says, obviously picking up on my discomfort. 'She's obsessed with all things baby at the moment and wants to convert everyone. She's going to have a tough go with me.'

I can't help smiling, thinking how much Lucy and Rachel are like Kate and me – or how we were, anyway. Kate sang hymns about the wonder of babies, but her words were slightly contradicted by the spit-up on her clothes, the bags under her eyes and the vacant expression on her face . . . at least for the first few months. I watched in horror as her innocent babe transformed into a red-faced, screaming demon for hours on end each night, wondering who in their right mind would willing *try* for a baby.

I miss Kate and her no-nonsense, tell-it-like-it-is (or how *she* thinks it is) attitude. From marriage to children to moving to the suburbs, she's always been right beside me. But she can't follow me to where I am now, despite her attempts. A memory floats into my head of one of the few conversations we had, about six months after Milo's death. I'd managed to drag myself from the depths of my bed and over to her house, hoping that would convince her to stop calling every God-given hour – not that I answered. I sat carefully on the sofa, avoiding the menagerie of soft toys as if they were ticking bombs, and drifted away as she told me it would all be okay, that I'd come to terms with a 'new normal'.

I don't need a 'new normal'! I wanted to shriek. *I need my son back!* Instead, I nodded mutely, burrowing even deeper inside myself as I watched Kate's daughter streak across the room and into her mother's arms.

And that was the last time we spoke – or rather *Kate* spoke. She tried and tried to reach me, continuing to knock on my door and ring day after day. But how could I bear to be with someone who still had a family, who could breathe in the sweet scent of their child every second? Watching would be pure torture.

Maybe I could have told her that, tried to make her understand, instead of shutting her out. Maybe if I really had talked to her, we'd still be friends. Guilt niggles now that I never once returned her many messages. Maybe there were times she needed *my* support. Once upon a time, I knew everything about her life – and vice versa. But once upon a time, we had no idea life could be so cruel.

'You don't want children?' I ask Lucy, realising the silence has stretched a bit too long and they're waiting for me to say something.

Lucy shakes her head so hard her fringe flies back and forth. 'Oh, God, no. I don't want to be responsible for anything other than myself. And I like my freedom way too much. I don't want to be tied down, you know?'

I nod. I do know, because I felt exactly the same way, before I realised that being tied down – having someone to depend on, and who depends on you – isn't necessarily a bad thing. Scary, yes, but strangely comforting. 'You know, you get used to it. It's a huge lifestyle change, but you have this new little person in your life, and even though it's hard, it makes the trade-off seem . . . not easy, but worthwhile.' I smile, remembering what a big adjustment it was. I can't even remember the last time Edward and I had a big night out. I strain my mind, sieving through the last several years. Maybe . . . maybe before Milo was born?

After he came, we always talked about getting a babysitter, but we never did. I might have followed through, but Edward wasn't keen to entrust him with anyone for long, even my mum. If you'd have said to me, back before I got pregnant, that I wouldn't go out with my husband for almost two years, I'd have deemed you crazy – that there was no way a baby would change my life that much. But it does. It changes everything.

Suddenly I realise the two women are staring at me in confusion.

'Wait, I thought you said you didn't have kids?'

Oh God. I jerk to my feet so quickly the table wobbles, the water sloshing dangerously in the glasses. I can't do this. I can't go there. Without even saying goodbye, I rush off the crowded terrace and back onto the street, feeling the baffled gaze of the two women following me as I go.

I sink down on a bench, trying to avoid the dots of pigeon poo as I catch my breath. That conversation with those two strangers was the first time I've spoken about Milo since his death, even in such general terms. I know that's hard to believe, but I couldn't. *I couldn't.* It was as if just opening my mouth and bringing out the words would let the pain in – the pain I've been trying so hard, so unsuccessfully, to avoid.

But I haven't self-combusted. I'm here. I've opened up a tiny little piece of me and I'm still breathing.

Barely.

23
ZOE, AUGUST 2010

Edward's been gone a month now, and I still can't believe we're not together. One second we're celebrating our anniversary, the next . . . we've split. Just goes to show I was right about forever: you never know what might happen the next week, the next day, the next second. Being right is providing little comfort, though.

What really kills me is that our break-up isn't because we don't love each other, because someone cheated, or something that went wrong between us. If possible, things had been getting even better with time. No, our split is all down to the fact that I won't swear to something that's impossible to fulfil, and Edward can't do without it.

So, that's it. He moved his things out one day when I was at work. Pain rushes at me as I remember turning my key and opening the door, revealing empty spaces on the wall where his posters had hung, and empty drawers in the bedroom that had cradled his clothing. No matter that I'd hated his IKEA-style posters – black and white trees pretending to be arty – or that his super-neat way of rolling socks was a constant source of bemusement. The flat felt hollowed out, and for that first evening, all I could do was sit on the sofa and stare at the space. I used to love my own place, but now, I'd give anything to hear the whine of Radio Four in the background or the laughter from *The Big Bang Theory*.

So many times I picked up my mobile to ring him, but so many times, I put it down again. What could I say?

Kate thinks I'm crazy, of course. Over a bottle of wine (for me – she's still breastfeeding) in a corner of a noisy Tex-Mex restaurant on the South Bank, she asks me how the hell I could let someone like him go – and lose a year of my life in prime conceiving years – just because I won't commit.

'But I *will* commit,' I say, swilling the wine around my mouth. 'That's the thing. I'll commit with everything I have right now. I just . . .' I set the glass on the table. 'How did you know for sure that you could be with Giles for the rest of your life?'

'I didn't.' She shakes her head. 'Hell, right now, I'd happily divorce him.'

My head snaps up at Kate's answer. That definitely wasn't what I expected from my uber-romantic friend. 'What? Is everything okay?'

She shrugs. 'Yeah, I guess. Having Olivia . . . well, it's been hard. A screaming baby doesn't exactly do wonders for a relationship, and then the constant *tiredness* . . . Add to that the bickering over who did what and who got less sleep, and the last thing you want to do is even see each other's faces at the end of the day. Forget date night. I just want to be *alone*.'

Wow. I can't imagine feeling that way about Edward, although right now, I wish I did. It'd certainly make things easier.

'Anyway.' Kate gulps her water, eyeing my wine like she's been in the Sahara for years. 'I'm exaggerating, of course. But the thing is, no relationship is always going to be one hundred per cent happy all of the time. Things will change and develop. But you have to believe in the other person, and that your love is strong enough to get you through all of that. It's kind of like taking a leap of faith.'

Hmm. *A leap of faith.* That's exactly what it's like, and after crash-landing with Ollie, I couldn't get out on the diving board again. But now that Edward's gone, I wonder . . . I wonder if I made a mistake. After all, I'm not the same person who said yes to Ollie. I'm different, and Edward's different. Maybe it is time to put myself out there again. To have a little faith, like Kate said.

'Oh my God.' Kate lowers her head.

'What? Have your boobs sprung a leak again?' She's always going on about needing to pump before they erupt in a milk water-fall. Ah, the joys of motherhood.

'Edward's over there.' She nods in the direction, her voice dropping to a whisper.

Oh Lord. A mix of nerves, angst and excitement go through me, and my insides feel all shivery. I knew there was a reason we had to come to the South Bank tonight. Of all places . . . I don't know what I'm going to say to him, but I know I can't leave this place without talking.

'Zoe—' Kate lays a hand on my arm, but I'm already on my feet and pushing back my chair.

Fuck. My feet freeze and my blood turns leaden. He's not alone. He's with a slender redhead, a delicate little thing whose model-like proportions make me seem like an Oompa Loompa. It's obvious by the way they're talking that they're on a date. He's grinning in a cheeky way that's so familiar, resting his hand on top of hers.

Blood starts moving, racing around my veins so fast I can almost feel it, see it in the white of my eyes. Didn't take him much time to move on, did it? So much for forever. If I was really the one he wanted to spend his life with, surely it'd take him longer? God, I haven't even been able to *think* about dating anyone else.

Well, screw him.

'Zoe? You okay?' Kate's looking up at me with a concerned expression.

'Fine.' I spit out the word through gritted teeth. I will be fine, anyway. Before I can even think about what I'm doing, I head to the raucous section of the restaurant that's part bar, part salsa dance floor. I push my way through the gyrating bodies and over to a muscly man in a tight black T-shirt.

'Hi,' I say, forcing a smile and swivelling my hips in time to the music. The loud beat and trumpets fill my ears, and I try to let it replace the hurt and anger in my heart.

'Hey, baby.' The man puts an arm around my waist and pulls me against him, and I breathe in the scent of spice and sweat, so unlike Edward's fresh, clean smell. Our bodies move together in time to the music, and when the man lowers his lips to kiss me, I lean into him even more. Out of the corner of my eye, I see Edward's stricken face as he leads his date past the dance floor and out the door, and I feel something inside me break. That's it. That's the end of us.

Well, it was anyway, right?

24
EDWARD, SATURDAY, 7 P.M.

I push through the Saturday night shoppers, feeling like my head has a big neon sign floating above it, pointing to the carrier bag and telling everyone I've bought lingerie for someone besides my wife. I shove the bag behind me, feeling idiotic but unable to stop myself. In an odd way, this reminds me of the time Zoe rejected my proposal and I started dating . . . what was her name? Eva. She was beautiful and smart, the same age as me, and according to my friend who'd fixed us up, 'gagging to get married'. I wanted to move on so much that I rushed into dating someone else, even though I was nowhere near ready.

I sigh, remembering that month away from Zoe and how betrayed I felt, how broken. I'd truly believed she'd marry me – that she'd be my wife, and we'd spend our future together. I walked miles those few weeks, trying to accept that it wasn't going to happen. That if Zoe didn't want to get married, then she wasn't the one for me. All those steps, and I still couldn't come to terms with it. Watching her grope a random bloke was the last straw.

But this is completely different, I tell myself, spritzing on cologne at the perfume counter. For a start, I'm several years older, and my naive notion of forever has been broken into a million jagged pieces that'll never fit together again. Spend forever with Zoe? The thought makes me shudder. I'd rather spend forever in an igloo – at least it'd be warmer.

My mobile rings, and I slide it from my pocket. It's Fiona. God, I can't wait for her to come.

'Hi, there,' I say when I answer. 'What's the latest?'

She sighs. 'It's looks like we'll be stuck here for a few hours yet. They're saying now we can expect to arrive after midnight. So you'd better be awake!'

'Oh, I'll be awake, don't you worry.' My flirtatious tone surprises me – it's been a while since I've used it. I rarely sleep more than a few hours at night anyway. I twist and turn, flipping and thumping the pillow, but no matter how hard I try, I can't get comfortable. It didn't take long before Zoe suggested I sleep in the guest room, and I was more than happy to oblige. Lying so close beside my silent wife each night made the distance between us seem even further.

Fiona hangs up, and I gaze at the clothes arranged like ornaments on glistening hangers. Might as well get kitted out while I'm here. There are still a few hours to kill, and if I keep busy, keep moving, I won't have time to look back.

25
ZOE, SEPTEMBER 2010

Ever since that night at the restaurant, I've avoided the South Bank like the plague. I don't want to see Edward again – it's too much, especially if he's with another woman. My heart constricts painfully at the memory of him chatting so easily with his date, of that smile he used to give me. When I managed to unpeel myself from the man on the dance floor, Edward was gone. I staggered back to the table, barely able to breathe. What the hell just happened?

I sank into my chair, and Kate reached across to grip my hand. She didn't say anything – she'd said it all anyway; what else was there to say? – but poured me more wine, then handed me a tissue as the tears streaked down my cheeks.

That night was a definite low, and for the past few weeks, I've either been holed up at work or sitting at home, knitting like a crazy thing to keep my hands and mind busy. There's a huge pile of socks sitting on the side table, socks I know I'll never wear but just have to keep making. I guess I'll donate them to charity or something. Kate's been trying to get me out to a pub, over for supper, *anything*, but I always turn her down.

The fact that I feel like absolute shit makes it easy to reject anything to do with the outside world, too. People sometimes say if your heart is hurting, your health suffers too. Well, that's definitely the case here. My stomach churns at just the thought of food, I wake up with blinding headaches, and all I want to do is sleep. I'd see a doctor if I wasn't so obviously depressed.

I'm about to stitch together yet another pair of socks when the buzzer sounds. My heart jumps that it's Edward – in my mind, I've replayed the scenario where he comes to say forever doesn't matter and he just wants to be with me so much, it's practically worn out. But when I hear Kate's voice, I let out a laugh and shake my head. Of course Edward won't come round. Why would he, after my little display at the restaurant?

I buzz her up, wondering why she's here. I certainly haven't invited her.

'Christ, you look like shit.' She hugs me when I open the door, then pushes her way into the flat. 'Has a yarn bomb exploded in here?' she asks, surveying the room. 'Is this what you've been doing every night – sitting here in front of the telly making socks? What are you, seventy years old?'

'Hello to you too, dear friend.' My tone is snarky, but I can't help smiling. She's right: it does look like a yarn bomb exploded.

'Sit down and let me get you a cup of tea or something.' She pushes me gently onto the sofa. 'You're practically skin and bones! Haven't you been eating?'

I shake my head. 'Not much. My stomach's been acting up a bit. I'm just not hungry.'

'I think that's the first time I've ever heard you say that!' Kate laughs, then leans in to study me. 'You do look kind of pale.'

'Yeah. I'm just tired all the time, and I keep getting these awful headaches . . .' Yesterday's delightful migraine felt like someone jabbing my temples with a pointy instrument of pain.

'How long has this been going on for?' Kate calls from the kitchen, where I can hear the kettle whistling as it boils. It's a comforting noise, and I can't help closing my eyes and letting myself drift off a bit. God, I am so tired.

'Zoe!'

I jerk upright at Kate's voice. Did I actually just fall asleep? I yawn and rub my eyes. 'Sorry, what?'

Kate hands me a cup of tea, then moves a ball of yarn off the sofa to sink down beside me. 'I said, how long has this been going on for?'

'Um . . .' I cast my mind back over the past few weeks. It all feels like a blur, but I don't think I've eaten properly since seeing Edward that night. 'I guess about a month. It's just depression, I'm sure.'

'Well, it could be, but usually you eat when you're upset, not the reverse.'

'True.' I struggle to sit upright so I don't fall asleep again, remembering the countless times I'd gorge on chocolate cakes from Iceland or shovel in crisp after crisp, emptying the whole bag in one sitting.

'Nausea, headaches, fatigue . . .' Kate pauses. 'Do you think it could be something else?'

'The flu?' I shake my head. 'Not for this long.'

She stretches out her legs. 'When's the last time you had a period?'

I shrug, my mind working. Being with Edward meant I never had to contemplate an accidental pregnancy, to constantly monitor my periods and my body the same way I had with other boyfriends. Worry jangles inside as I realise I haven't had a period for . . . two months, maybe?

Shit!

'You don't think I'm pregnant, do you?' Even saying the words out loud makes me want to gag. 'It's not possible! You know I haven't shagged anyone since Edward, and it's not like he knocked me up.'

'Is there any possibility – even the slightest – his tackle could be functional after all?'

'His *tackle*?' I shake my head. 'I don't think so, no. I'm sure he would have told me if there was the slightest chance. I know he really wants kids, and he was afraid I'd take off when he told me he couldn't have them. Surely if there was a possibility he'd have let me know.'

'Well, maybe he doesn't know himself. I mean, stranger things have happened. There was a couple in our antenatal group who were told they'd never have children. And then – hey presto! – she was preggers.'

Horror courses through me. 'Oh my God.' Any remaining colour drains from my face.

Kate lays a hand on my arm. 'I don't want to scare you, but I do think you should take a test, just to be sure. If you're not pregnant, then you can put it out of your mind . . . and see a doctor, because something's not right.'

I feel sick just at the thought of taking a test. Like I said to Edward way back when, I'm not against the idea of children, but I'm nowhere near ready. And certainly not now, without a man even in the picture!

Kate's shoving on her shoes. 'I'll run out and grab one. You sit tight here.' The door slams, and I hear her feet thumping down the stairs to street level.

I grab my needles and start casting like crazy, as if the faster I knit, the faster I can run away from the situation. The needles move frantically back and forth, back and forth, as my brain whirs. I can't be a mother – a single mother. I can't! I can barely take care of myself, let alone a helpless newborn. What would I do about work? Would I have to move back to my parents, do the walk of shame as an unwed mother? I know I'm thirty-one years old, an independent woman, and all that, but where my parents live they might as well be stuck in the nineteen-fifties.

And . . . what about my *life*? My future?

The needles whir faster. *Calm down, calm down.* I take deep breaths. I might not even be pregnant. You can miss a period for any reason, and I've certainly been stressed and off-kilter lately. Headaches, tiredness . . . that could be anything.

'I got the test.' Kate slams back in with a Boots carrier bag and lobs the box at me. I'm tempted to move aside and let it fall on the floor instead of catching it. 'Here. Do it now, so you can get it over with.'

My friend knows me well. Left to my own devices, I'd probably stare at it for hours, convincing myself I don't need to do the test, that everything is all right, and pregnancy is a laughable concept when it comes to my body. But I know I need to bite the bullet.

I haul myself up, clutching the box in one hand, and head for the loo. The pressure on my bladder means I need to pee again anyway, and my heart starts beating fast as I realise I've had to pee a lot lately.

Just do this and get it over with, I tell myself, opening up the box, then the foil, then sliding off the cap. I lower myself onto the toilet and try my best to pee onto the stick, almost hoping I'm missing my target and putting off the result.

I replace the cap, set the test on the window ledge, then wash my hands. Seconds tick by and I can't bear to look. As if in a trance, my feet carry me back out to where Kate is sitting on the sofa.

'And?' she asks, her head snapping up as soon as she hears me enter.

I shake my head. 'I don't know. It's in there.' I jerk a thumb towards the loo door as if it's contaminated.

'Do you want me to go see?'

I nod. 'Please.' I don't know why, but if the news comes from Kate, it will almost feel cushioned . . . filtered through another reality. If the result is positive, of course. While my brain knows it could be negative, my body is telling me a different story.

Kate nods, then strides purposefully into the bathroom. There's nothing but silence – no sharp intake of breath, no 'hurrah!' of relief – and my fingers furiously work a sock as I hear her footsteps come back into the lounge.

She sits down on the sofa beside me, and I tilt my head slowly to meet hers. I can't make out her expression.

'Well?' I ask finally, when I can't bear it any longer.

She takes my hand, and I know, even before she tells me, what the answer is.

'I'm pregnant,' I say, and she squeezes my fingers. 'I'm going to *kill* Edward.'

26
ZOE, SATURDAY, 7.15 P.M.

My feet burn from walking so much. Liquid seeps from broken blisters, where my shoes have rubbed them raw. I've only been in Paris a few hours, but it seems like days. I feel . . . I pause, trying to get a grasp on my emotions, and a muttered French curse drifts over my head as the person behind me steps past. I don't know how I feel, exactly, other than I don't feel like me. At least, not the 'me' who got off the train this morning.

Although the evenings are lengthening with summer approaching, I know it's only an hour or so until darkness falls. I should be panicking at the possibility of spending the night on the Paris streets alone, but I'm not. Not yet, anyway. I'm suspended between the past and present, not caught in either, and still unable to envision the future.

I felt this way when I was pregnant with Milo, too: incapable of believing I was actually going through with it, knowing my past was behind me now that I was a mum-to-be, yet the future as a mother seemed completely unfathomable. That first pregnancy is a no-man's land, where you're neither a person in your own right any more or a mother yet. I wish now I'd enjoyed it more, instead of wishing it away – anxious to finally meet the baby growing inside of me.

I used to laugh when people told me to enjoy the newborn days, the toddlerhood, because 'they grow up so fast'. Some days – when Milo had colic or screamed like a banshee because he hated his buggy – time seemed to stretch for hours.

But in the end, those people are right. It *does* go fast. And when you only have that child for two years, it seems like the blink of an eye. His little face – the face that was fading slightly, like a photo greying over time – bursts into technicolour. I close my eyes, trying to imprint the sharpness of the image on my brain before I lose it again. For just a second, it feels like he's right there in front of me. I can almost smell the mix of baby wipes, yeasty bread and earth his body gave off, and the rush of love overwhelms me. Memories whoosh through my mind, from his red-faced newborn days all the way through to his mischievous expression when he grabbed the forbidden TV remote.

It's hard for me to think now that I almost didn't have him. That I almost missed out on . . . well, to call it *love* feels trite. It's more than simple love. It's a fierce, visceral emotion that resonates from every cell, the feeling that you'd do anything for this tiny being you brought into the world.

Because, I realise, no matter what else happened – how my fairy tale fell apart – I wouldn't give up having that love for anything. For the first time since Milo's death, I want to hang on tightly to the memories instead of blanking them out, to remember every minuscule detail of his life. I can take solace in that, I discover. It will never wipe away the blame, but right now, the comfort outweighs the pain.

27
EDWARD, SEPTEMBER 2010

'Just a second,' I call over my shoulder to Eva as my mobile starts ringing. We're on our way out to dinner with her friends who, thankfully, I've clicked with. I really hit the jackpot with her. All right, so we don't have that spark I had with Zoe – the all-encompassing, all-in emotion. I'm more than okay with that, though. I like how safe this feels, the slow pace it's moving along at and the fact that, this time, I'm sure where it's going.

It's pedestrian rather than a car race, and that's just what I need right now.

My brow furrows when I spot the caller's name on my phone, and I move into the bedroom.

'Kate?' I close the door softly. My head is telling me I should have let the phone ring out, to keep everything in the past at bay. Too late now.

'Oh, thank God you answered.' Her voice sounds strained and frantic.

'Is everything all right?' A thought pings through my mind and fear grips my heart. 'Is Zoe okay?'

'In a manner of speaking.' Kate's tone is grim, and my heart drops. We may not be together any more, but I can't bear to think of anything happening to her. 'Look, I don't even know if I should be calling you. Giles thinks I should just leave it alone. But . . .'

'But what?' My voice rises a notch, and I clear my throat.

'Zoe's pregnant.'

Kate's words hit me like a bullet between the eyes. Zoe? *Pregnant?* Jealousy rolls over me with such intensity I need to sit down. It's obviously not my baby. So why the hell is Kate ringing to tell me this? Some kind of post-break-up torture?

'Thanks for the update,' I say, my voice cold. 'But I don't need to know what's happening in Zoe's life.'

'You do, Edward.' Kate pauses, and I'm very tempted to hang up the phone. To break the connection, to stop the pain. 'The baby is yours.'

I shake my head so hard my neck cracks. Christ, didn't Zoe tell Kate I can't have kids? Now I have to explain that, too? 'It's not. I can't have children, so whatever's going on . . .' I swallow. 'Just wish Zoe well. Bye, Kate.'

'Wait!' Kate's voice emerges like a squawk. 'I know you can't get someone pregnant. But Zoe hasn't been with anyone else, so . . .'

'Not even that bloke at the restaurant?' I can't help asking.

Kate snorts. 'All that was just for your benefit. As soon as you left, Zoe ditched the guy.'

Silence stretches between us as her words swirl around my mind. *Could* I get someone pregnant? All my life, I've taken that GP's words at face value – that fathering a child would be next to impossible. My jaw tightens. Could he have been wrong? Did I somehow misunderstand? Much of that time is a blur of hot sweats and pounding head – not to mention the pain, horror and embarrassment of swollen testicles as a complication of my illness.

'Look, I know this is a shock,' Kate's voice breaks into my thoughts, 'but I had to tell you now. Zoe's, well . . . she's not sure what to do.'

'She might not have it?' My voice comes out high and thready, and I clear my throat again.

'She's confused, I think.' Kate pauses. 'But listen, I know you two still love each other. Or, at least, I know she still loves you. I've never seen her like this, in such a state after you two broke up – not even with her last fiancé.'

Last fiancé? What the hell? After everything she told me – after breaking up because of it – Zoe was engaged to someone else?

'All that business about getting married . . . well, now there's something else involved. A baby. *Your* baby. I really think you two need to talk. Soon, before she does anything.'

I hear a child wail in the background, and Kate sighs. 'I'd better go. Zoe's going to murder me when she finds out I've told you, but I couldn't let her do this on her own. Whatever happens, whatever you decide, I really think you need to do it together.'

'Thanks, Kate.' I hang up and stand, rubbing my eyes. My limbs are heavy, weighed down by layer after layer of information I can't digest. *Zoe was engaged before? She's pregnant, and it's my baby? I might be able to have children after all?* It's so unbelievable, it feels like I've stepped into another reality.

'Edward! Come on, we're going to be late!' Eva's bell-like tone rings through my head, and I take a deep breath as astonishment peppered with joy sweeps through me. I need time to think about all this, to somehow try to wrap my brain around it all. I roll my head in a circle, trying to ease the tension in my shoulders as thoughts race through my brain. I want forever, yes. That will never change. But Kate's right: there's someone else involved now. And if having a child isn't the ultimate bond, then I don't know what is. Besides . . . if Zoe committed to someone once, maybe she will again. If it's just a negative experience that put her off, perhaps that can change. A flicker of hope leaps up inside. Perhaps Zoe and I *could* work after all. An image of the two of us, smiling down at our pink newborn the same way Kate and Giles did flashes into my mind, and desire almost knocks me over.

Think practically, I tell myself, willing my pulse to slow down. I can't just barge into Zoe's, even if I wanted to. I need to find out if it's possible that I could get someone pregnant. I don't doubt Kate's good intentions, but she's tied up with her own child half the time, and I know she and Zoe aren't as close as they used to be. I couldn't bear it if I turned up to see Zoe, ready to claim my family future, only to learn it isn't mine.

I'll see my GP first thing tomorrow morning, and then I can figure out what to do.

28
ZOE, SATURDAY, 7.30 P.M.

The sky is turning pink now, with thin, bluey-purple clouds forming floating crosses. I watch them come together then drift apart, thinking it's been a while since I gazed up at the heavens. By this point in the evening, I'm usually crawling under the duvet. It's a very early bedtime – so different from the days when I'd stay up until midnight, knitting, reading or just lolling about on the sofa – but I want the day to be done. I'm not sure why, since the next one only brings more of the same. But I love sinking into the darkness of sleep, when everything is blotted out . . . except for when the nightmares kick in.

For the first few months after Milo's accident, sleep was my saviour. I could doze anywhere: at the table, on the floor, even while Edward was talking to me. But then— I shake my head, unable to think of that day. Then, I stopped sleeping, fighting with the pillows and blankets as if they were to blame for what happened, not me.

I fled to the GP, desperate for pills to blot the demons from my mind, and they worked for a while. But once my doctor refused to renew my prescription, saying they were only a temporary measure, the dreams started up. Piercing screams. The grind of metal, and a slap-bang as Milo hit the ground – and blood. Crimson blood, streaming like a river. Streaming from my baby's head, from my womb. In reality, none of that happened. In reality, there was just . . . silence. Silence, and a slow trickle of red signifying everything's over. Finished, before it even started.

Then I jerk awake in bed, my curls plastered to my face, legs slippery with sweat, and reach out for Edward before remembering that he's not there. He's never there, not any more. I'd hardly got out the words asking him to sleep in the spare room when he'd practically raced over there, and he's been there ever since.

My parents think I should talk to someone. Mum even rang up a grief counsellor and made an appointment. Back in the beginning, when I was desperate for anything to make it better, I went along. I tried, but I couldn't talk. I ended up sitting for almost an hour in silence, focusing on the inane painting of a deserted beach above the counsellor's head. Forget counsellors; I can't even talk to my husband, let alone a stranger.

'Madame?' A voice pierces my thoughts, and I realise I'm standing stock-still in the middle of a doorway. A man is standing there, keys in hand, obviously eager for me to move on so he can close up shop. 'Would you like to come in?' He motions inside, where I can see various toys dotting the shelves, gleaming under bright lights.

'Oh no, that's okay,' I mumble, but my eyes have locked on something, a soft toy from my past – from my son's past. It's a brightly coloured butterfly, complete with crinkly wings covered in mirrors and buttons that squeak. Kate gave it to us after Milo's birth, and in a feat of stunning originality, we christened it Bob. Milo was a solemn, watchful baby, but Bob never failed to make him laugh, even at his grumpiest. I can't help smiling as I picture Edward and me, in our tiny cramped lounge, camped out on the floor. I'd hold Milo on my lap – a delicious lump of warm, soft baby weight – and Edward would swoop Bob into us, squeaking and crinkling. Milo would wiggle and squeal, and Edward and I giggled too. Delighted at our creation, delighted at *life*. Full up with laughter and love.

'Please, come inside. Have a look.' The man beckons me into the shop again, but I shake my head. I've seen everything I need to.

'No, thanks. I need to get going.' I shoot him a brief smile, then force my legs forward. For the first time since arriving in Paris, I feel like I *do* need to get going. These past few hours of talking again, of feeling again, have unlocked a bit of me . . . the bit that used to be a mother. I actually *want* to talk to Edward, my son's father. Out of everyone, of all the people who surrounded us after Milo left, he is the only one who really *knew* Milo – knew every inch of him. He's the only one who's a part of him.

He's the only one who really knows what losing our child feels like.

29
EDWARD, SEPTEMBER 2010

My leg jiggles as I sit on the cracked plastic chair in the doctor's office. It feels like my future is in his hands – like he can either give me everything I ever wanted, or condemn me to my present.

'I don't have access to your history, so it's impossible to give you an answer now,' the doctor says, tapping away on his computer. 'But infertility due to complications with mumps is quite rare. A low sperm count, maybe. Were both testicles swollen?'

I nod.

'And did your GP refer you for any additional tests?'

I bite my lip, trying to remember. All I can recall from that time is mortification from having to show so many people my balls, along with discussions of my 'sperm count' and 'fertility'. After I recovered, I wanted nothing more to do with doctors. I vaguely recall Mum trying to force me back for a follow-up, which I refused. Eventually she dropped it, and I just carried on through life with the knowledge stuck in my brain I couldn't have kids. It was never an issue, actually, since Zoe was the first woman I ever considered marrying.

'He might have done. I'm not sure,' I say now.

'Well, you'll need to have a few tests before we can say either way. I'll refer you to the nearest fertility clinic.' He clacks away on the computer. 'The earliest availability is the end of October, the sixteenth. Is that okay?'

'Is there anything before that?' I don't want to leave any room for Zoe to end her pregnancy before I find out for sure – if that's what she's thinking about doing.

The doctor shakes his head. 'No, sorry. I'll put you in for that date then, shall I? You'll receive a letter in the post with all the details.' He shoots a none-too-subtle look at the clock on the wall above my head.

'Okay, great,' I mumble, getting to my feet. Things are only slightly clearer now than yesterday. My head is swimming and I still don't know what to do. I like things in black and white, with no margin for uncertainty. You either commit, or you don't. It's my child, or it's not. Is Kate right, and Zoe hasn't been with anyone else? Will she want to be with me and have our baby – if indeed it is that?

'Are you all right?' The doctor's voice is tinged with impatience. He's clearly keen to get me out of his office and move on to the next patient.

'Fine, fine. Thanks.' I walk from the room and close the door behind me. *I want to be there for you through thick and thin.* The words from my aborted proposal come to mind, and I shake my head. Did I really mean that? If so, perhaps now is the time to prove it – marriage or not.

I'm not ready to give up on us, I realise now. If Kate is right and that is our baby, I'm ready to trust in our love and our future.

I need to see Zoe.

30

ZOE, SEPTEMBER 2010

It was surprisingly easy to make an appointment at the clinic. A quick call, a chat with a counsellor who makes sure, I guess, that you know what you're doing, then a text from an anonymous number with your appointment date: 20 September. I don't know what I'm doing; of course I don't. I change my mind a hundred times each day. But in a way, it's comforting to have something firm, an end date for all this torment.

I don't know where the past week has gone, but somehow it's the night before the procedure. I hate to think of it as an abortion, with all the ugly connotations that brings up: protestors thrusting plastic foetuses in women's faces as they dodge the throng towards a faceless clinic; stabbing pain and scraping; bright-red blood.

My hand slides down to my stomach, which is still as soft and curved as ever. It's hard to believe there's a baby inside there, curled up in the cushiony sponge of my uterus, frantically dividing in a bid to become human. Because it's not a person yet, right? It's just a group of cells.

At least that's what I keep telling myself. And while the thought of being a single mother makes me want to run away screaming and tearing out my hair, I also feel like these cells, which somehow ended up in me, deserve a chance: to multiply, and become a baby, a person, after all. Despite my fears and downright horror, I can't help picturing this tiny baby's hand wrapped around my finger as I cradle it on my chest.

But that's just one snapshot, I remind myself, mentally turning the album pages of dirty nappies, piercing screams and relentless feedings. Am I up for that – alone?

Not a chance.

This time tomorrow, the whole saga will be over. I lean back on the sofa, trying to analyse how that makes me feel. Relieved, yes, but also . . . sad, and a little empty, I guess because having this thing inside me is a physical connection to Edward, a tenuous link to what we had – what I wish we still had. After tomorrow, that will be gone.

Kate has been at me every day to talk to him. She thinks I need to tell Edward, seeing as how it's his baby too. And, she added, to at least let him know he *can* have kids. I know she's right, and I will . . . eventually. Right now, I'm too angry. Angry at him, even if it's not really his fault. Angry that this happened to me; angry he didn't *know* it could happen. I need someone to blame: someone to make sense of it all, even though underneath, I still love him. I love him as much as I did the day he proposed.

But love isn't enough, is it? Our future isn't together. He made that pretty clear by moving on so quickly – probably to the woman who'll give him the wedding he's craving, plus the 2.4 children. And even if Edward does support this baby, ultimately, it's still my responsibility. I'm still its mother. This won't be our baby; it'll be my baby. And I'm just not ready to take that on.

The buzzer rings, and I haul myself off the sofa, nausea roiling over me. That's one thing I won't miss. Kate promised to come over tonight and keep me company, and for once in her life, she's early.

I punch the intercom to let her in, then plod back over to the sofa and close my eyes. God, I feel like I've run a marathon today.

'There's pizza in the fridge if you're hungry,' I say, when I hear the door swing open.

'I'm not hungry.'

My lids fly open at Edward's voice. *What the—?* I swing around and meet his steady gaze, drinking in his familiar face. There are bags under his eyes and he looks like he hasn't shaved in days. He's wearing the old T-shirt with a little hole under his armpit, and I close my eyes against the tide of memories washing over me.

'What are you doing here?' I press down on the curls spiralling up from my head, then swipe a hand across my face. He could have told me he was coming so I could try to transform myself from swamp creature to human!

Edward sits down beside me, and the familiar scent of mint and vanilla wafts over. 'Kate told me you're pregnant.'

My mouth drops open. *What?* Oh my God, I'm going to strangle her. My mind whirls and I try to come up with something to say, but I can't.

'Is it . . .' He takes a shuddery breath. 'Is it mine?' His eyes laser through me, and time stops. I can feel the heat from his leg and I move away. If I touch him, I'll dissolve. I want him so much; every cell in me is dying to reach over and stroke his face, poke my little finger through that hole in his T-shirt like I used to. It would be so easy to say yes – to have someone else make this decision with me, to not feel so alone, so *responsible*. To have him back in my life again, even if just for the next few days, even if it's not as my boyfriend.

But I can't. What's the point? I've made my decision not to have his baby. I'm not going to complicate things – or even *hurt* him – by telling him about something that, by this time tomorrow, won't even exist. Our lives will continue on their separate tracks. That's the path we've started down, and the one we need to stay on.

'No.' The word emerges as a whisper, and I clear my throat. 'No, it's not yours.' I manage to get out the sentence without my voice breaking, but not my heart. Pieces jab at my ribs, my gut, like sharp glass.

He flinches like I've slapped him, then gets to his feet, his movements jerky. 'Oh. All the best, then,' he says stiffly, then shuts the door behind him.

Silence falls and I double over on the sofa, sobs shaking my body. A headache pounds at my skull, and bile inside starts rising.

What the *hell* am I doing?

31
EDWARD, SATURDAY, 7.30 P.M.

I touch this shirt and that as I wander through the men's department, not really sure what I'm looking for. I want something new, something untainted by my previous life. By the grief, the heaviness that wraps itself around your neck like a leaden tie, by the memories like hand grenades, chucked at you when you least expect it.

That's why I shop so much lately. The old me would have snorted incredulously at the time I've spent in trendy stores, buying clothes I normally wouldn't have been caught dead in: jeans I can barely get my foot through and paisley-printed shirts. With my hair slicked up with product foisted on me by my stylist (I even defected from my regular barber) sometimes I barely recognise myself in the mirror. And that's exactly what I want.

Fiona seems to like my makeover. When I first turned up at work with my new jeans and crisp shirt, she told me she'd been dying to get me into some decent threads for years – after I caught her ogling my arse. It was nice to have someone actually notice me after feeling invisible at home for so long. I know that sounds egotistical, but there it is.

A wave of fatigue sweeps over me, and I look for somewhere to sit down – just for a second. As I scan the space in front of me, I spot a small kiosk with a sink and a chair, offering shaves and trims. I run a hand over my chin, feeling the scrape of tiny bristles and the wiry brush of my goatee. It's been a long day, and in the rush of hustling to the train this morning, I didn't shave. I could really do with one if I don't want to scratch Fiona's face to hell. Plus, a good sit-down for ten minutes or so will revive me for the night ahead.

I push between the rails and inside the small glass area, some-how managing to explain to the man what I want. I've just finished my pathetic attempt at speaking French when an idea hits: *why not shave off my whole goatee?* I started growing a beard just after Milo was born – not intentionally, but life was hectic, I was tired, and it was too much effort to shave. And when he got older, he loved rubbing his head on my chin and laughing at how it felt against his skin. His bubbling giggle echoes in my head and that hand grenade of pain explodes inside.

'Take it off,' I say to the man, making hand gestures so he fully understands. 'I want it off.'

The man nods and points to the chair. I lower myself into it, cursing the skinny jeans that make crossing your legs very uncom-fortable, if not impossible. I close my eyes and try to clear my brain of everything except for the rasp of the razor as it traverses my face and the spicy scent of the shaving foam.

I wonder if Zoe will notice? The thought sneaks into my head, and I snort with impatience. It doesn't matter if she notices or not any more. She's made it quite clear she's through with me. In fact, I'm starting to wonder if she ever really wanted me in the first place. The old anger – anger I'd managed to bury under layer upon layer – bubbles up again as I remember her looking me straight in the eye, saying Milo wasn't my baby. I still don't understand what changed her mind: what made her decide to have Milo and marry me, but I was so happy she finally agreed to marry me that I didn't question it.

I let out a small snort now, and the barber shoots me a quizzical look. *Finally* agreed to marry me, shit. How pathetic that my wife needed convincing, needed to be pregnant, before succumbing to marriage. I want to shake the old me for being so naive, so eager.

Slowly, without looking down or opening my eyes, I jimmy the wedding ring off my finger and slide it into my pocket. My hand and my heart feel lighter, and I flex my fingers as the barber scrapes the past two years from my face.

32

ZOE, SEPTEMBER 2010

My eyes are gritty, my mouth is dry. An invisible hand grabs my guts and twists, trying to force my meagre breakfast up and out of my throat. I'm in the waiting room of the clinic – a nondescript space stuffed with women of all ages. As I sit here, I try not to think about what's going to happen in the next few hours. I try to focus on the end result: that everything will be fixed and back to normal. But everything won't be fixed, will it? I won't have Edward.

The nausea rises again as I remember the look on his face when I said the baby wasn't his. I spent all night with my hand on the mobile, bringing up his contact, staring at the phone, and desperately wanting to ring yet desperately *not* wanting to. For the millionth time, I tell myself this is for the best – for us both. And for the millionth time, I wonder if it really is.

Is Edward with that woman? Is there a chance . . . a chance he still loves me? At the very least, I should have talked to him, to see why he came by. That must have meant something, right? The pain and confusion and emotion all swamped my mind, driving me to put an end to it all. What if there's another path to take besides this one – a path we could take together?

I grab my knitting needles and force myself to move them, back and forth, back and forth. The girl beside me raises an eyebrow at my frantic movements, but I don't care. I want to lose myself in the motion, to forget everything. But even as the needles click, the feeling that I'm making a mistake grows and grows.

And it's not just about Edward. It's about this thing inside my body, this baby. It's a part of me; it's depending on me, in a way no one else ever has. Although the thought scares the hell out of me, I also feel incredibly protective – as if I'd never, not in a million years, let anyone harm it . . . ironic, given where I'm sitting at the moment. I feel, I guess, like a *mother*. All the future angst, the frustration and the dirty nappies in the world can't compete with that. I always wondered how Kate could complain for hours on end about having a child, then finish off by saying, 'It's all worth it.' Now, I can kind of understand.

Okay, so I'm not sure. About a baby, about the future, about anything, really. But like Kate said, no one is ever sure – not one hundred per cent. Relationships are a leap of faith. *Life* is a leap of faith. My hand slides down to my belly, and I let out a puff of air. If nothing else, this is a reminder that you can't control things. Stuff happens, and the best you can do is try to get through it – with the people you love. Pushing them away because you're scared of losing them doesn't solve anything. I know that now.

Will Edward still want me, though? Will he forgive my terrible lie that the baby's not his? And will he believe me now when I tell him it is his, after all?

'Zoe, we're ready for you now.' A nurse appears in the doorway, beckoning me forward.

I get to my feet and walk towards her, my heart pounding. But instead of following her through to the examining room, I push past, up the stairs, and out the door into the crisp, sunny morning.

I take a deep breath, and get ready to jump.

33

EDWARD, SEPTEMBER 2010

I've dragged myself into work today, but even though we have a project deadline looming and I should be frantically coding, I can't focus on the screen. Not surprising, given I hardly slept last night. After seeing Zoe, I stayed up for hours with my flatmate, Gus, drinking beer, talking cricket (slightly challenging, given my lack of knowledge), and trying to forget what happened.

But I can't block out the look on Zoe's face when she said the baby wasn't mine – the way she just tossed the word 'no' out there, like it didn't – wouldn't – mean anything to me. Like she couldn't see then that I would have gladly given up the legal ties of marriage, just for the chance of being with her – and our baby.

A snort escapes and I want to punch myself for being so stupid. I'd like to give Kate a piece of my mind, too, but I'm way too tired to even form a coherent sentence right now.

Somehow the day passes, and I lurch back to the flat after dodging several phone calls from Eva. Part of me wants to go to her, to bury myself in her and forget everything else. But despite my attempts, there's too much Zoe in my mind to even think of being with another woman right now. All I know is that I haven't got Zoe pregnant. I haven't got Zoe, either, but then, I should be used to that. After what Kate told me about her former engagement, I'm starting to wonder if I ever did.

As I climb the dusty stairs to our door, I can hear the low rumble of Gus's voice along with the higher tones of a woman's. My heart drops. The last thing I feel like doing right now is playing Gus's wingman like I normally would, lobbing him jokes and making him seem a thousand times more charming than he is in reality. I'll grab a beer, say a quick hello, and head out again. I really need to find a place of my own and soon.

I fit my key in the door and swing it open, my jaw clenching when I see who's inside. It's not some random woman Gus picked up.

It's Zoe.

'What are you doing here?' My voice sounds like a stranger's, cold and husky.

'Er, I'll just give you guys some space.' Gus holds up his hands and backs slowly out of the room, looking only too happy to get out of there.

His door slams shut and it's silent for a minute except for the hum of the ancient fridge. I lean against the wall, not wanting to even sit down. 'Well?'

Zoe leans forward, pushing her curls behind her ears. Even they look like they're low in energy, hanging limply instead of their usual crazy spiral. 'Please, can you sit down? You're making me nervous twitching like that.' Her voice is unnatural, too, high and shaky.

I take a seat in the broken armchair across from her, the springs squeaking as I sit. She's even paler than last night, if that's possible, and sweat coats her face.

'Edward . . .' Her voice cracks and she clears her throat. 'I lied. Last night.'

I shake my head. I really can't take much more of this. 'You lied? What, you're not pregnant?'

'No, I am.' Her hand slides down to her belly and I can't help following its path. She looks just the same as ever – perhaps even a bit skinnier. She takes a breath and her belly rises too. 'I'm pregnant. I didn't lie about that. But . . . it's yours.'

The words fly at me, gripping my throat. I lean back as disbelief rolls over me, quickly followed by a shot of anger so powerful my chest tightens.

'So why the fuck did you say it wasn't mine?' My leg starts jiggling and I stand and pace across the room, trying to work off the emotion flooding through me. How could she even think of doing that to me? She knows I thought I couldn't have children. Was she really going to let me carry on believing that? And if she did decide to have the baby, was she going to deny me access to my own child?

Christ! Does she hate me that much?

She leaps up and grabs my hand. I let her tug me down onto the sofa, drained now, feeling numb.

'I'm so sorry. I was confused, and I didn't know what to do.' She pauses. 'I thought I wasn't ready to have a baby, so there was no point telling you.'

'*No point?*' For a split second, I want to shake her. 'You mean besides the fact that I thought I couldn't have kids?'

Her cheeks flare red and she bites her lip. 'I would have told you eventually. After . . . everything.'

'Oh, gee, thanks.' My tone is so sarcastic and bitter, I hardly recognise it. I've never spoken this way, not to anyone. But Zoe, well, she just brings out all these emotions the way no one else does.

'So why are you telling me now?' I can't help looking at her stomach again, see-sawing back and forth between incredulity and relief. Curled up inside her is my baby, the child I never thought I'd have – the child I realise now I desperately want. I'm not infertile after all. After everything, I'm almost afraid to let myself believe it.

'I know you're angry with me and I don't blame you.' She takes my other hand, and my fingers automatically thread through hers, despite myself. 'But I do want to have this baby.'

I nod slowly, trying to absorb everything, my heart pounding. Just last night, I was ready to take on the role of father and partner. Then I had everything yanked away. Now Zoe's here, telling me I'm going to be a dad after all. An intense longing sweeps over me to be there for this child. To cradle it in my arms, to be its whole world.

'And I want to have it with you.' She draws in another deep breath and squeezes my fingers. 'I want to marry you, and make us a family. I'll never lie again, I promise.'

My eyes lock with hers and I sit here, stunned. She wants to be with me. She wants to get *married*? A million questions float around my mind, like whatever happened to her allergy to forever? Why didn't she tell me she was engaged before? And I can't just dismiss her cruelty at lying about the pregnancy, like it was nothing. It's huge, and she was playing with my life, my future happiness.

But . . . I love her. I do, for better or worse, and she's just removed the very reason we broke up in the first place. She's willing to commit to forever, and I know that's a big step. And even if she wasn't, there's something else: something that trumps all other factors.

We're going to have a baby.

I want to do this with her. I want to do this together. My simmering anger at her lie, the unanswered questions – none of that is important. Not now. An image of Giles and Kate staring beatifically down at their newborn comes to mind, and happiness flickers inside. I can have that after all. We can have that. A *family*.

'Edward?' Zoe's staring at me, and I realise I've been sitting in silence for a while.

'Just a second.' I peel my hands away from hers and head to my room, where most of my things are still in boxes. I rifle through a jumble of clothes, tossing aside trousers and pants. I know it's here somewhere, if I can just find it. I should have returned it, but for some reason, I couldn't. My fingers touch the black velvet box and I pull it out, then head back out to the lounge. Zoe's exactly as I left her, frozen in place.

When she sees what's in my hand, her face breaks into a huge smile. God, I've missed the way her eyes crinkle like that. Before I can say a word, she kneels down.

'It's my turn,' she says. 'Edward, I love you. I want to be with you . . . forever.' Her voice shakes on the word, but at least she's managed to get it out. 'Will you marry me?'

I tug her up and take the box, opening it up and grabbing the ring. As I slide it on her finger, I can't help thinking I'm a lucky man.

In this one moment, and for the rest of my life, I have everything.

34
ZOE, SATURDAY, 8 P.M.

As the sky darkens and night-time falls on the streets of Paris, I ponder how I can find my husband before it gets much later. Wandering around in the day might have been all right, but it's probably not the best option at night. It's funny; now that I want to reach Edward, suddenly my senses feel heightened, like the world has come into focus. I notice the groups of men pushing by me, the empty alleys looming darkly and the shards of broken bottles, and my desire to reach my husband heightens. I'm not exactly sure he's a safe place either, and I don't know what I'll say to him. I just want to reach out, to connect to him and our son in a way I haven't for years.

I run my tongue around my lips, tasting the salt from the long day in the sun. I used to adore lounging outside for hours, ignoring all health warnings. My skin would go brown – unlike Edward's, which turns lobster-red at the hint of light – and I'd soak up the warmth, feeling it reach my very core. Now, though, my face feels tender and sore, as if this exposure is its first in years. In a way, it's exactly how I feel inside too.

I turn the corner onto yet another unknown street, eyes scanning the pavement for someone I can ask for the way to the Marais.

I still won't know which hotel Edward's at, but at least it's a start in the right direction . . . and maybe I'll spot a phone box on the way. I'll call collect and tell him what's happened. Despite the distance between us, he must be worried. I know that much for sure.

The sultry sound of a saxophone floats through the night air, volume rising as my legs plod down the street. I stop outside a heavy wooden door, making out the accompanying sounds of laughter, the clink of glasses, and the low hum of countless conversations inside. I lean against the glossy wood, breathing in the scent of paint and polished brass.

The door is cold on my sunburned back, and I'm just about to push off it and continue on my way when my weight clicks it open, revealing a quiet courtyard. Golden light spills out onto cobble-stones, and before I know what I'm doing, I step through the door and into the light. Through another door, I can see into a grand townhouse and out to the garden, where a party is in full swing. Guests mill about on a manicured lawn, and elegantly dressed wait-ers circulate with plates of food and drink. My mouth waters at the thought of consuming something – anything – and I realise that I've hardly eaten since . . . I can't even remember when.

The band switches to an upbeat number, and couples swirl and twirl to the music on a dance floor in the corner of the garden. Even though I'm dead tired, I can't help swaying back and forth to the beat. God, it's been so long since I even *listened* to music. The last time was—

The memory hits me and I catch my breath. The last time was at Milo's funeral. I can barely remember those first few days after the accident. It's the disbelief, the strangeness of it all, as if you're living in a dream and someone, sometime will wake you up and tell you it's all just a nightmare. I still feel that way most of the time.

Anyway, since I couldn't do anything but sleep, Edward organ-ised all the details. I couldn't bear to. Dealing with practical things meant the nightmare was real. It was a wonderful funeral – everyone said so, as if funerals were things that could be graded on a scale of one to ten. As if a boy's life after two years could be celebrated. For God's sake, he'd hardly even *lived*.

But Edward was thorough. He dug out all our photos and put together a slide show, he chose Milo's clothes, and the song . . . My eyes ache with the pressure of waiting tears as the notes of 'Sweet Child O' Mine' float into my head, tender and slow like a lullaby. In those first few months, when Milo would morph from a happy baby to a screaming demon between the hours of four and seven, Edward would endlessly croon that tune to him, over and over, until his cries finally subsided in one big, long, shuddery sigh and he drifted off to sleep. We'd gaze down at Milo's angelic face, saying how lucky we were. And now I know how much that's true. We *were* lucky, but our luck ran out. The best thing that happened to us was taken away, leaving only us: a broken version.

I cringe, thinking how hard that must have been for Edward. To do it all himself, all alone. To pack up his son's belongings while his wife slept on, and on and on. He *did* reach out to me, I realise now. I remember the bed sagging as he sat down beside me, clasped my hand, and tried to break into my haze. He tried to talk, but I just . . . couldn't. I couldn't even deal with my own emotions, let alone his.

The band stops and a smattering of applause echoes around the garden. I rub my eyes, the urge to speak with Edward growing bigger and bigger, until it's almost a compulsion. I push blindly into the house and out to the garden. Surely someone there has a phone they'll let me use, if I explain the situation? My foot catches on the raised edge of a cobblestone and I tumble forwards, only just stopping myself from falling over. I straighten up, running a hand through my curls and hoping I don't get chucked out before I can borrow someone's mobile. Among these elegantly dressed guests, I stick out like a sore thumb in my jeans and T-shirt.

I catch a bit of English floating across the perfumed air, and I edge my way towards it. My cheeks colour as I hover beside a middle-aged, posh couple discussing this year's opera season.

'Um, excuse me?'

Their heads swivel towards me with identically raised eyebrows, and my blush deepens. This really is a ridiculous request – they're hardly going to hand over their mobile to a complete stranger – but I might as well ask. What do I have to lose?

'I've been mugged and I lost my phone and wallet. I wonder if I might use your mobile to ring my husband?' I try to make my voice as posh as possible.

'Oh, my.' The woman puts a hand to her chest. 'Are you all right? Have you reported it to the police?'

'I'm fine,' I say, 'and no, not yet. I just need to reach my husband and everything will be all right.' I know it won't be – it will never be all right – but for the first time since Milo left, I have a feeling it might help.

'John, give her the mobile,' the woman says.

John casts his eyes over me. 'Wait a second. Do you know Florence and Guillaume? Have they invited you here?'

Oh, shit. Trust me to find the suspicious Englishman. 'Well . . . I don't know them personally, no,' I say. 'But—'

The wife rolls her eyes. 'Oh, for goodness' sake, John. Just let the poor woman call her husband. You can see she's been through an ordeal!'

I gaze down self-consciously. Yes, you can certainly see that.

'Oh, all right.' The husband removes a gold-plated mobile from his pocket. 'How about you tell me the number, and I'll dial it for you.'

Thank God. I reel off Edward's number, the digits flowing automatically from my tongue.

'It's ringing.' John hands me the phone.

My heart beats as I wait for Edward to answer. In a way, this feels like the first time I've spoken to him for years – the first time I've really wanted to, anyway. *Come on,* I say inside my head, my foot tapping on the soft grass. Surely he'll pick up soon. He must have his phone on hand, knowing I'm missing. Right?

'Hello, you've reached Edward . . .'

My heart drops as the phone clicks through to voicemail. Why on earth isn't he answering his phone? What else could he be doing than looking for his wife? I clear my throat and get ready to leave a message.

'Hi, Edward.' Just saying his name feels different. 'It's me. I got mugged at the train station and my mobile and wallet are lost. I don't know where we're staying so I can't find you.' I swallow, wondering what else to say. I can hardly tell him to ring John's phone and stick around here all night waiting, can I? Judging from the evil eye I'm getting right now, I'd better wrap things up. 'Anyway, I'm borrowing someone's phone to make this call. I'll try to find another way to contact you.'

I hang up and hand the phone back to John, disappointment swirling inside. I know we've been distant lately, and that Edward's pretty much been living his own life – as have I. But I guess I still believed if I ever really needed him, really wanted to talk, he'd be there . . . like he always was. Fear pricks my gut. Has that changed? *Has* he bowed out?

'Dear?' The woman is looking at me with concern, and I shake my head again.

'I'm okay.' I force a smile to show them I'm not a lunatic. 'Can you just . . . tell me the way to the Marais?'

John nods. 'Go out the door and turn left, then walk for about ten minutes. You'll come across Rue des Quatre-Fils. Turn left on that one, too. That should take you to the centre.'

'Okay.' I try to imprint his instructions on my brain. 'Thanks for the phone. Have a good evening.'

John nods again and takes his wife's arm, and the two of them disappear back into the night. I retrace my steps out through the townhouse and across the courtyard, pushing open the heavy door. The street is emptier now and the music fades as I leave the party behind me. Even though every muscle in my body aches, I quicken my pace.

I don't know where you are, Edward, I say inside my head, as if I'm sending a telepathic message. *But I'm coming to find you.*

Finally.

35
EDWARD, SATURDAY, 8 P.M.

'Okay, monsieur. All done.'

My eyes drift open as the barber's voice cuts into my very pleasant fantasy – soon to be reality? – of me and Fiona in bed. I lift a hand to my chin and feel nothing but smooth skin.

I sit up and take the mirror the man's handed me, eyebrows rising in surprise at the reflection. It's me all right, but I don't look the same as I did before I grew the goatee. My image stares back, and I flinch at what I see: not the wide, youthful gaze of the young man I once was, but a man with slightly saggy jowls to match the bags beneath my eyes. I might have removed the hair, but I can't remove the years. Still, it's something different, and that's what I want.

I pass the mirror back to the barber. 'Thank you,' I say, giving him a few euros.

He nods and picks up a towel to tidy up, and I head back out to the shop floor where assistants are starting to usher shoppers towards the exits. The huge clock on the wall reads almost eight: four hours to kill until Fiona's train arrives. I have to say, this day seems endless. Usually, with work and meeting friends – and Fiona – the hours fly by in a comfortable blur. One day to the next, moving me further and further away from the events of the past. But now, without my regular schedule, it feels like time is suspended.

Outside on the street, the cafés and restaurants are packed with Saturday night punters. I pass a couple gorging on a huge plate of oysters, and my stomach growls, remembering when Zoe introduced me to them. I was dubious at first – they looked more like something you'd chuck in the rubbish than ingest. But once I tried one, I couldn't get enough. God, it's been ages since I had some.

Does Fiona like oysters, I wonder, tearing my thoughts from Zoe and back to the woman at hand. She'll probably be starving when she finally arrives; perhaps we can find a place that does them. I try to imagine Fiona sitting across from me as we down our oysters, but all I can see is Zoe once again.

Maybe I'll grab some champagne for later, I think, nodding at the man behind the counter as I enter a shop. I choose a cold bottle from the fridge and peel off a few notes, then slowly make my way to the hotel, trying to take as much time as possible.

Back in the hotel, I place the tissue-wrapped lingerie on the bed and my phone bleeps. I dig it from my pocket, noting there's a missed call and a voicemail. Strange that I didn't hear it ring, but then, Parisian streets aren't known for their silence. The call is from a number I don't recognise, but the country code is for the UK. I dial into my voicemail, fingers tapping on the duvet as I wait to see who it's from.

'Hi, Edward, it's me.'

My fingers disconnect the call, like they have a mind of their own. I stare at the mobile, almost as if Zoe's going to leap from it and into this room . . . the last thing I want right now. I don't know why she's calling from a different number – is she with someone else, back in the UK, like I'm about to be here? Given how little I know about her life now and, as I've just discovered, how she spends her days, it's certainly not out of the realm of possibility. I've no idea why she's ringing, but I really don't care. I want this weekend for me, without the complications and sadness of the past few years.

I slide the phone back into my pocket, vowing to answer only if Fiona calls.

36
ZOE, OCTOBER 2010

As soon as I open my eyes, the knowledge hits me: today I'm getting married. Today, I will promise to love, cherish and honour Edward, until death do us part. The words roll around in my head and I haul myself upright, nausea making me groan. But I know it's not nerves for the impending ceremony; it's the baby inside. Now that I've accepted that my future is written, all my anxiety about forever has stopped barking in my brain, like a small yappy dog you've finally made friends with.

I shake my head, swinging my legs over the side of the bed. If I'd have known vanquishing my marriage phobia was that easy, Edward and I never would have broken up in the first place. But in a strange kind of way, I'm glad we did. It only confirmed how much we want to be together, even if it did take a baby to get me to push the final button.

My hand moves to my stomach. It's still early days – I'm about three months along – but I'll always be grateful to this little one for bringing me and Edward together again. Who knows what would have happened if I hadn't got pregnant? I'd like to think we'd have found each once more, but the outcome might have been different.

Funny how I thought a newborn was the ultimate death knell for a new marriage, back when Kate told me she was pregnant. Now, it's been our saviour. And although I'm still terrified, I'm so excited to meet this baby, this perfect mix of Edward and me. Kate will be there every step of the way too – I've already warned her to expect frantic phone calls morning, noon and night. Thank goodness she had her baby first so she knows what to do. Watching her with Olivia, I know it will be hard . . . but I also can't wait to feel my child's chubby arms clutch me tight, or to rock it gently off to sleep.

'You're getting married today!' Kate jumps on my bed, and I groan again as it bounces up and down. I swear, she's more excited than I am, even though it's not the ceremony she would have wanted. In fact, it's the opposite of her elaborate affair. With just a month of planning – call me vain, but I still wanted to be able to fit into a size twelve – we've decided on a small ceremony room at Islington Town Hall, with only Kate and Giles, along with our parents, as guests.

I smile, thinking of when we first told our parents we were getting married – and having a baby. Of course I'd met Edward's mum and dad before: lovely, but a little distant and cold, as if they don't want to get too close to you (Edward's mother even does air kisses). I'd hoped the news of a grandchild might melt them a bit, but they kept their composure as always as I babbled on about due dates and morning sickness. My own mum and dad couldn't have been more different. Mum couldn't wait to touch my belly, advising me on everything from stretch marks to heartburn. She used to drive me crazy with unwanted advice, but now I was drinking it up.

'Right, let's get you ready!' Kate's chipper voice is a little too chipper for this time of morning, and I cover my ears.

'We still have hours,' I complain, tempted to flop down again.

'Yeah, and have you seen the state of you? It's going to take that long to have you looking less Bride of Dracula and more, er . . . well, more like something Edward would want to marry.'

A few hours later, I've been primped, poked and made-up to within an inch of my life. My curls are lacquered with several layers of hairspray, my lashes coated with heavy mascara, and my lips can barely part, they've got so much sticky gloss on them. But when I gaze in the mirror . . . *wow*. I look like a proper bride, even if my gown is just a fitted, vintage-style dress I picked up at the local second-hand shop.

'You're gorgeous,' Kate says, eying my reflection. 'And I'm not just saying that because I'm afraid of the pregnancy hormones I know are racing around your body right now.'

I laugh, because it's true: my emotions have been a little heightened lately. Edward keeps joking that he'll buy me a flashing light to signal when he should stay away. I wonder what he's doing right now. One thing's for sure: it's probably nowhere near this level of preparation. I'll be lucky if he shaves and trades his baggy jeans for some hole-free trousers.

I turn sideways, examining my profile in the mirror. Thankfully, my stomach is still relatively flat – well, as flat as it ever was.

'All right, little one,' I whisper. 'Let's go get married.'

37
EDWARD, SATURDAY, 8.45 P.M.

I'm out on the street again. I couldn't stay in that coffin-sized hotel room more than ten minutes on my own. The second there's silence, thoughts descend like stinging wasps: how Zoe shut me out; how she lied; how she's been the one making all our decisions. I'll sit at a café and have another pint, watch the street life filter by . . . anything's better than staying inside alone.

I lower myself into a wicker chair at one of the many places lining the street, sipping my beer when the waiter brings it to me. I don't usually drink this much, but there's little else to pass the time here waiting for Fiona. Besides, I want to be relaxed and chilled out for her, not tightly wound from thoughts of my absent wife. I jiggle the change in my pocket, wondering if I need to get more euros from the cashpoint. As I slide the contents of my pocket into my hand and pick through them, I realise my wedding band isn't there. I check the other pocket, but it's not there either.

Shit.

I paw through the assortment of coins, keys and random Tic Tacs, but the ring is nowhere to be found. Have I really lost my wedding band? I stretch out my legs as the knowledge sinks in. I knew my marriage was over – removing the watch Zoe gave me signalled that decision – but this seems like a final judgment from above. A mix of nostalgia and sadness washes over me. However far we've drifted now, that ring was a reminder of what we had, of what we promised: love, forever. Now that reminder's gone. It shouldn't matter, but somehow it does.

My mind flips back to our wedding – the best day of my life right up until Milo was born. Part of me couldn't believe it all: Zoe as my wife, and my very own child. I couldn't get the wedding band on her finger fast enough. As she slipped on my ring, I gazed down and marvelled how, until the day I died and probably even after, that ring would still be on my finger.

Until death do us part.

Sounds about right – except it wasn't my death, or Zoe's.

My throat tightens and emotions push at my chest. I take a huge swig of the beer in front of me. I'll talk to Zoe as soon as I get home, I decide, and tell her I'm moving out. I'm sure she won't mind – she feels the distance as much as I do. Hell, she's the one who created it. I'll crash at my parents' until I find somewhere to live. Maybe a flat, back in London again. I can't wait to get out of that village, where the trees and flowers and quiet – things we moved there for in the first place – now feel like they're suffocating me. Give me noise, give me shrieking sirens and late-night partiers.

Give me *life*.

38
EDWARD, NOVEMBER 2010

I've seen this scene in films so many times, but I never thought it would happen to me. Today is our very first ultrasound, when we get to see the little baby growing inside my wife.

My wife. I can't say that enough. I love how it rolls off my tongue, and I take every opportunity to throw it into conversation. Zoe rolls her eyes and laughs, telling me 'I do still have a name!' but I can see by the glow in her eyes that she likes it too – despite all her protests. Marriage has elevated our relationship, giving us a new status.

And the next step? Parents. I shake my head as Zoe climbs onto the examining table, remembering her words on what feels like ages ago. *Us as parents? Can you imagine?* And now, here we are, just six months away from having a baby. I can't wait. I bought Zoe a huge stack of pregnancy books and although I'd never admit it to my mates – most of whom are still down the pub each night sinking pints – I've read most of them too.

I know it's a lot for Zoe to handle. After all, it's her body ballooning out, her womb cradling the baby, and her milk that will feed it. She's the one this child will call out for when it's ill, when it awakens in the middle of the night, and when it scrapes its knee.

She'll be its *mother*, the ultimate figure in any child's life, the ultimate comforter and protector. No father can compete with that sacred bond, although I certainly intend to be a very close second.

'All right, can you lie down, please?' The sonographer picks up her instrument, and Zoe scoots down, the paper beneath her crinkling.

'I'll just lift your shirt, and spread this gel on your stomach . . .'

I clasp my wife's hand, my eyes tracing the contours of her tummy as if I'll be able to see what's in there. Zoe squeezes my fingers, and I can tell by the look on her face that she's still worried. I spent most of last night trying to quell her doubts.

'What if there's something wrong with it? What if they go to check the heartbeat, and it's not beating any more? What if . . .' She shook her head, her usually animated face pinched and pale.

'It'll be okay,' I said, over and over, pulling her into my arms. I'm not sure how I know everything will be fine, but I just do. I know this child, this surprise baby, is somehow meant to be. It's brought the two of us together, and it'll continue to do that as a family.

The screen comes to life as the sonographer moves the probe up and down Zoe's stomach, and Zoe grimaces. She was so afraid the sonographer wouldn't be able to see anything that she downed litres upon litres of water, and she was desperate for the loo half an hour ago. I can't even imagine how she's feeling now.

'All right. There's your baby.'

Zoe lifts her head and I lean forward to stare at the screen. There in front of us, curled up like a frankfurter with tiny appendages, is our child. My heart starts pounding and I squeeze Zoe's fingers. Even though it looks more like a tadpole than anything human, a wave of pride sweeps over me.

'Is it okay?' Zoe's tone is anxious.

'Everything looks on track so far,' the sonographer says. 'I'll just take a few measurements.' She deftly moves the probe and does a few clicks, then smiles over at us.

'Do you want to know the sex?'

'You know already?' I ask, raising my eyebrows. 'I thought you couldn't tell until much later on.'

'Well, sometimes. But I'm quite sure now.'

I meet Zoe's eyes. 'Do we want to know?'

She nods. 'Hell, yes!'

'It's a boy,' the sonographer says.

'A boy! We're going to have a boy!' A huge, goofy grin lifts my lips, and Zoe grins back at me too. I'd be happy with whatever gender, but secretly I was hoping for a little boy. Someone to kick around the ball with, to take to games when he's older, to have that special father-son bond as he grows. If I was excited before, now I'm bursting.

This child is the most important thing in my world – in *our* world – and I'm going to make his life the happiest, the most fulfilling it can be. That's my promise to him, and I'll have to fall down dead before I break it.

39
ZOE, SATURDAY, 9.15 P.M.

I spin in a circle in the busy street, half-tempted to shout Edward's name and see if he magically emerges. I've followed John's directions to the letter, and I've been wandering around what should be the centre of the Marais for what feels like forever. But I still have no idea where to go – of course I don't. How stupid to think I'd be able to stroll through the blocks and find him.

Even though I've no idea where Edward is physically, emotionally I feel closer to him than I have in ages. Yes, there's still plenty separating us, and I know you can't breach years of silence with just a few words, but . . . Milo is gone, but his memory still links us. Shutting out Edward means shutting out a lot of good memories with my son, memories with the family I once had. I can see that now.

Right, time to hunt down a phone box and make a collect call. Surely this time he'll answer. First, though, I need a second to catch my breath. I was on a mission to get here as quickly as possible, as if by erasing the blocks between us, I could tear down the walls. I'm so bloody tired my body is practically vibrating. I can feel a headache brewing, gathering momentum in my temples and pressing its thumbs on my eye sockets.

I lean against a shopfront, then sink down onto the stone step. The streets here are bustling, and the night is alive around me. The murmur of voices and the honking of horns remind me of London, of all those times I'd drink in the city's electricity – just pounding the pavement and revelling in the possibility that the night could take you *anywhere*. Underground clubs, midnight sing-a-longs at the cinema, fringe theatre in the back of beyond: London was my playground, and I loved everything about it. I loved showing Edward all it had to offer too. God, that girl – that couple – seems so far away now.

The quirk of London's scene feels far away too. It's a beautiful evening featuring all those Parisian clichés I loved to hate: laughter from diners at countless cafés floats on the warm air, people stroll by holding hands, and street lights glow like torches against the starry sky. I shake my head, remembering how I told Edward not to even consider Paris for our honeymoon – no way would we succumb to that kind of stereotypical romance.

I want to turn back time now and tell that girl to be softer, maybe. To not resist so much, to wring every second of enjoyment from being a wife and mother . . . while it lasts, even if it does mean sacrificing nights out and embracing a few stereotypes. Funnily enough, this gorgeous street scene is exactly what I would have loved when Milo was young, back before a dingy pub was the highlight of my day. I wasn't the girl who'd stay out until dawn any longer. Time changed me; parenthood changed me. Grief has changed me, too, but right now, I can't help coveting that huge plate of oysters on the table across from me, the way the man lightly touches his partner's arm then smiles like she's his world.

My tummy growls and my hand slides down and across the scar on my stomach, the one physical reminder that I gave birth. For months after Milo's accident, I couldn't look at the faint white line on my stomach. I'd tug my clothes on as fast as I could, afraid I'd melt if I caught sight of it. But now . . . my fingers touch my skin. Now, I'm glad I have it: proof that my son existed, proof that my body *did* nurture him and bring him life – even if I brought him death too.

40
ZOE, APRIL 2011

'Zoe!'

Edward's voice jerks me awake, and I sit up in bed. 'Ugh,' I say, touching the damp covers beneath me. It feels like I'm sleeping on one giant wet spot. 'Did you spill something?'

Edward laughs. 'No. I think that's coming from you.'

'From me? No,' I say drowsily, lying down again. 'I didn't bring a drink to bed. Not this time, anyway.' Edward's always complaining about my collection of empty mugs and glasses on the bedside table.

'Zoe, wake up.' Edward's shaking my arm. 'I think your waters have broken.'

My pulse starts racing almost instantly. Of course that's what it is – how could I not have known? Just one of the many things it took me ages to clue into over the past nine months. Thank God for Kate and her encyclopaedic – if often a little *too* much – knowledge of pregnancy.

'Oh, shit.' I sit up in bed again and gingerly get to my feet, plucking my wet pyjamas from my skin. I guess those contractions I've been feeling since this morning weren't Braxton-Hicks, after all.

Edward's got my hospital bag and is tugging on his trousers. 'Come on, get dressed. Let's head over to the hospital now.'

I shake my head and laugh. 'Relax! There's no need to go until I have stronger contractions. At the moment, they just feel like period pains. If we go now, they'll send us home again and tell us to come back later.'

Edward shakes his head. 'I don't care. Come on.'

I shrug, knowing it's useless to argue with him when he has that stubborn look on his face. Besides, part of me wants to get to the hospital as quickly as possible to make sure there's plenty of time for that epidural. Memories of Kate's face and her screams of pain enter my mind for the countless time, and I shudder. There is *no way* I'm going for a natural birth.

At the hospital, I lie back on the examining table, trying to breathe through the pain gathering momentum in my abdomen.

'Is everything okay?' I ask, as the midwife prods my nether regions, then attaches a monitor around my belly. Instantly I hear my baby's galloping heartbeat, and excitement goes through me. I can't wait to meet him!

The midwife stares at the numbers flashing up on the screen, her brow furrowing. 'Just let me grab the doctor, and I'll be right back.'

Edward and I stare at each other, and he squeezes my hand. 'What do you think that means?' I ask him. 'She wouldn't have to get the doctor if everything was fine, right?'

'Let's just wait and see what the doctor says,' Edward says in a firm tone, but I can tell by the way his jaw tightens that he's worried too.

After what feels like forever, a harried-looking consultant arrives. She takes one look at the monitor and the printout, then glances down at me. 'Your baby is in distress for some reason – the heart rate is dropping. We need to deliver it as soon as possible. I'm going to ask the nurses to prep you for a Caesarean.'

My mouth drops open. '*A Caesarean?*' I'd expected the whole birth thing to take a long time – at least a day, if not more. That didn't bother me. It was like I needed the time and the process to transition from being me to being a mother. The thought of it all happening in one fell swoop is jarring.

But none of that matters when it comes to keeping our child alive. I glance up at Edward, and he's nodding.

'We'll do whatever we need to, to have a healthy baby,' he says, echoing my exact thought. It strikes me how lucky we are that we *did* come to the hospital early, that I didn't try to fight Edward and stay at home like they told us to. Guilt sweeps over me that, if I'd had my way, I might have put my baby at risk . . . even if I didn't know then what I know now. Why wasn't I the super-protective one?

As I'm wheeled into the delivery room and the bright light blinds me, I screw my eyes shut and make a silent vow that from now on, I'll do everything in my power to keep my child safe.

41
ZOE, SATURDAY, 9.45 P.M.

My eyes fly open at the sound of voices passing by me, my heart pounding fast. God, did I really just nod off? I clamber to my feet, my muscles protesting at every move. As tired as I am, I can't let myself doze on the pavement in the middle of a foreign city – not that I have anything of value left to steal. Not in monetary terms, anyway. I'm starting to feel that despite everything, maybe there *is* something inside me I can hang on to. A tentative sense of hope that perhaps I can move forward, make my way into life again.

I force my feet forward as the vivid image of Milo's birth runs through my head. The way he gazed at me from the midwife's arms, as if I was the one thing he knew in this strange new world – the one thing that made sense in the swirl of new senses working, air tearing at his lungs.

The vow I made to protect him. The vow I broke.

I round a corner, and a crowd blocks the pavement. I can't hear anything, but by the way they're craning their necks, I can tell they're watching something. I dodge my way between the tightly packed bodies, trying to get through. All of a sudden I catch sight of a man and a woman clad in black, dancing on the pavement in a silent performance. They move in a straight, narrow line like they're on a tightrope – they wobble, they fall, they glide back together. Their limbs twist around each other so they're indistinguishable, and then they fling themselves apart, balancing on their separate section of tightrope once again.

It's mesmerising: the kind of thing I'd take Edward to, back in the pre-Milo days. I smile, remembering how he'd leave countless shows and ask me what on earth all that was about, then tell me he enjoyed it. I'm not sure he did, but he kept going anyway . . . for me. I wonder if he'd do that now? I can't even remember the last time we saw a show, even before Milo's accident. I'd be lying if I said I didn't miss it, but having a child gradually fills in all those empty spaces until it becomes your life. At least it did in our case.

As I watch the dancers bend and swoop, I can't help wondering what would happen if someone lobbed a baby their way. Who would catch it: the man or the woman? Would it throw them off balance, or would the baby melt into them seamlessly? How would they embrace again – the same, all-encompassing way – if one of them always had to hold the child? They would never move with such abandon again, not as a couple.

The thought unearths a memory of Edward and me, the first couple of days in the hospital after Milo's birth. It was a mad blur of painkillers, trying to breastfeed without him pressing on my incision, and desperately trying to get my head around the fact that I was now a mother, now responsible for this tiny, crying, helpless thing. Funnily enough, Edward seemed to have no problem, cradling Milo like he'd done it a thousand times before and changing nappies like a pro. I was terrified about breaking the baby and still trying to figure out which was right side up on the nappies.

But even with all the doubts and uncertainty, locked up in a hospital room with only our baby and each other, those first few days were like a honeymoon with our new family. We were happy just to be there, to watch Milo sleeping, to gaze at him in wonder that he was the combination of us in living form.

'Just remember, before there were three, there were two,' a midwife said, smiling as she watched us moon over the baby, like he was the only thing in the world. *Our* world.

Well, he was. And that midwife was wrong. Sure, we'd been together before Milo, but he brought us back together. From my proposal, from the wedding, from the beginning of our forever, he was there with us. Of course we loved each other, right from the day we met. But Milo was knitted into the fabric of our marriage from the very first stitch.

I suppose that's why we didn't mind all the inevitable changes having a baby brings, adjusting quickly to the dynamic of three. Our sex life screeched to a rather dramatic halt for a while, but whose doesn't after having a baby? And sure, we didn't go out like we used to – okay, we didn't go out, full stop. And while I might have itched sometimes to leave the flat, plastered now in baby things, for the most part I was content to stay in and make sure Milo slept soundly. Looking back, it's possible I felt a little smug at how life had fallen so neatly into such a wonderful pattern, stitch after stitch forming a warm, cosy blanket we wrapped around us. Milo *did* melt seamlessly into our twosome. I adored the world we'd created, and I wanted to stay cocooned in it forever. I believed it was possible.

I pause now, trying to catch my breath as the pain shudders through me once more, making my insides vibrate like an internal earthquake. *Before there were three, there were two.* Can we go back to being just two, resume our dance as lovers, not parents? Do we even know how to do that? The people who first met on the South Bank all those years ago don't exist any more. We have changed, that goes without saying. We'll never move with abandon like we used to, child or no child.

I shake my head, remembering my conversation with Kate, right after Edward and I broke up, when she told me that you have to believe in the other person and that your love is strong enough to get you through. I let out a puff of air, wondering if I still believe that, if the faith I once had in us only functioned as a family. I don't have the answers, but it feels kind of good to be asking questions – to be *present*, instead of wandering in a fog.

Cheers and claps ring out, and the two dancers bow. I move away, scanning the street for a phone box. If Edward doesn't pick up, I'll ring my parents. Since this trip was their gift, they must still have the hotel name somewhere. But ten minutes later, I still haven't found one, and I'm starting to flag. Do phone boxes even exist any more? It's properly dark now and, apart from the string of cafés, most of the shops are shuttered, their windows glowing with shiny wares. Up ahead, a door opens and light spills down the steps of a large stone building. I squint, my heart leaping when I spot the word 'police'. They'll let me use the phone when I explain what happened, right? They'll have to.

A small smile curves my lips as I hurry up the stairs. I'm seconds away from talking to my husband. This time, I'm sure he'll answer.

42
EDWARD, SATURDAY, 9.45 P.M.

I'm officially drunk. My brain is foggy, my face is numb, and my vision is blurry. It feels weird but nice, as if I've been removed to another place where nothing can touch me; nothing can penetrate this haze around me. Is this how Zoe feels, I wonder, when she disappears into her own space? If so, I can kind of understand.

Not that it makes things any better, I think, my hand going down to my empty ring finger. I touch the skin where the ring once resided, noting how it feels soft and sensitive. There's a slight white circle and the skin is a little indented, but that will fade with time.

Christ, it's almost ten! Where the hell is Fiona? I pick up my mobile and dial her number, fingers tapping on the table as I wait for her to answer.

'You're not going to fucking believe this,' she says when she picks up. Her tone is tight with anger and annoyance in a way I haven't heard before.

'What?'

'They've just announced they're going to take us off the train and bus us out to the middle of the arse-end of nowhere, and put us up in hotels for the night. They're hoping to get whatever's wrong sorted out in the next few hours, so we can be there early tomorrow.'

LEAH MERCER

My heart drops as my plans for the night disintegrate before my eyes. Shit! She won't be here until tomorrow morning? What the hell am I going to do knocking around Paris on my own? Going back to that tiny hotel room is like dying an early death. I cringe at the thought.

'That's awful, Fiona,' I say, really feeling for her. What was supposed to be a fun, quick jaunt to meet me is turning into a nightmare. 'I'm so sorry. Do you have everything you need?'

'Well, apart from pyjamas.' She laughs.

'Listen, I can totally understand if you want to just turn around and head home tomorrow,' I say, thinking maybe I can ditch this place now and go back too. But then . . . going home means facing Zoe and the impending conversation and . . . I need a little more time to get my thoughts and plans in order.

'I'm not going home,' Fiona says firmly. 'I'm coming to Paris if it kills me! Anyway, if I do arrive early tomorrow morning, we'll have all day together before we need to go home. Let's make the best of it.'

I smile, loving her optimism and drive. 'All right. Keep me posted on your arrival and I'll meet you at the station. Have a good sleep.'

'You, too. See you soon.'

She hangs up and I slide the phone back in my pocket, a sense of urgency building inside me. I have a whole night to kill, and I know I won't be able to sleep – at least not easily. What I need is more alcohol to dull the senses.

I motion to the waiter to bring me another, then down the drink in one go.

148

43
ZOE, SATURDAY, 10 P.M.

I pull open the door and walk into the blazing light of the police station. I blink as my eyes adjust to it, making out a scruffy, marked counter, behind which sits a moustachioed man who couldn't look more bored if he tried. It's Saturday night, and Parisians must be very well behaved if this deserted station is anything to go by.

For just a second, I pause. Doing this, being found again, means facing the cold, tense place and the pain I've been hiding out from. Am I ready? I take a deep breath as the answer filters in: yes. The past few hours have shown me that I don't need to take cover. That I can think of Milo without breaking into bits, and that it's all right to *feel*. Blame will always sit on me, bags of sand pressing down on my chest. But maybe . . . maybe I can breathe a little deeper, let my lungs fill with air.

'Excuse me,' I say after marching over to the desk.

'Yes?' The man meets my eyes, and my heart lifts that he does indeed speak English.

'I was pickpocketed in the Gare du Nord, and I lost my mobile and my wallet.'

The man sighs and takes out a piece of paper I can only assume is a police report. 'When did this happen?'

'Um, earlier today, about noon.' How bizarre that it was, in fact, still today. It feels like it happened years ago.

The sergeant's white eyebrows fly up. 'And you waited until now to report it?'

I can feel my cheeks start to colour. How to explain that I didn't want to be found, to seek help? Suddenly I realise that was part of my problem after Milo left us: I wouldn't let anyone help – not Kate, not my parents, and not Edward. That felt like cheating, as if leaning on them would make my grief easier to bear. *Why weren't you watching him? Why didn't you stop him? How could you let this happen?* The refrain rang in my head, reminding me that I didn't deserve easy, didn't want easy. If anything, I wanted to make it harder.

He shakes his head. 'I'm sorry, Madame, but the chances of finding your things are practically impossible.'

'That's all right,' I say. It hadn't even occurred to me they could find them, actually. 'I just need to contact my husband. Could I please use your phone?'

The sergeant nods and asks me to write down the number. Then he dials it and passes me the grey receiver, which looks like it might have been white in a former life. I listen to the tinny ring as my brow furrows. I know Edward's been annoyed with me lately, but surely he's anxious to hear where I am? Even if he's not out on the streets or trying to find me, he must at least be keeping his phone nearby. Why the hell isn't he answering?

'Has my husband been here?' I ask, hope darting through me as I hang up. 'Edward Morgan. We lost each other this morning when we first arrived, and had no way to get in touch. He may have reported me missing.'

The man flicks through a few papers, then shakes his head. 'No, there's no police report about you or your husband,' he says.

'Oh.' Okay, then. But no matter how much I may have pissed him off, I can't believe he's not doing *something* to find me. You'd have to be pretty callous to not care if your travelling companion – let alone your wife – disappears in a foreign city, right?

Time for Plan B: my parents. I write down their number and hand it over, knowing I'm probably going to wake them up. As long as I can remember, they've gone to bed at 10 p.m. sharp, except for those terrible few nights just after Milo's accident, when Mum sat by my bed for hours, dozing in the chair where I used to breastfeed, just to be there in case I woke up from my slumber.

Pain jars through me as I think about how I pushed them away these past few years, to the point where I can't even remember the last time I called them. Bad daughter, bad mother . . . bad wife. *God*.

'Hello?' Dad's voice is gruff with sleep.

'Dad, it's me. Everything's okay,' I say quickly, before he moves into emergency mode. 'It's just, Edward and I got separated, and he's not answering his mobile. I just need the name of the hotel we're booked into, if you can find it.'

There's a pause on the line, and I can imagine Dad sitting up in bed and shaking his head as he tries to compute what I've said. 'You're in Paris?' he asks, and I can hear Mum in the background asking him what's wrong.

'Yes.' I tap a finger on the counter. 'Where else would I be?'

'Edward rang earlier today,' Dad says slowly. 'He said he thought you might have come back here and asked me to check. So I went down to the house, and all the lights were on, and music was blaring. You didn't answer the door when I rang, but . . .'

I bite my lip as guilt filters through. He doesn't need to finish that sentence; I know exactly what he's going to say: I hardly ever answer the door. It's easier to hide away than face people, even if those people are my parents.

'That was probably the cleaner,' I say. After Milo was born, Edward decided to hire a cleaner to ease the pressure on the two of us – and to make sure our house didn't descend into a plague pit of germs that could infect our infant. Even though there's no reason to have her any more, we never cancelled. I asked her to come today so I wouldn't have to face her steady gaze, the inquisitive eyes wondering how I'm doing and why the hell I can't do this myself.

'What do you need? What can we do?' Dad's voice rises, and I hear Mum pick up the other line.

'Zoe, are you okay?' Her voice vibrates with concern and love, and my eyes well up. For the first time, it really hits home how worried they must have been about me all this time – all these *years*. And I did nothing but repel every attempt to help. I swallow back the emotion, conscious of the sergeant's eyes on me.

'Hi, Mum. I'm all right. I just need the name of the hotel, and then I can go there and meet Edward.'

'Sit tight and I'll get it.' Dad puts down the receiver and I hear his footsteps as he strides away.

'Honey, you've been lost until now? What on earth have you been doing?'

I shake my head. How to explain? 'Nothing, really.' Although it feels like I've lived a year.

'Okay, I've got the file right here.' Thankfully Dad saves me from having to elaborate. 'It's . . . Hotel Le Marais.'

I ask the sergeant for a pen and scribble it down. 'Thanks.'

'Please call us when you're safe and back with Edward, all right?' Mum asks.

'I will.'

'Promise?'

I nod, wishing I could propel myself down the line and into their arms, squeezing them tightly like I did as a little girl. I can't remember the last time I hugged either one. 'I promise.'

'Okay, then. Take care, and be careful. Talk soon.'

'Bye.' I give the phone to the sergeant, who glances at the hotel name on the notepad.

'Let me get an officer to take you there,' he says, motioning for someone from the bank of desks behind him.

'Oh, no, that's okay, I can walk,' I respond, every though the soles of my feet feel like someone's jabbing them with daggers every time I put weight on them.

He shakes his head. 'It's late and it's dark, and I am not sending you out there on your own.' A man joins him at the desk. 'Come, Sergeant Pelletier will drive you.'

I'm too tired to argue, and the thought of the bed awaiting is way too tempting. 'Okay.'

A short ride later, the police car turns onto a narrow street then slows in front of the hotel. At first glance, I can see it's the kind of place Edward hates: small, tucked away, with genuine features and cramped corridors that make it feel like you're staying in an old aunt's house in the country rather than twenty-first-century Paris. I can't help grinning just imagining his initial reaction.

I nod my thanks to the policeman, then climb from the car and heave open the door. Inside, the receptionist eyes me curiously, no doubt wondering why I've turned up with a police escort. But I'm not about to waste time explaining. I just want to get to the room and see someone familiar. See Edward.

Nerves curl through me at the thought of facing him. It's been so long since we actually touched; since he tried to touch me. Will he push me away? Or will he wrap his arms around me and pull me close, the way he has countless times in the past – the past before Milo's accident? Will he be happy to see me, or disappointed I'm not miles away, like he thought?

I take a deep breath and try to stay calm as the lift judders upwards. The doors slide open and I make my way down the dimly lit corridor, then swipe the key card in the door. I push open the door, wondering if I should knock, then tell myself not to be silly. We've lived together for ages – of course I don't need to knock. But in a way, this feels like a first date again, or the first meeting after a very long time apart.

'Edward?' I call as I walk inside, listening for any noise or sign that he's there. But the room is silent save for the muffled traffic noise filtering in through the window, and I sink down onto the bed, savouring the comfort of the soft – if lumpy – mattress beneath me. After everything that's happened, it's hard to believe I'm finally here. I found the hotel, even if my husband isn't in it.

Where could he be? I shake my head as my mind runs through the endless possibilities. If he thought I wasn't coming, he could be anywhere. He's never been a big drinker, so it's unlikely he's out on the town. He's probably taking a walk, stretching his legs and breathing in the night air before coming back to bed. I remember how he used to walk for hours – *we* used to walk for hours – by the river in London, and then around the village paths with Milo in his buggy.

I sink down onto the bed, memories of sun filtering through newly green leaves, the crunch of the pram's wheels on gravel, and how Milo's dark eyelashes grazed his pink cheeks as he slept, cocooned in blankets. I stretch out my arms, as if by extending them I can let the memory in further, and my hand touches a package wrapped in tissue paper. I sit up, wondering what's inside. Edward's never been much of a shopper – well, until recently, when he started appearing with those godawful skinny jeans and laddishly bright shirts. I wonder what he's bought?

I tear open the tissue paper, eyebrows rising in surprise as my fingers touch delicate satin and lace. *Wow,* I think, as I remove the garment and shake it out. Did he bring this from London? Or buy it here, especially for me, before he thought I went home? And does that mean he wants to make things better again? This is the first thing he's bought me since . . . well, since those first few months after Milo's accident, when he'd bring home flowers, and my favourite perfume, and chocolates, as if appealing to my senses would bring me back. The flowers wilted, the perfume went unopened, and the chocolates grew mould. And then he stopped buying me things.

Hope rushes through me as I hold the nightgown up to my body. Okay, so he's not got the size spot-on and this is a little too frumpy for my taste, but it's the thought that counts – a thought that shows me he does still care, at least enough to buy me this. Perhaps . . . perhaps we do have a shot at figuring out how to be a couple again. It will be different than what we expected – the dream house filled with our children – but *we're* different now too.

I spring from bed, remembering my lank hair, sweaty body and not-so-sweet odour. I don't want to sully this garment with my grime. I race across the room and duck into the tiny bathroom, turn the shower dial as hot as it can go, then stand under the steam and scrub, watching as my skin turns red in the blissful heat and the dirt washes away.

44
EDWARD, OCTOBER 2011

One year. One year of husband and wife. A year ago today, we exchanged vows, exchanged forevers. I raise my flute of champagne in the air, marvelling at how quickly the year has gone. I know everyone says it, but time really does fly once you've had a child. It's a visible reminder of how quickly things change and grow. I can't believe Milo is six months old now, flailing and grunting as he tries to crawl. He's a persistent little guy who doesn't give up, which usually results in tears and screams until I manage to distract him. Zoe finds it hard, I know, but that trait will serve him well later in life. The persistence, I mean, not the tears.

I smile, meeting Zoe's eyes across the sofa as she sips her drink. It's been a wonderful year full of firsts, and nostalgia stirs in my stomach that this is the end of that year. Being jammed in a tiny flat in the heart of a noisy city doesn't exactly make things easy, and having a baby has definitely put an end to us going out – but our little boy makes it all worthwhile. We're a family, a solid unit of three, and I love how having Milo has connected us in a way nothing else could. I can't wait for the next chapter in our lives.

'Oh, that tastes so *goooooood*.' Zoe takes another sip of her champagne, eyes rolling back in her head in bliss. After a difficult start, she's still breastfeeding, so she doesn't drink nearly as much as she used to. 'You know, this is just as good as going out. I don't think I have the energy to even comb my hair, let alone leave the flat.' She yawns and drains her glass. Milo's teething and was up half the night. We were too, taking shifts of endless rocking and walking until he managed to drift off. I feel like a zombie, but excitement darts through me when I think of what I've organised for this evening.

A knock on the door makes me jump from the sofa. Right, time to put the plan into action.

'Who's that?' Zoe's brow furrows. 'Did you order dinner already?'

I shake my head as I cross the room. 'All will be revealed,' I say in a mysterious tone.

'Hello! Happy anniversary!' Zoe's parents cram into the tiny space, her father nearly tripping over Milo's walker.

Zoe unfurls from the sofa. 'What are you two doing here?' she asks, giving them a hug.

'Babysitting duties, and that's all we're allowed to say.' A smile creases her mother's face, and Zoe raises her eyebrows at me in surprise. Over the past year, we've thought about getting her parents to babysit so we can go out – just for a meal, after Milo's down at night. But . . . I couldn't. I couldn't bring myself to leave him with others, even if it was his grandparents. What if he cried? What if he needed to be put back to sleep, in that jiggling/patting way with the song only we know? It didn't take much to bring Zoe round, and so we've basically kept the takeaway companies in business this year.

I'm still uneasy about leaving Milo, but this . . . well, this is for all of us. This is for the next stage of our lives. It's a bold move, but I think Zoe's ready. I know I am. We've talked about it loads, and I think she's come round to the idea.

'Babysitting? Really? Well, in that case, come in!' Zoe ushers her parents into the room, whisking toys and other baby paraphernalia out of the way. She turns to me with a grin. 'I know I said I was too tired, but it *would* be nice to go out and do something. Thank you, honey.' She puts a hand on my arm, and I bite my lip. Yes, we're going out, but it's probably not exactly what she thinks. 'Just let me get changed and throw on something that hasn't been peed or drooled on!'

'You always look good,' I say, meaning it. No matter how tired she is, or what she's wearing, Zoe has a way of lighting up a room. 'Anyway, you don't need anything dressy. What you're wearing is fine.'

'For our first night out in bloody forever?' Zoe shakes her head. 'No. No way. Give me ten minutes. I'll be right back.'

I chat with Zoe's parents for a bit, filling them in on Milo, his latest accomplishments, and what to do if he wakes up.

'Okay, ready!' Zoe appears in a cloud of her favourite perfume. It's been so long since I've seen her wearing make-up and 'normal' clothes that my mouth drops open. God, she looks sexy. I can't wait to get her back here tonight.

'You look fantastic.' I kiss her glossy lips.

'Very nice, darling,' her mum says. 'Now, you two go off and have a good time. I've got the mobile right here and we'll call if we need you. Go!'

Zoe laughs as she shoos us out the door. 'You don't need to tell me twice. Come on, Edward!' She grabs my hand and tugs me down the stairs. 'God, it feels so weird not to be carrying Milo or any of his stuff! So, where are we going, anyway?'

I wag my finger in the air. 'No questions. Just wait and see.'

'Okay . . .' She takes my arm, and we walk down the busy pavement towards where I've parked the car. Now that the plan is underway, doubts start to creep in. Maybe I should give her a heads-up; tell her where I'm taking her. She thinks we're going to dinner, or the theatre, or any of our old haunts. Where we're going is new territory for us both.

'Ooh, the car! So it's somewhere outside the neighbourhood. Hmm.' She climbs in, and I close the door and start the engine, navigating the packed roads as we cross the city.

'Where are you taking me?' Zoe asks several minutes later, when we've left London behind us. 'Is it one of those country pubs? Or a country home with a fab restaurant? Come on, Edward, give me a hint.' She pokes my side.

I squint at the satnav. 'Almost there. I think. Just around this roundabout . . . ah, here we are.' I smile as I navigate the narrow country road into the village of Cherishton in deepest, darkest Surrey. The village has great transport links, with a fast train into Waterloo. That's one of the reasons houses are so pricey around here, I reckon, but I've found one I'm sure Zoe'll fall for. I certainly have. Putting in an offer without talking to her first was risky, but it's not binding and I didn't want to lose the house to anyone else. This place is perfect for us.

'It's pretty here, isn't it?' I glance sidelong at Zoe as we enter the chocolate-box village, complete with thatched cottages lining the road, a village green flanked by a pub, a church and a post office, and even an organic shop and café. Making their way down the pavement are two mums laughing and chatting, each pushing a buggy. The trees glow yellow as the sun sets, and I can see by Zoe's expression that she's impressed too.

'It's like something from a postcard,' she says. 'But why are we here?'

'Just wait.' I turn onto a small side street past the church, and right at the end is my dream home. *Our* dream home, I hope. In estate-agent speak, it's an old stone farmhouse, built in the mid-1800s and recently renovated to a high standard. There's a huge kitchen with an island and breakfast stools, a separate dining room, and a homey lounge with a massive fireplace. Upstairs, our master bedroom with en suite is at the front of the house, and at the back are two bedrooms, another bathroom and a box room that Zoe can use as her office.

But best of all is the garden, accessible through French doors from the kitchen. It's at least an acre, completely enclosed by mature trees and bushes, so Milo can run around safely with no chance of escape. Already I can picture a slide, some swings and maybe even a trampoline for him to work off that excess energy. Milo tearing across a dappled garden, chasing a ball. A kitchen where more than one person can enter without having to perform a manic version of Twister.

Bloody amazing.

I pull in to the driveway, the gravel crunching under the car wheels.

'Why are we stopping here?' Zoe asks, slicking on more lip gloss. A woman inside waves through the bay window, and I wave back. 'Who's that?'

'Well,' I take a breath. 'You know how we've talked about getting a bigger place, but we can't afford to buy in the city?'

'Yes . . .' Zoe tilts her head, her eyes darting from me to the house and back to me.

'I signed up to an estate agent's website a while back. They've been sending me alerts whenever new properties come up. I just wanted to get a sense of the market – not seriously look or anything – but then I saw an email about this one. I managed to get a viewing yesterday after work, and, well . . . it's incredible.'

Zoe's mouth is opening and closing. 'You want to live *here*?' The way she says the word, it's as if I've asked her to pack up and move to the Sahara. 'I know we talked about moving further out, but this is the freaking countryside!'

I swallow. 'Okay, so it's not right in London, but it's not far, either. We can still come in whenever we want. And wouldn't you like to have your own office? And a garden for Milo to run around in? Just . . . room to spread out?'

Zoe's eyes meet mine, and I can see the wheels spinning in her head. It is a lot to absorb, but once she sees the inside of the house, I know she'll be won over.

'Extra space would be nice,' she says finally. 'But—'

'Come on.' I lean over to kiss her and undo her seat belt. 'Don't say anything more until you see the rest of it.'

'The outside is pretty,' she says, somewhat grudgingly. Stones line the walkway, and trees arch overhead. The glossy red door looks like it's beckoning us in.

I take her hand and together we walk up the pathway. Then I bang the heavy knocker against the solid door, waiting for the estate agent to open up. The door swings open, and I try to keep the excitement off my face when I take in, once again, the wide corridor with solid oak floors, the skylight letting in the last rays of sun, and the lovely cream walls. If possible, I like it even more than I did when I saw it yesterday.

'Come on in,' the agent says, ushering us into the warm interior and out of the crisp autumn evening.

Half an hour later, we've poked into almost every nook and cranny, and the agent is looking at her watch.

'I hate to rush you, but I have a viewing across the village in just a few minutes,' she says. 'I'll let you know as soon as the vendor tells me anything about your offer. They're overseas so it's always hard getting in contact.'

I nod, wincing as I catch a look of surprise on Zoe's face. I wanted to be the one to tell her about the offer I put in, and perhaps – perhaps I should have talked to her before making it. But I was so confident she'd like this place . . . I can't tell a thing from the carefully neutral expression on her face right now. I've tried to catch her eye all through the tour, but she wouldn't meet my gaze. I bite my lip, hoping I haven't been wrong.

'So what do you think?' I say to Zoe when we're back in the car.

She clicks her seat belt closed and shifts in her seat. 'What did the agent mean about your offer? You already made one without talking to me first? Shit, we haven't even looked at other places yet!'

'I know, I know, but this house . . . well, isn't it ideal? There's been a lot of interest, and I didn't want to lose out. Anyway, we can always pull the offer if you don't like it. Of course we'll make the decision together.'

It's so quiet in the car that I can hear the muffled song of birds outside.

'Look, I know this is a huge change for us,' I continue, 'but think of how brilliant it'll be for Milo. The roads are safer, we'll actually get to know our neighbours, and the estate agent says the primary school is outstanding.'

Zoe sighs. 'It's a wonderful house,' she says finally. 'Great space, lots of original features, and I love the garden. Obviously you've already made up your mind.' She pauses. 'It's just so far away from what we know, from our life now. We love the city, popping out with Milo to the café around the corner, or hopping on the Tube to central London.'

'And that's fine at the moment,' I say, 'but what about when Milo can walk? He'll want space to run and play, not cafés and museums. This move isn't about us, it's about him – our family.' A family I really, really want to grow. What's that saying: new house, new baby?

'You know what? You're right.' Zoe smiles, but I'm not sure it reaches her eyes.

'Really?' I'm almost afraid to ask in case she changes her mind, but I want to be sure. The last thing I want is for her to be unhappy because she thinks she's making *me* happy. I want this to be our dream together.

She nods. 'Yes. It is a beautiful house, and it'll be great for Milo. The garden is amazing, and really, if we do want a night out, there's that fast train, right? Anyway, it's not like we go out a lot now. It'll be an adjustment for sure, but I'll get used to it. *We'll* get used to it.'

'I love you, Zoe. This is going to be perfect.' I put my arms around her, pulling my wife as close as the seat belt allows. I've loved living in Zoe's flat – there's so many memories there – but a place we own outright, a space we can make our own?

I'll finally feel like I'm home.

45
EDWARD, SATURDAY, 10.45 P.M.

Through my alcoholic haze, I'm vaguely aware of my mobile ringing. I glance down, noting it's Zoe's parents, then see that an unknown French number has rung me at some point, too.

Ah, whatever. I slide the phone into my pocket again and stand, the night swinging around me. Now I remember why I don't drink much: beer gives me the spins, and I know I'll spend half the night with one foot on the floor praying to get off the self-induced merry-go-round. Zoe used to call me a lightweight, and compared to how she used to be, she was right. Before she had Milo, she could down tequila shots like water, then carry on as if nothing had happened. I'd have one shot and stagger around for the rest of the night. Talk about role reversal.

That wasn't the only role reversal in our marriage, I think, lurching towards the pavement. I was the one pushing for our dream house, I was the one wanting another child. And with Milo, I was the one seeing danger at every turn, the one who'd get up when he cried while she slept through. I reckon if men could breastfeed, I would have done that too.

I'm not complaining. I loved that time with my son, the early mornings when the house was still and the sky outside was just beginning to lighten. I'd wipe his tears and scoop his warm limbs from bed, cuddling the limp, barely conscious body on my lap, rocking him back and forth until he felt ready to face the world with a huge yawn and a wiggle.

A shot of anger darts through the layers of alcohol I've wrapped around me. Why couldn't Zoe have watched him more closely? Why couldn't she have held his hand with just that much more strength? Is it really so hard to keep a child – *our* child – safe? I know I said I don't blame her, and I don't . . . for the most part. But even though I told her it could have happened with me, it wouldn't have. Not a chance.

I forgave her . . . or did I? Every so often, like right now, when I'm not expecting it, rage ambushes me, swarming over me like an army of biting ants, making every bit of me prickle and sting. She lost our child. She let him go. Sometimes I can't bear to be near her. Most times, lately. I can't wait to sell that house and get back to the city, back to the river where I used to walk for hours.

Back to the life I had before.

I lurch towards the hotel and my bed, the anger I felt at Zoe propelling me forwards. Suddenly, my rage is focused on her, like she's the lightning rod for the horror and pain of the past few years. I want to track her down, to shout and let loose all my fury, to vent in the face of her indifference. My life is shit, and it's all her fault.

I'm about to pull open the hotel door when I change my mind. The last thing I want is to lie on the bed and watch the room spin for hours. I'm solidly drunk, and I need to wait for that to wear off. Besides, my anger has given me a spurt of energy so intense I swear I could run a marathon without stopping.

A group of blokes about university age swarm past me, laughing and shouting in American accents about some all-night club that's supposed to be nearby. I've never been one for clubs, but right now, I'll take anything that'll give me a chance to work off this buzz. I'm drunk enough not to care how ridiculous I look when I dance.

'Hey!' I raise a hand, and their heads swing back towards me. 'Can you tell me where this club is?'

A few of them lift their eyebrows quizzically at the sight of me, and I'm suddenly aware I'm old enough to be their father. Well, maybe not, but I probably look that way to them.

'Sure thing.' One of them beckons me forward. 'Come on, we'll take you there.'

I fall into step with them, trying not to show how drunk I am. Their easy banter fills my ears, everything from picking up hot chicks to . . . more hot chicks. I smile and shake my head, feeling every minute of my forty-one years. It seems like aeons since I was single and out drinking with my mates. Being a husband, father-hood and tragedy all create an ocean between me and them.

But these blokes don't know any of that. All they can see is an old guy who wants to have a good time. And damn it, I'm going to if it kills me. I'm sure tomorrow that I'll feel like it will, but I'll deal with that later.

'It's right here.' One of the blokes points to a nondescript door down some stairs. I can already hear the bass booming, and I follow them down the steps and hand over crumpled notes to the man at the door. Inside the club, the air is dank, and I blink against the strobe lights flashing at a blinding pace. The music is so loud I can feel it vibrating my insides, and I'm constantly jostled as people push around me. It's everything I would have hated a few short years ago, but now I welcome the assault on my senses.

I fight my way to the bar, then order two tequila shots. I down them both and head out into the crowd again, onto what I think must be the dance floor. As the alcohol slowly burns its way down my throat and into my gut, I feel my body start to move as the beat takes hold, like something primitive inside me is responding to a tribal call. I shake my head back and forth, and everything blurs in front of me.

46
ZOE, SUNDAY, 12 A.M.

The small clock on the bedside table says it's midnight, and after the long day in the sun and all the walking I've done, I'm struggling to stay awake. Freshly showered, smelling of soap and not sweat, and with neatly curled hair, I'm perched on the edge of the bed, waiting for Edward. I'm afraid to lie down in case I drift off, and anyway, this nightgown thing he bought me itches like mad if it presses on my skin. It looks rather hideous on me, but I'm touched by his effort . . . an effort I haven't made for years. No wonder we're in such a state.

I glance at the clock again, wincing when I notice only a minute has passed since I last checked. Where the hell is he? I've used the room phone to call his mobile several times, but each time it goes straight to voicemail without even ringing first. I tap my fingers on the duvet. I hope he's okay. How ironic that I'm now worrying about him after being lost myself.

A loud growl from my stomach surprises me. I can't remember the last time I was hungry. Usually, I force myself to eat some cereal, or a slice of bread, or just anything to keep me going. The time when fantasising about dinner was the highlight of my day is long gone.

Edward and I used to go out for lunch every Sunday, a tradition we continued even after Milo's birth, even after moving from the city. It was impossible to confine our son to a high chair once he started walking, but the village pub had a huge garden he could run in. We took it in turns to play with him, shoving steaming food in our mouths when we could. It may not have been the most relaxing lunch – and it couldn't have been further from the trendy glass-and-chrome places we used to frequent – but somehow it felt right. My memory fills with laughter, spilled wine on wooden tables and the way Edward would pat my belly once I'd cleared my plate, even though he knew I hated it.

There's hardly any belly to pat now. Where I used to have curves is now stiff and bony – what I would have died for, about ten years ago. My boobs have deflated, thanks to a combination of breast-feeding for over a year plus the weight loss. My body is one of the many reasons I don't make love to Edward any more. I see the way he looks at me now. Where once his gazes were hungry – as if I was a delicious dessert he couldn't wait to devour – now he seems repulsed.

I remember how sex used to be, back in the early days. I remember the way Edward's tongue felt against me, how his lips moved on my neck, the way he slid into me. A charge goes through me, forcing my lids open in surprise. I can't recall the last time I felt turned on by anything. My body aches with longing and a kind of restless urge to . . . I'm not exactly sure. Have sex? Eat? I don't know what could satisfy the stirring inside of me right now.

I stand and yawn, desperate to stay alert, trying to envisage what'll happen when he walks through that door. He'll be surprised I'm here, that's for sure – surprised in a good way, I hope. When he sees me wearing what he picked out, that should send the right message: that I'm *here*, I'm present. It feels weird to be receptive to my husband after tucking myself away for so long.

But I'm ready now – maybe not for sex, not just yet – but ready to talk, ready to touch.

Waiting for Edward to walk through the door reminds me of when we first moved into the new house, leaving our old life behind but not yet adapting to our present. I'd cut down my workload to make the transition easier, and without the banter of my clients, the familiar hum of traffic outside my window and the comforting wail of sirens, the place felt . . . oppressive, as if Milo and I were alone in the world, with no one around. The lovely back garden eliminated our need to hit the cramped play areas with rusted equipment like we used to, joining countless other city mums desperate to escape their tiny confines. The one café in the village opened only from eleven until two, and the buggy wouldn't fit through the door. There was no library to decamp to on rainy days, no raucous soft-play centre, and no ridiculous music class during which I could trade eye-rolls with other mums while Milo mouthed the maracas. The dads magically disappeared to their city jobs, and while there were plenty of mums around, I'd yet to really connect with them.

So the days seemed endless. Around four, I'd start to crave human interaction (beyond baby talk), and count down the minutes until six, when Edward would walk through the door if the train was on time – never a guarantee. Once he was home, hugs traded with Milo and kisses with me, I could feel contentment creep over me like sinking into a hot bath. It was those times he was late or had a meeting that I'd itch to get away, run off to the city and submerse myself in cinema or theatre, or just walk down the busy streets.

But I adjusted – or I was starting to, anyway, when Milo's accident happened. I got to know the other mothers in the village through my daily strolls with Milo, my parents moved nearby, work picked up again and the minutes ticked by faster. Slowly, the house that had seemed so grown-up, so adult, so foreign, began to feel like a fit. And slowly, we both wanted more – more family, more love, more life to fill it.

And then, in just a minute, the home we'd made together was wrong. Every time I entered it was a reminder of what we'd lost: the idyllic life I'd baulked at.

How I long to have that back now.

I sink down on the bed, willing away the tears pushing at my eyes. I've cried more today than I have in two years. That life is gone, and I've only myself to blame. I don't know where to go from here, or what Edward wants. Stay put? Sell the house? Move back to the city?

We can talk about all this later, I think, finally succumbing to the urge to lie down. The most important thing now is to just . . . *connect*. I let out another yawn and my eyes sink closed, and the last memory that floats through my mind before everything goes black is Edward, Milo and me, pushing open that red door to our new home.

47
EDWARD, OCTOBER 2012

This time last year, I was showing Zoe the house. Now, we've settled in nicely, and at the risk of sounding smug – okay, at the *certainty* of sounding smug – life is brilliant. More than I ever imagined, even. It feels like tempting fate when I think that, but I can't help it. Married two years now, with a wonderful son.

I shake my head, thinking it couldn't be better . . . well, maybe with another baby, but we'll get to that. I hope, anyway. I want another child. I want us to be an even four and not a lopsided three. I want Milo to have a sibling, the way I never did. If I could get Zoe pregnant once, I'm sure I can again.

I glance around the kitchen as I open the fridge to get out the champagne. I love this place. It feels like we've lived here forever now – like this is where we're meant to be. Milo adores the space, Zoe's settled into the kitchen table, despite me telling her to move to the box room, and to my surprise, I've actually started gardening – and I'm enjoying it. We may have become fully fledged adults, but it feels right, and I can't wait to spend the rest of our lives together here.

I hand her a dewy glass and she lifts it to her lips. 'So, I've been thinking.'

'Uh-oh,' she jokes. 'I know that look! Last year you sprang this house on me. What do you have planned this time?' She reaches out to take my hand, and I glance down. Our wedding rings slide against each other as our fingers intertwine, and happiness gushes through me as I remember that moment two years ago when she finally said 'I do'.

Milo's cry squawks through the baby monitor, and Zoe and I both laugh.

'Perfect timing,' she says. 'As usual!' It's a running joke that whenever I open my mouth to say something important, or we try to have sex, or just close our eyes for an instant, our son starts wailing.

'I'll go.' I put down my champagne glass and start to get up, but Zoe presses on my arm.

'No, *I'll* go,' she says, springing from the sofa and heading up the stairs before I can protest.

I watch her leave, sipping from my flute as her croons and soft murmurs drift from the monitor. It's been wonderful watching Zoe adapt to being a mother. She was hesitant at first, unsure what to do and how to occupy that space. But now it seems so natural to her, and I love witnessing the connection between mother and son. She doesn't even seem to miss the city, which only goes to show how moving here was the right thing to do.

'Okay.' Zoe settles onto the sofa again and picks up her glass. 'I think he's all right now. What were you going to say?'

'Well.' I swing round to face her and take her hand as I draw in a breath. 'Milo's getting easier now, and we have an extra room . . .'

'You want to try for another baby,' she finishes with a smile, and my eyebrows fly up that for once, we actually seem to be on the same page.

I nod. 'I'd love another one. There's no guarantee, but it hap-pened once—'

'It can happen again.' Zoe squeezes my hand. 'We may have to try a lot, but it's a sacrifice I'm willing to make.'

'Really?' Excitement builds inside at the thought of a newborn nestling in my arms, of running in the garden playing football with my two little children. I'm surprised she didn't need a little more convincing, but I love that we're in tune.

Zoe nods. 'Yup. In fact, why don't we start now?' She slides a hand down my leg. 'There's no time like the present.'

A shudder of desire runs through me. 'Happy anniversary,' I say, as she lowers her body onto mine.

48
ZOE, SUNDAY, 6.30 A.M.

My eyes open slowly and I stretch out on the bed, taking in my surroundings as my mind whirls, trying to place where I am. The arches of my feet cramp and my legs ache, and the strangeness of yesterday filters into my consciousness. I jerk towards the other side of the bed, but Edward's not there. Judging by the first rays of light coming through the crack in the thin curtains, it's still very early in the morning. Where on earth could he be?

I grab the room phone and dial his mobile for the countless time, but again it goes to voicemail. I hang up, drumming my fingers on the bed. It's not like him to stay out all night – at least, I don't think it is. Not the Edward I know, anyway. Is it possible he came here, saw me, and left? No, he wouldn't do that. We did come here to Paris together, after all. I shake my head, wondering if this is how Edward felt when I disappeared: confused, anxious, yet hopeful I'd turn up any second.

He *will* turn up, I tell myself, quashing down the familiar worry rising inside, unwilling to let myself go there again. There's no way I can sleep now, so I peel off the awkward-fitting nightgown and lay it neatly on the bed, saving it for another time . . . maybe tonight? I open the case to throw on some fresh clothes. The sight of my jeans and T-shirts nestled up to Edward's shirts and socks makes me smile, and a jolt of hope goes through me. We have spent years together and been through so much. Can we somehow make our marriage work again?

I hop into the shower, rinsing off the sleep and drowsiness, then make myself a strong cup of instant coffee with the kettle in our room, my lip curling as I sip the sour taste. It's absolute rubbish, but I crave the caffeine. Today, for the first time in ages, I want to be awake, alert. I want to be *alive*.

I pull a chair over in front of the window and lever it open, breathing in the sharp coldness of the morning air as the first rays of sun bathe the building opposite. The street is quiet and the shop-fronts shuttered, but even after my long day yesterday, I don't want to stay inside and wait. In a way, I feel like I've spent the past few years doing that . . . Waiting for what, I don't know. The pain to ease? The blame to shift? Now I want – I need – to do something, even if that something is just a walk through the streets as the city awakens.

I grab the hotel pen and notepad, and scribble a note for Edward outlining what happened, that I'm here, and I'll be back soon; to please please *please* not go anywhere without me. I bite the end of the pen, wondering if I should write more: that I want to talk . . . that I'm sorry. I shake my head, staring down at the expectant paper. I can't write that here. Those are words that need to be said face-to-face, when I see him again. I add two kisses under my name, hoping they'll signal my state of mind, then slip on my dusty shoes, grab a cardigan from the suitcase, and head out the door.

My footsteps echo on the street as I walk under the archway and into a beautiful square with arches waving down each side. The last time I was out this early – stayed out this late – was . . . no, I won't think of that now. I open my eyes wide, drinking in the sights. The sun hits the top of the buildings, highlighting their glorious symmetry. In the middle of the square, a fountain gushes water, glistening in the morning sun. *Edward would love this,* I think, wondering if he's seen it yet. Automatically my head swivels left and right, as if I'll spot him leaning under one archway, but of course he's not there. The square is deserted except for one poor punter, obviously the victim of too much drink, being helped by a hotel porter as he heaves in the corner. Ah, the aftermath of Saturday night, I think, shaking my head. It's the same the world over.

I head out of the square and down a street I'm sure I walked on yesterday. Everything looks different in the early morning, when the age-old beauty of the buildings isn't clad in darkness and the pavements are peaceful and calm. It's as if the city is recovering from the long night, gearing up to embrace the day and all its potential. In a way, I feel like that, too.

I'm about to turn and head back when the sun hits something in a crack in the pavement, the reflective rays almost blinding me. *Just a coin,* I think, as I squint to get a better look. But it's not a coin, I realise, leaning closer. Jammed between two broken paving blocks, it looks like a ring. I stoop down, the muscles in my legs screaming, as I try to jimmy it out with my finger. It *is* a ring, a thick gold one, like a man's wedding band.

Actually, I think as I turn it this way and that, it looks remarkably like Edward's wedding band. But there's no way it could be; that ring is glued to his finger. He refuses to take it off to give it a proper clean, even when it got splashed with paint when he was doing up Milo's room. A memory floats into my mind of him, swiping at his finger with white spirit, and laughingly saying I'd have to kill him first if I wanted to get this ring off his finger. I just rolled my eyes, thinking how I removed the ring when I did the dishes, at those silly baby swim classes, when I showered . . . how it wasn't the ring that symbolised the health of the marriage, but rather the connection between two people. For him, though, that ring was everything.

I lean against the stone wall and lift it to my eyes to get a better look, then run my fingers along the inside to see if it's engraved. I know it's impossible that this is Edward's, but the resemblance is so uncanny, something inside me is driving me to just . . . check. The scratch of engraving meets my fingertips, and my stomach flips. Slowly, I lift it even closer to my eyes.

E & Z. Our own happy ending.

I stare at the letters, feeling a thousand times older than the woman who first laid eyes on them, even though it's only been a few years. Back then, we thought our happy ending would be a house filled with children and laughter. *Can* we find our way to another ending – together?

I take a deep breath, my fingers closing around the wedding band. I don't know, but I want to try. To talk, to finally open myself, and see if there's anything still inside. We've both changed; both been through so much, but I hope there's something between us worth saving.

I head back to the hotel, his ring biting into my palm, I'm clutching it so hard. Now that the shock of finding his ring has passed, a little dart of worry flies towards me, piercing the balloon of anxiety I managed to quash earlier. The Edward I know – I *knew* – wouldn't willingly take this off. So how on earth did it end up on the pavement? Is he all right? Has he been mugged, and his ring dropped by the muggers by mistake? Does this have something to do with where he's been all night?

I quicken my steps through the square, crossing my fingers he's back in our room. Inside reception, the air is heavy now with the scent of coffee and warm croissants, and I cast a quick look inside the tiny dining area, but he's not there. Too anxious to wait for the lift, I take the winding stairs two by two, my breath coming in puffs as I near the top. When I swing open the door, my heart is pounding and I feel lightheaded, but I'm not sure if that's from the burst of exercise or my nerves.

I cock my ears for the shower, for the splash of water in the sink, for anything telling me he's there. But my note rests on the pillow just where I left it, the curtain's fluttering in the breeze of the window I threw open, and there's no sign of him.

Where are you? I want to yell out the window like they do in the movies. I picture my voice floating over the potted chimney-tops and grey-slated rooftops, wrapping around the Eiffel Tower and sliding off the dome of Sacré-Coeur.

Is it daft to think that somehow, somewhere, he can hear me?

49
EDWARD, SUNDAY, 6.30 A.M.

My vision is blurry, I'm cold although I'm drenched in sweat, and the pounding music and flashing lights are making me queasy. I've no idea what time it is, but I know one thing: I need to get back to the hotel room and crash. It was good to go crazy in a way I haven't done for years – maybe ever – but I'm too old to keep it going.

I stumble towards the club door and up the stairs, grabbing onto the railing to stop from falling over. Outside, light is slowly creeping into the dark night sky, and the first rays of sun are touching the pavement. I shut my burning eyes, then quickly open them when the world starts spinning. Christ, what have I done to myself?

Right, which way to the hotel? I wasn't paying attention when I followed the Americans to the club, but I don't think it was too far. Anyway, maybe walking a bit will help me work off the spins. I start to move hesitantly down the pavement, feeling as if I'm moving through treacle.

One foot, then the other. One foot, then the other.

If I concentrate on that, I'll get there eventually.

After what feels like forever but is probably only a few minutes, my eyes widen – as much as they can, anyway – as I spot a fountain through the arches. This is the square around the corner from the hotel. Somehow, I've made it back, and not a moment too soon because my guts feel like they're about to expel themselves through both ends. I quicken my pace as much as my muscles will allow, across the grassy bit, past the fountain, and—

My breath leaves me in a *whoosh* as I crash into one of the many arches. A sharp pain comes from my temple, and I dazedly lift a hand to my head. My fingers come away covered in blood.

'Monsieur?' A man is at my side, taking my arm. 'Monsieur, are you all right?'

I can't even bring myself to answer or even nod, the pain clutching my head is so intense. *Good thing I'm drunk*, the thought bubbles up in my brain. *Otherwise this would really hurt.* I want to laugh, but my stomach is starting to shift, and I'm afraid any movement will make me vomit.

Too late. All the beer and everything I've eaten splash in a waterfall on the pavement. The man moves away, his face registering disgust. *I'm disgusted too, mate,* I want to say. I can't believe the state I'm in. I've never been sick from drink, and starting in my forties is downright pathetic.

'Sorry,' I croak, wiping my face with a hand. He takes my arm again and beckons me over to an empty bench. I slump down, feeling like absolute hell. I can feel a line of blood snaking down the side of my head, and the throbbing is getting worse, like someone's jammed an ice pick in my skull.

'I have called an ambulance,' the man says. 'You sit here. It will come soon.'

'No, no.' I try to shake my head but it hurts like hell. 'I don't need an ambulance. I'll just rest for a minute and then I'll go to my hotel. It's over there.' I wave an arm in its direction.

'You fell very hard into the wall,' the man says in an authoritative voice. 'And that cut on your head looks like it needs stitches. You must wait here.'

I want to argue but I can't find the words. I can't find the energy to move either. When the ambulance comes, they'll see it's a wasted call and send me on my way. I lean back and close my eyes again, praying for the world to stop moving.

50
ZOE, APRIL 2013

I stare at the blood on the loo roll, the knowledge sinking in as instantly as my PMT arrives: I'm not pregnant. Outside the bathroom, Milo is banging on the door, calling 'Mama! Mama!' so insistently you'd think I'd buggered off to Mars instead of treading the few steps from the lounge to our downstairs loo. I used to think those mums who said they'd give anything to go to the bathroom in peace were slightly demented. How hard can it be to leave a child and pee? Now, I'd give anything for a little bit of headspace to absorb that, yet again, we haven't conceived.

It's only been a few months. Six months, in fact, since Edward and I started trying. And even though I know that's not very long, and that it likely won't happen easily, the very fact of *trying* makes me long for an outcome. I've never been good at waiting around, believing in fate for a positive outcome. To that end, I've been doing everything I can to get pregnant: taking those horrific vitamins, giving up booze (!!), and even checking my temperature to confirm when I'm ovulating. Still . . . nothing.

It's so funny that when I didn't want to get pregnant, didn't think it could happen, I did. And now, when we're actually ready, I can't. Even though I know where the problem lies, I can't help feeling it's somehow my fault. Or my body's fault, rather, since I'm starting to feel like it's not my own property any more. Kate (now living in a madhouse with two children, a dog and three hamsters) keeps telling me to relax, that it will happen, and to enjoy life with one child while we can.

And we are, of course we are. No one can claim motherhood is easy, and sometimes my head aches from the relentlessness of it all. But just like I imagined, those little moments every day – the moments when your child flings his arms around your neck, or when his giggles burst like bubbles in the air – make the hardship fade away into oblivion. I can barely remember my life before him; it feels empty somehow, without this weight of love and emotion.

Edward's trying to be calm about the whole thing, but I can see the disappointment and longing in his eyes when I tell him, month after month, that it hasn't happened. He nods, gives me a hug, then just says we'll keep trying. I want to ask how long – how long all this will go on for, because I don't think I can bear year after year of failure. Instead, I clamp my lips closed, breathe in his scent, and tell myself that if it doesn't happen, it's fine. We have our family, we have the world's most wonderful boy, and anything else is just a bonus. Perhaps we're being greedy wanting more. Perhaps we *should* just bask in what we have. It's hard, though, when desperation pours from Edward's every cell.

'Mama's coming!' I call to Milo when the banging and shouting reaches such epic levels, I'm afraid the door will cave in. Sighing, I pull up my knickers and wash my hands, gazing at my reflection in the mirror.

Anything else is just a bonus, I repeat like a mantra, opening the door and gathering my wiggly son in my arms, breathing in his little-boy scent. He bites my nose and squirms away, and I lever myself into a sitting position just as the front door swings open.

'Daddy!' Milo breaks free and streaks towards his father, throwing his chubby arms around Edward's legs.

'Hey! Good day?' Edward ruffles Milo's soft brown hair, then bends down and kisses me. 'Any news?' He knows my period's due today, and I try not to seem too anxious as I shake my head.

'No. Not this time.' I look away from Edward and over at Milo, unable to stand the disappointment etched in Edward's face. 'Come on, little boy. How about you tidy up before you trip on a toy?'

We both watch as Milo runs to his toy box and proceeds to empty the rest of it rather than the reverse. Edward laughs, and I let out a big sigh. It's only funny when you haven't been tidying toys all day.

'Come here.' Edward pulls me up and over to the sofa. God, it feels good to sit on something cushioned rather than the hard floor I've been playing with Milo on all day. I lie back and shut my eyes, feeling myself relax now that Edward's home and the weight of responsibility for Milo has been lifted a bit.

'I've been thinking . . .' Edward's voice cuts into my haze, and I reluctantly lift my lids. 'I know we haven't been trying that long, but maybe I should get some tests done, just to see what the picture really is.'

I sit up and rub my eyes. 'Yeah, that makes sense.' If it makes him less anxious, I'm all for it. 'What do you need to get the process started?'

'I'll see our GP,' Edward says, stretching out his long legs. I make a face, eyeing a hole in the seam of his jeans. I really need to take him out shopping soon. 'The last time, it took about a month to book me in for testing, so I'd expect the same again.'

I swing towards him. 'The last time? What do you mean? You had the tests done before?'

Edward shifts on the sofa. 'Well, no. I didn't actually go.'

My brow furrows and I try to straighten it out. Mum keeps telling me I'm going to get wrinkles, and she's right. 'Why not? When was this, anyway?' I cast my mind back over the past couple of years, trying to remember if he ever told me he was going to get tests done, but the results come back blank. And why would he not tell me, anyway?

'It was after Kate told me you were pregnant. I wasn't sure what to think – if it was even possible – so I went to see the GP, who booked me in for the tests. But then when you told me it wasn't mine, then it was, and everything, well . . . there really didn't seem to be much point.'

'Ah.' Both of us are staring at anything other than each other. It's the first time we've ever spoken of that terrible chain of events – of the terrible thing I did. Looking back, I can't believe I told Edward that Milo wasn't his. I can't believe I lied like that to the man I loved, the man whose son was inside of me.

But I'm not the same person. I'm not that woman who baulked at forevers, at filling in the blanks of my future, at building a life full of love. Hell, I even want more of it, despite what that means – more sleepless nights, even less freedom and even more juggling.

I'm not afraid any more.

51
EDWARD, SUNDAY, 7 A.M.

The wail of an approaching ambulance cuts through the wall of pain that's imprisoning me. I try my best to turn in its direction, but it hurts even more. I must have hit my head really hard.

'English?' The paramedic asks when he reaches me, accompanied by the man who first helped me.

'Yes,' I say through gritted teeth. Even speaking that much is agonising.

The paramedic tries to turn my head and a sharp yelp escapes me. I'd be embarrassed, but honestly, I'm still too drunk to care and it hurts like fucking hell.

'You come with us to hospital,' the paramedic says. 'A doctor will need to stitch this.'

'No, no, no,' I say. 'Can't you just put a plaster on it?' Suddenly, a thought enters my mind. What time is it, anyway? Fiona's train will arrive this morning, and I'm in no fit state to meet her. I can only imagine how she'd embrace the winning combination of booze and vomit. At the very least I need a shower. A trip to the hospital – a French hospital, at that, where I'll have no clue what's happening – is not on the agenda.

But the paramedic has other ideas. He's already taking my arm and helping me up. 'You don't get that stitched, you'll have a big . . . what do you call it? Scar. Plus risk of infection. Come. It won't take long.'

Yeah, right. Since when have hospitals been known for their speed? But Fiona still hasn't rung, and I don't want a scar or infection either. Sighing, I let the paramedic lead me into the back of the ambulance and position me on a stretcher. The doors slam closed, the engine starts up, and my eyes close as it pulls away.

The clang of the doors opening again jerks me back to consciousness. I try to sit up but the pain is blinding, so I lower my head. As the paramedics carry me into the hospital, the bright lights and the smell of antiseptic, dust and the musky scent of people crowded together hit my senses.

All of a sudden, a wave of memory sweeps over me so quickly I don't have time to push it back.

It's the day of Milo's accident, and Zoe's just rung. She's in the back of the ambulance with him, she says, in a voice so flat and lifeless, it sounds like a stranger. Sirens blaring in the background, she asks me to meet her at the hospital, then hangs up. I try to call her back, but the mobile signal at the godforsaken location my company's holding their corporate retreat is so weak, I can't get through.

Why the fuck has this happened on the one day I'm miles from home?

I hastily make my exit and grab a taxi to the train station, praying to God the next train is soon. For once, my luck is in. A train pulls in with a screech and I hop onto it, my heart beating fast. At this time of day, there are plenty of seats, but I can't bear to sit. Instead, I stand in the doorway, as if being right there at the ready will make the train go faster. All the while I dial Zoe's number over and over, but it just keeps ringing, then goes to voicemail.

As the rows of suburban houses and chimneys flash by, my mind fills with images of Milo, lying in the back of the ambulance – if they could get him to lie down, that is. We always joked he'd need to be sedated before anyone could get him to be still; putting him to bed could sometimes take hours. Maybe it's a broken arm, or a twisted ankle? A knock on the head needing observation? Perhaps he's sitting up, tugging at the cords and banging on the wall. I pace back and forth across the narrow space, trying to speculate on the nature of the accident and cursing my wife for not telling me more.

Finally, the train pulls into the station. I press the door release button over and over, willing it to hurry up. When the doors hiss open, I dash off the train and down the platform, then up the stairs and over the bridge to the waiting rows of taxis.

'Royal Surrey Hospital, please,' I say, barely able to speak after my burst of exercise. I try to ring Zoe once more, the mobile phone sweaty in my grasp. Still no answer.

I throw a few notes at the driver as the car pulls up to the hospital, then slam the door and hurry into A&E. We've been here once before, a few months ago when Milo had croup. Christ, that was scary. Just listening to him struggling to breathe put the fear of God into my heart. Seeing him in pain made me physically sick, and in that one night, I realised I couldn't bear to lose him.

I push past a huddle of tired-looking people towards reception. Normally I'd be mortified to queue-jump – I'm a proper Brit that way, Zoe always jokes – but now, I don't even care.

'My son was brought in by ambulance an hour or so ago,' I say, wiping the sweat off my brow. 'Milo Morgan. Please can you tell me where he is?'

She looks like she's about to order me to the back of the line, but something in my face must have communicated my desperation, because she asks for his date of birth, and then clacks away on the computer.

'Have a seat right here,' she says, her tone brisk, but her eyes have softened. 'I'll get someone to bring you to him.'

I move a few steps back but there's no way I can sit. I run a hand over my face again, and once more it comes away slick with sweat. Somewhere inside this huge behemoth of a building is my son. I need to see him, to hold his hand and to kiss his chubby cheek. I need to make sure he's okay, or that he's going to be soon. I need him to know that Daddy is here.

'Mr Morgan?' An orderly appears at my side. 'Come this way, please.'

I follow him through a set of swinging doors and down a corridor, the only sound the squeaking of his shoes. As we move away from A&E and through yet another nondescript hallway, my brow furrows. Where are we going? Has Milo been transferred to another unit? I want to ask, but I don't want to slow the man down. I just want to get to my family as fast as possible. The orderly is moving quickly, thank goodness, and I churn my legs to keep up. I'd run if I could.

He ushers me into a lift, then presses a button and the lift shudders into action. As the doors slide open, a blue sign with white letters meets my eyes. It takes a while before the letters actually gel together to make a word, and when my mind understands what that word is, my feet refuse to move any further. They can't move any further. I'm not going there. That's not for me – not where Milo is. They've somehow got it wrong.

The sign says 'Morgue'.

The orderly is halfway down the hallway, the squeak of his shoes even louder now in the silent corridor, before he turns around and sees I'm not behind him.

'Mr Morgan?'

I'm still rooted to the ground, my muscles shaking now as the tremor that started inside me spreads through my body. My head shakes back and forth too. Every part of me, every cell, rejects where this man is taking me.

'I'm looking for my son,' I say, my voice somehow emerging from the desert that is my mouth. 'My son. Milo Morgan.'

The orderly steps towards me, and uncertainty mixed with panic flashes across his face. For the first time, I realise how young he is – he's probably not even twenty.

'Er, yeah, I'm sorry, reception told me to bring you here,' he says. 'For the boy that came in by ambulance, right?'

I nod, and the orderly bites his lip.

'Please follow me.' It sounds more of a timid request than anything else, and even though I still can't believe I'm in the right place, in a strange way, I feel compelled to help out this young man. I force my legs to move towards him, then around another corridor, until we stop outside a room. There's a small window with a curtain drawn across it, and I can feel my breath catch in my throat.

'Your wife is inside here, along with your son,' the orderly says, then turns and walks quickly down the corridor again, the squeaks increasing in frequency as if he can't wait to escape the scene.

I still can't believe they've got it right, but I need to allay the dread and fear inside. Like something in a nightmare, in slow motion I raise my hand and knock on the door, my heart pounding as I wait for whoever's inside to open it. *Please let it not be Zoe. Please let it not be Zoe. Please let it not be Zoe.* A desperate kind of prayer runs through my head as footsteps approach.

I see the door handle twist, and then Zoe appears, and everything inside me goes black.

52
ZOE, SUNDAY, 8.30 A.M.

There's no way I can stay in this hotel room and just wait for Edward to appear. I need to move, to do something. My days of drifting around waiting for the time to pass are over.

I slip his wedding band in my pocket, then thump down the narrow stairs and over to reception.

'Could you tell me when you last saw my husband? Edward Morgan?' I ask the receptionist. It's a small hotel, so there's a chance she might remember. She gives me a pitying stare, likely wondering what kind of pathetic marriage we have that I don't even know where he is.

'I haven't seen him this morning,' she says, 'but I've only just started my shift.'

Ah, of course. 'If you do see him, can you please tell him his wife is looking for him? There's a note in the room,' I say, not wanting to go into details. She's already starting to look bored.

'Of course. And may I remind you that checkout is at eleven?'

Cheeky cow, I think, as a flash of panic goes through me. What if I don't find Edward before checkout? How will I get home? It's funny that now I actually want to go back. I've spent the past two years trying to get away.

But I'll find Edward again. Of course I will – all his things are still here. Unless . . . My fingers worry the ring in my pocket. Unless something's happened to him.

He's a big boy, I remind myself, pushing back the niggling fear. I'm sure there's a perfectly reasonable explanation for why his ring was on the pavement. I bite my lip, thinking that maybe I'll call a few hospitals . . . just in case. I never told Edward, but it's something I used to do whenever he came home late from work, in that first year after Milo's accident. Life – or death – had shown me how easily something could be yanked away, how quickly someone you loved with all your being could just disappear. And even though I wasn't hanging on to Edward during that time – I couldn't, I didn't have it in me – there was still a part of me that feared losing him. I called so much that the hospital refused to answer my queries, and eventually I stopped. But I don't think my fear ever did.

But this isn't the same thing, not even close. We're in a strange city, he hasn't been here all night, and his ring was on the pavement. I know in my heart of hearts that something isn't right. I head back down to reception, knowing she's going to think I'm crazy and not even caring. I gave up caring what other people think about my state of mind long ago.

'I'm worried about my husband,' I say to her now. 'It's not like him to be out all night. I'd like to call the hospitals just to make sure he's not there. If you could give me the number—'

'I do it,' she says, surprising me with her responsiveness. 'It will be easier if I do it.'

'That would be great, thank you. His name is Edward Morgan, he's tall and thin with dark hair . . . He should have his ID on him.' I bite my lip again, thinking that if his wedding ring was missing, maybe his wallet is, too. What are the chances of us both getting mugged in this city?

She nods and looks up a number on the computer. I hold my breath as she dials it, then asks the operator something in rapid French. I catch Edward's name, and then she nods. 'I have called the nearest with an emergency department. I am on hold; they are checking admissions now. It could take some time.' She looks pointedly at a chair in front of the desk, but there's no way I can sit.

He'll be fine, I tell myself. He has to be. After everything I've been through, there's no way I could lose him, too. Not like this.

The receptionist lets out a stream of French to whoever's on the other end of the line, then turns to me. 'He's at hospital Hotel Dieu,' the receptionist says, and my heart jumps.

'Is he okay? What happened?'

'They wouldn't tell me anything,' she says, dialling another number and shooting French into the receiver. 'I've called you a cab, and it should be here in a minute. It will take you there.'

'Thank you.' The words emerge in a trembling voice. My legs somehow carry me to the door, my heart beating against my ribs like it wants to get out. This can't be happening. Not again.

I won't let it.

53
EDWARD, SUNDAY, 8.30 A.M.

'**M**onsieur?'

My eyes fly open at the sound of a voice. A doctor is hovering over me, poking and prodding at the wound on my head. Christ, that hurts.

'You will definitely need stitches,' he says, turning away and pulling open a drawer where the torture instruments await. 'One moment, please.' He slides open a curtain and I rest my head against the hard mattress again with a soft groan. My skull is pounding so hard it's practically levitating off the pillow with each throb, and the less said about the state of my digestive system, the better. What the hell was I thinking, drinking so much?

My eyes drift closed again, and Zoe's face flashes into my mind, exactly how it looked that day at the morgue: not my wife, not someone I know, someone frozen . . . someone locked inside so firmly she could barely move. I should have hugged her, or tried to, anyway, but I couldn't. All I could see, once my vision cleared, was Milo.

I'd never seen him so still. Even when he was sleeping, he was a whirlwind, constantly twisting himself up in blankets and falling off the bed. His face was chalky like he'd been into Zoe's face powder once again. One cheek was scraped and bruised, and his lips had two deep marks. But other than that and some dirt on his jeans (par for the course), nothing could tell me what happened.

Zoe explained in that same flat tone, gripping Milo's hand the whole time as her voice filled the small room. I remember staring at her, seeing her lips move, yet all the while not taking it in. Desperately trying to find something – someone – to make it not true.

A cry bursts from me now that has nothing to do with my head. Grief rolls over me, and this time, I'm powerless to stop it. It fills every pore of my being, soaking into all the cracks and empty spaces, until I feel like my body is almost solid with sadness, like concrete weighing me down on the bed. I want to get up, to escape, to move away from it like I usually do, but I can't – I'm pinned. It presses on my lungs with such force I can barely breathe, or even form thoughts. A low wail leaves my throat, a sound that's so animalistic, it doesn't even seem human.

I don't know how long I lie like that, inert on the bed, as sadness crashes inside me like physical blows to my guts. Each hit takes my breath away, as image after image of Milo lying on that gurney assaults my mind. I silently beg for my brain to stop, but I've lost control. I've no choice but to give in.

In the midst of all this, Zoe's stony face fills my mind. Is this how she feels every day? Is this what she lives with – a sadness that isn't just a passive passenger but a violent hijacker, grabbing your life and the will to live? If so, I can understand now why she's had such a hard time moving on. If this is the norm, just getting through the hours must be torture. No wonder she couldn't talk to me, couldn't respond to what I thought was my help and support.

A stab of guilt pierces me as I picture the times – the many times – I tried to move her on, and the frustration I felt when nothing seemed to work. Packing up Milo's room, encouraging her to get more clients . . . even asking to try for that baby again. I wince, remembering her stricken expression. If someone tried to chivvy me along right now, I'd haul off and hit them. I was only doing what I thought was best, but can I really say my method of moving forward has served me well? Have I ever even allowed myself to grieve properly for him, for my son? Feel the soul-deep sadness engulfing me now for longer than a few seconds, without batting it away?

I slide my hand down to my ring finger, where the skin still feels strange and naked, then up to my recently shorn chin. Here I am, trying to make myself into something I am not, turning back time by shaving and trying to lose myself in alcohol. Here I am, about to cheat on my wife and the mother of my child with a woman I like but – let's face it – don't love, and probably never will. I'm forty-one years old, and I'm lying in bed at the emergency department of a foreign hospital after splitting my head open from drinking too much. Pathetic.

And none of it has helped blank the memory I'm trying to dodge. I'm still a man whose son has died, and whose wife has left him too. And while I may understand that a bit better now, no matter how hard I try, nothing will erase that.

Not even sleeping with Fiona.

I force my eyes open and look at my mobile. Fiona still hasn't texted her arrival time, but it must be soon. I'll get fixed up here, head to the hotel, and see when she's coming. I'll meet her at the train station and tell her I'm sorry, but I need to return to London – I can't go any further with her. I don't want to disappoint her, especially after the long train journey, but I can't keep this up any longer. I don't want to be a tourist in this town; I don't want to try to keep forcing myself to look ahead.

I just want to be home, even if I don't know where that is any more.

54
EDWARD, MAY 2013

I'm sitting in the doctor's office, willing myself to stay calm as I await the results of the fertility test. I know I'm not infertile – obviously, since Milo's my son – but if we need extra help to conceive again, it's best we find out now. I hate the look on Zoe's face, month after month, when she discovers she's not pregnant. I hate knowing it's because of me that we can't complete our family yet, to give Milo a brother or sister. I want Zoe and Milo to have everything, but my body won't play ball. The weight hangs heavy on me every day, a constant rebuke in the background of our happy life.

And so, as much as I detest the thought of jerking off into a tube, then handing it over for analysis, I've done just that. If there's something I can do to kick-start my balls into functioning properly, I'm on board.

'Edward Morgan?'

I follow the doctor into his office and settle into the chair, thinking back to this time a few years ago. It feels like another century, but I can still remember the confusion and uncertainty whipping around my brain as I tried to figure out what to do – and then how it all fell apart when Zoe told me the baby wasn't mine. I try not to think about that now, because there's no point recalling the absolute pain, the hurt, and then the relief yet disbelief when she told me the truth. We are happy, life together is wonderful, and dredging up old memories achieves nothing. Besides, Zoe promised never to lie again, and I believe her.

'We have the results from your test.' The doctor leans back in his chair, and my heart picks up pace. 'Your sperm count is certainly on the lower side, likely as a result of your illness as a child, but there's no reason why you shouldn't be able to conceive naturally. I'd say give it another six months, then come back if you're still having trouble. All right?'

I let out the breath I hadn't even realised I was holding. 'So everything is fine?'

The doctor nods. 'It should be, yes.' He shifts in his chair, a subtle signal this conversation is over.

I nod, say goodbye, and make my way through the corridors and out into the warm spring day, feeling curiously flat inside. I should be happy: the doctor's just told me I'm okay; nothing needs fixing. But maybe I *wanted* fixing, a helping hand to lift this burden. Instead, I'm stuck with a low sperm count and a wife I still can't get pregnant – at least, not this time.

I pause on the pavement outside the clinic, picturing six more months of Zoe's false cheery tone when she tells me no, not this time. I know she's covering the disappointment she really feels . . . covering it for me, of course, since I'm the one to blame. I'm the one who can't give her what she wants for the first time in our marriage, and it kills me.

I envision her face, lit up with optimism and hope as I come through the door, only for me to tell her that I don't have a solution, I don't have an answer. All I have is me and my faulty sperm. And how the hell can a man apologise enough for that?

I turn in the opposite direction of home, away from my wife and son.

55
ZOE, SUNDAY, 9 A.M.

As the taxi makes its way to the hospital, I lean back on the seat and take a deep breath. So many thoughts are running through my mind it's impossible to even consider closing my eyes, despite the fact I've only had a couple of hours' sleep.

Is Edward all right? What happened? Is he lying unconscious, or sitting up being polite and apologising for the inconvenience, like he normally would? I shake my head, my curls pinging off my flushed cheeks. If only I knew something about his condition I wouldn't feel so tense, so cast out into the unknown, flip-flopping between terror and a roll-of-the-eyes at the trouble he got himself into.

For the first time, I can understand how hard it must have been to be on the other side of Milo's accident – not as hard as me, obviously, since I'm the one who caused it. I didn't mean to leave Edward in the dark, of course I didn't, but I could barely speak myself. Even just finding his contact on my phone took five minutes; the numbers kept swimming in front of my eyes. And I'd hoped . . . I'd hoped that Milo might make it. *Hope* is such a feeble word to express how I really felt. If I said I'd scald myself, freeze myself, endure any form of torture for my son to live, I'd have done it in a heartbeat. Less than a heartbeat, even.

That look on Edward's face when he opened the door to the room where Milo was lying – it's something I can't ever forget, like a void had opened up in front of him and he was falling in. I should have moved to comfort him, but I'd already fallen in myself – the only thing keeping me conscious was holding onto Milo's hand, his chubby fingers gripped in mine, the way they should have been earlier that day. And once I let go, I plummeted.

When I told Edward what happened, and he hurled those words at me, those words I'll never forget, then burst out of the room, opening the door with so much force it banged against the wall, well . . .

Why weren't you watching him? Why didn't you stop him? How could you let this happen?

I shut my eyes now against the sun streaming from the sky. I don't blame him for his actions, for his words. I would have prepared him if I could, but how can you prepare your husband for his son's death? I couldn't even come close to absorbing it myself. I don't blame him now for his distance either. He tried to haul me out of the pit I was in, but it wasn't his hand I wanted. It was Milo's, and I couldn't bring myself to reach to anyone else.

But now . . . now, I want to come out of this cave. I *need* to. If Edward and I can endure two years of what we've just gone through and stay together despite it all ('together' being relative, of course), then there must be something worth saving. There's a reason we've both hung in there, why we both agreed to come on this trip in the first place. There is an *us* we need to find again. It won't be the same – neither one of us is. But maybe it can still be something special, something we can rebuild together.

I swallow hard. If we're going to do this, we need to be open and honest . . . no secrets. And that means telling him what happened, that awful day I disappeared a few months after Milo's death. I can already picture his incredulous expression, the shock I never told him. I cross my fingers, praying he'll understand, that he'll be able to understand. I need to take that blind leap of faith and, for once, trust that our relationship is strong enough.

'This is it, Madame.'

I look up at the imposing stone façade of the hospital, then gasp as I realise I have no money. *Shit.* I'd followed the receptionist's command without even thinking about it. I make a big show of rifling through my pockets, pretending to look for notes as the cab driver releases a very Gallic-sounding sigh.

'I'm so very sorry,' I say, desperate now to be out of this car and into the hospital. 'I can't seem to find my money.'

'No money?' In the rear-view mirror, I can see the driver's raised eyebrows.

'I'm sorry, it's just, my husband's in emergency here, and I rushed over . . .' I cross my fingers he understands English well enough to grasp my halting explanation.

'Go, go.' He makes shooing motions with his hands, and I slide from the seat before he changes his mind.

Inside the hospital, the same smell of antiseptic and polish meets my nose and I push away the memories clawing at my mind.

'Excuse me,' I say to a harried-looking older woman with a neat grey bob sitting behind a desk. 'Do you speak English?'

She nods quickly, as if her head is on a string. 'Yes.'

Phew. My nerves can't take trying to speak French right now. 'I'm looking for Edward Morgan. He was admitted sometime last night, I think.'

'One minute.' The woman slides on her glasses and spends what feels like an endless amount of time clicking on the keyboard. My heart is racing and every muscle in my body is set to 'twitch' as I await her response. *What unit will he be in? How long will he need to stay?* I watch her mouth for any sign of movement.

'He's just been released,' she says finally, and relief sinks into every cell of my body. Released. He's all right. Oh, thank god. I still don't know what happened, or why he had to go to hospital, but none of that matters. What matters is that my husband is okay.

'Thank you.' I nod, feeling a smile grow on my face, a glimmer of hope and excitement circling my belly for the first time in . . . well, that night before Milo's accident, I guess. I turn from the desk then race across the polished floor and through the heavy doors, spinning from left to right as I realise I don't have the cash for a cab ride back to the hotel. I'll have to walk.

My legs churn and I force them faster and faster, unable to wait any longer.

My husband. God, how I've missed him.

56
ZOE, JUNE 2013

'More, Mama! More ladybird!' Milo struggles to sit up in bed, grabbing my hand.

I lean down and tuck his blue blankie under his arm. If I need to make up yet another story about the ladybird we saw in the park today, I'm going to lose it.

'No, sweetheart. It's time to sleep now.'

'No . . .' The protest emerges in a low howl from my son, and I kiss his soft cheek as I try to extricate my hand from his grip. Normally Edward's on bedtime duty, but he's off in the wilds of Buckinghamshire on a corporate retreat. After a busy day of park, park and more park, I can't wait to settle down in front of the telly with a glass of Cabernet – although I may need to rethink the wine. I might be wrong, but my period was due a few days ago, and there's been no sign of it. I'm also feeling a bit nauseated, the kind of sickness that sits on your shoulder and refuses to budge.

I say goodnight to Milo and creep from the room, praying he falls asleep quickly. As I pad down the stairs, my hand slides to my stomach. Could there be a baby growing inside me? Another little one to complete our family – finally? I pray to God there is, at the very least to bring back my normally happy, solid husband.

Usually I'm the moody one, but ever since he got those test results, he's become increasingly stressy. It's as if the doctor increased the pressure on him to get us pregnant, instead of easing the strain of thinking there might be problems. I dread the day my period arrives now, because I know he'll stalk out the door and walk for hours, returning only when I've gone to bed.

He's even started asking me if I'm open to fertility treatments. I want another baby, but the cost of those treatments is astronomical, and there is still a chance we can conceive naturally – a very good chance, if my suspicions are accurate. Plus, I'm not keen on injecting myself with hormones day after day, not to mention having my womb 'harvested', like it's some kind of pick-your-own. I want this baby to happen naturally, as if it was meant to be. Not to be coaxed into being with needles and drugs.

But all this is irrelevant if I am pregnant right now. I take the packet from the Boots bag and rip open the foil. Then I carefully close the bathroom door so I don't disturb Milo, who I swear has supersonic hearing. As I aim for the stick, I can't help thinking of that day when I first found out I was pregnant with my son. So much has changed. I'm a wife, a mother, and I live in a small village in the sticks. If you'd have told me then what my life would turn out to be, I'd have said you were crazy – and crazier still if you said I was happy.

Because I am, I think, sliding the cap on the test stick and laying it on the side of the sink to await the results. I am happy. It's taken a bit to settle in – both to motherhood and to our home – but I can't think of another life where I'd be happier. *Well*, I yawn, *maybe one with more sleep.*

I grab the stick off the sink, almost afraid to look. When I see the second pink line meaning I'm pregnant, a funny feeling flutters through me: excitement and hope, mixed with a little worry. What if I can't cope? What if two is too many? What if—?

I shake my head. I know from having Milo that you can never be prepared. That somehow, you just do it. I'll be fine. *We'll* be fine. God, I can't wait to tell Edward. He's going to be ecstatic! I'm tempted to pick up the phone and dial him right now, but this isn't something to tell him over the phone. I want to see his face, to see the spark in his eyes. He'll be back the day after next, and I'll have to try to keep the news under wraps until then.

In the meantime, I'd better prepare myself for even less sleep. I wrap my arms around my tummy, a smile curving my lips.

A baby!

Already I'm in love.

57
EDWARD, SUNDAY, 9 A.M.

I hobble from the hospital, feeling like I've aged fifty years. My head stings where the doctor stitched it, the throbbing – while dulled by several strong painkillers – still hasn't stopped, and my stomach is churning. I don't smell too great either. What I really need is a shower, some strong caffeine, and a bed, but if I lie down now, I'll be too comatose to meet Fiona's train. My heart sinks at the thought of telling her I can't do this, but once she gets a good look at me, she'll probably run off screaming anyway.

I squint against the bright sunlight and climb gingerly into a cab. 'Hotel Le Marais,' I say, my mind flipping back to yesterday when I uttered the same address. It feels like a million years have passed since then, that the person who said those words yesterday was someone else, someone who was climbing an endless ladder to escape rising black water threatening to engulf him. And now that it has engulfed me – now that it's finally caught up – I've discovered that I can deal with it. That it's all right to let in the dark every once in a while; that it can help quell the restless feeling too. And it's maybe even helped me understand a bit of what Zoe was feeling, that her coldness was nothing to do with me. It was about *her*, about trying to survive each day with the grief. Shame that understanding is too late now.

Or is it? I turn my head to take in the spires of Notre Dame Cathedral, my mind running in a million directions as images of the past two years float through my head. All the distance between us, the disconnection, the silence. Can we ever bridge that again? I can't even start to think about that through the pounding of my head.

The cab pulls up to the hotel, and I climb out into the fresh morning air. The street is alive now, the cafés unshuttered and windows cranked open. I open the hotel door and force a smile at the receptionist, even though just that movement makes my temples explode with pain. Her eyes widen when she sees me, and my cheeks colour as I realise how I must look.

'Did your wife find you?' she asks, smiling benignly.

My brow furrows. *Ouch*. 'My wife?' Am I hallucinating, I wonder? Has that blow affected my hearing?

She nods. 'Yes, monsieur,' she says slowly, as if I'm a three-year-old. Right now, a three-year-old would probably be cleverer. 'Your wife. She checked in late last night and she went to the hospital to find you. She has not returned.'

I move my head back and forth, trying to take in her words. Has Fiona somehow arrived early? Does this woman think Fiona is my wife? 'What does she look like?'

The receptionist tilts her head, likely now really thinking I'm a head case. 'Short, curly hair, pretty.'

Oh my God.

My mouth drops open. That's *Zoe*. But what the hell is she doing here? Did she change her mind and come back again? 'Thank you.' Despite my throbbing head, I charge up the stairs and scrounge in my pocket for the key. I slide it into the lock and open the door.

Sure enough, she's been here. The bed is rumpled, and a wave of guilt crashes over me as I notice the nightgown I purchased for

Fiona. Zoe must have thought that was for her. I sink down on the bed and lower my aching head into my hands, and that's when I spot a note. As I scan the lines explaining what's happened, my guilt spreads until it sinks into every pore. While I was drinking, shopping, shaving – Christ, *clubbing*! – Zoe was wandering the streets of Paris with nothing.

Suddenly I remember the missed calls from the foreign numbers, and I grab my phone and dial voicemail. Her voice comes through, plaintive and scared, and I sink down as emotions swirl over me: regret, self-loathing and despair at my actions. I did try to find her, but I didn't try hard enough. I didn't *want* to try hard enough.

My fist hits the bed. We may have grown apart, but I want her to be safe, to be happy, if she can. The anger I've carried towards her these past years has somehow drained away, like the plug has been pulled on a boiling cauldron inside of me. I just want to see her now, to hug her and tell her she's found.

And that I'm sorry.

My mobile rings and I jump. Could that be her?

'I'll be arriving in half an hour! Finally!' Fiona's voice chirps merrily through the receiver, its brightness like someone shoving a screwdriver into my eardrum. 'You'll be there to meet me, right? I was hoping we could get a late breakfast and then head to—'

Her voice cuts off sharply as the train enters a tunnel or something. I try to ring, but I can't get through. The last thing I want to do is leave the hotel room in case Zoe comes back, but I don't want to let Fiona wander around the station on her own either – not when she's expecting me, and not when I'm about to blow her off after inviting her here for the weekend.

I grab a pen on the bedside table and scrawl beneath the note Zoe's left me that I'll be back in about an hour and to please stay put and wait. Then, just in case, I peel a hundred euros from my wallet and place them on the bed, wondering how on earth she's survived the past twenty-four hours with no money.

As much as I don't want to leave, I head back down the stairs and ask the receptionist to call me a cab to the Gare du Nord. She gives me a strange look but does as I request. A few minutes later, a taxi pulls up in front of the hotel. I clamber in, and the driver pulls away.

I keep my eyes peeled for any sign of Zoe's curly head on the pavement, but soon the taxi is swallowed up by traffic on both sides and all I can see is other cars.

I'll be back soon, I tell her, hoping that somehow – even though I know it's ridiculous – she can hear me. *Stay put. Just please stay put. I'm coming back.*

58
ZOE, SUNDAY, 9.45 A.M.

My heart is pounding and adrenaline courses through my veins as I rush down the street towards the hotel. It's not far but the walk seemed to take forever. Finally, I'm here. Edward would have seen my note by now; he'll know I was mugged. I still don't understand what happened with him, but I just want to see his face, and maybe . . . feel his arms around me.

I dash into the hotel, and the receptionist glances up from the computer screen.

'Is my husband back?' I ask, my voice coming out breathless and reedy. After all my exertions, I can barely breathe, let alone form words.

She nods. 'Yes, he came back, but he left about . . . oh, fifteen minutes ago.'

My heart crashes so hard it hurts. 'He left?' I croak. 'He hasn't checked out yet, has he?' I hold my breath. Surely he wouldn't do that after reading my note.

'No, he hasn't checked out,' she says, and I feel like I can breathe again. 'He has gone to the Gare du Nord. I called him a taxi.'

I shake my head, trying to take in the words. The Gare du Nord? If he hasn't checked out, why on earth would he go there?

Unless . . . for some reason, he's gone to look for me? That doesn't make sense, though. Our tickets home aren't until this afternoon, and he has them both. Why would he think I'm there, of all places?

An incredulous laugh bubbles out of me. This whole thing is getting ridiculous, as if we're playing cat and mouse, popping into sight then hiding away again. I don't feel like going up to the room, sitting down and waiting patiently for him to return. He's gone to the station for a reason, and I'm going to go there, too – even if I have to sit and wait on the platform until our train home. In a way, it feels right, as if we've come full circle. Maybe we have.

I've no choice but to walk again, and the receptionist tears off a paper map and traces a route on the streets back to the Gare du Nord. I can't help wondering what she must think of this very strange couple, back and forth and all over the city without intersecting.

Sharp pain shoots through my feet with every step, as if each tiny bone is cracked. My shoes have rubbed my tender feet raw, blisters dotting my soles like fleshy polka dots. I don't care, because this is the final journey to find Edward. I don't know how I know that, but I do.

And so, after everything we have been through – and after everything that's still ahead of us, because I know life is never easy and I still have some burdens to unload – I step back onto the pavement and cross through the square on my way towards him. The fountain sparkles in the sun, the soft hush a lullaby to my tired ears. A man and woman, their faces deeply wrinkled and hair white as snow, nestle together on a bench. Despite fatigue pulling at my bones, I can't help smiling as the man gently tips his partner's head back to watch a flock of starlings take flight, their dark bodies a sharp contrast to the red rooftops. Hope swells inside as I take in the couple's upturned faces, swivelling in tandem as they watch the birds, and it strikes me that the beauty of this place – a perfect kind of beauty I used to scorn – is just what Edward and I need right now: untouched, unsullied, unmarked by our past mistakes.

The babble of the fountain is replaced by people chatting as they devour croissants on packed terraces, cars navigating the now-busy streets, and shopkeepers chatting over their wares. I catch a glimpse of myself in a shop's front window, and I jerk in surprise. My hair is a mess, I don't have any make-up on, and my T-shirt hangs off me, but I look . . . *alive*. It's the first time in a long while that I've looked that way.

I quicken my pace, hoping Edward will still be at the station by the time I make it. If I don't take a wrong turn, the receptionist said it should take me around half an hour. My breath comes in fast puffs and my mouth is dry, but I'm determined to get there as fast as I can.

I miss him, I think again. I didn't realise it; I couldn't feel anything other than the blackness inside of me. But now, I sense his absence as keenly as if he's been physically gone these past couple of years. I push past punters on the street, desperate to see his face. The closer that I get to him, the more I long to see him.

I plod on, the sun getting higher in the sky and the restaurants filling up even more. Finally, just when I think I can't take another step, the façade of the train station comes into view. I almost collapse in relief, but I force myself to cross the busy road and go through the door. I stand at the entrance, people rushing around me, as I wonder what to do now. Should I stay in one place and try to spot him, or should I move around and seek him out that way? Every inch of me is dying for a rest, but something inside urges me on. After the paralysis of the past few years, I can't be the one who stands still. I need to be the one who finds him.

As I circulate around the station, I can't help thinking back to yesterday, almost twenty-four hours ago now, when Edward and I arrived. One day – one day, and I feel so different. I actually *feel*; something inside me has been turned on again. I'll never stop blaming myself for Milo's accident. That jagged sadness will sit on me for the rest of my life. But I do want to have a life now, and I want that life to include Edward.

I walk up and down the concourse, wincing with every step, ducking into the shops I spurned the last time I was here. Where on earth would he be? I stop for a second as passengers stream from one of the platforms, swarming the concourse. I scuttle back towards one of the cafés. The scent of coffee floats through the air, and I breathe in deeply. I'd kill for some caffeine right now. I move closer to better inhale the scent when my heart stops. There's a man who, from what I can make out through the crowd of people, looks a lot like Edward.

Is it him? Could I have actually found him? Heart pounding, I squint to get a better look. He's shaved his goatee and he looks like he's been through the wars – there's a bandage on his temple, and his shirt is grimy – but it's *him*. Warmth builds inside and my lips curve in a smile as I try to cut through the crowd before him. I've no idea what he's doing here, but I knew I'd find him. And now I have.

'Edward!' I call out, but my voice is swallowed up by the buzz of people around me. I lift a hand and try to jimmy myself through the sea of travellers. I'm just about to step over a glittery suitcase when something stops me in my tracks.

Edward's not alone. Chatting and smiling by his side, nibbling on a croissant, is a slender woman with long blonde hair, the kind of hair I coveted as a child. He's nodding and gripping a pink case, resting beside them. Unable to move, I watch as she puts a hand to the bandage on his forehead, then draws him in for a hug.

I watch the scene unfold as if I'm in another place, behind a one-way mirror. My mind works furiously as I try to place the woman. I've seen her before . . . *ah*. It's Fiona, from Edward's work. I've met her a couple of times at company functions, and she's always been friendly with Edward – maybe a touch too friendly, although Edward and I laughed about it at the time. I attempt to unravel the chain of events, trying to understand why she's here. If Edward arranged to meet her, he knew she was arriving. But why – why would she come to Paris?

I swallow hard as thoughts run through my head. Edward didn't know I'd been mugged until this morning . . . he thought I'd gone back home. Did he ask her over, once I was out of the picture? A weekend with another woman, courtesy of his in-laws? Anger shoves out the glow inside me, anger mixed with hurt. How long has this been going on for? Is she the reason he's been spending so much time at work? I didn't think I could feel more pain, but apparently I can – pain and humiliation. My cheeks flush as I realise that nightgown, the champagne, weren't for me. They were for *her*. My fingers slide down to my pocket, where the ring is, and a bitter laugh emerges. I guess now I know why his ring was off.

I stare at my husband, my eyes tracing his freshly shorn face. He looks more than ever like he did when we first met, but he's a stranger. The Edward I know would never cheat on his wife. The Edward I know believed in family – in forever. Another stab of pain jolts through me, and nausea tears at my throat. The Edward I know is gone. How stupid, how naive, now absolutely *idiotic* to think otherwise.

I push blindly through the crowd, catching my foot on a suitcase and tumbling hard to the floor. As I fall, Edward's head swivels towards me and his eyes meet mine, as if I'm a homing beacon.

'Zoe!' I hear his voice as I scramble on the floor, trying to right myself amidst the forest of legs and suitcases. I jerk to my feet and keep my head down, desperate now to get away. I found Edward, yes, but he's not the man I want to find. And now, all I want is to crawl back inside myself, to put away the hope and let the familiar emptiness seep back in, blotting out the pain, the feeling, and leaving a void in its place.

'Zoe!' Edward's voice fills my ears again and I hurry dazedly through the crowd, joining the stream on an escalator, and going down, down, down into the depths of the city.

59
ZOE, JUNE 2013

After a morning of endless rain and desperate attempts to keep Milo entertained so I can get some work done, the sun has finally broken through the clouds. Everything outside is sodden, so I decide to take Milo to the playgroup at the church hall. The way he's literally bouncing off the walls reminds me of a caged animal, and his restless energy is doing my head in.

'Come on, Milo. Let's get your wellies on.'

Milo comes running, then plonks down on the floor as I wrestle on a boot. Whoever made these things so impossible to put on needs a good stint in purgatory. By the time I've managed to get on both wellies and his jacket, I'm sweating. I throw on my old mac and jam my feet into trainers, then grab my keys and open the door.

'Wait for Mummy!' I call as he races towards the front gate. The hall isn't far, but the narrow village road twists and turns, with no pavement to speak of. Milo gives me that cheeky grin, but he stops and waits, then holds out his chubby little fingers for me to take them.

I smile as I grip his hand and open the front gate, my mind full of my big news as we head down the grassy track at the side of the road. It's still hard to believe that this time next year, we'll have another tiny baby, and Milo will have a brother or sister. I gaze down at him, wondering how he'll adjust. Some jealousy, I'm sure, since he's pretty much had the run of the place – and us – since he was born. I slide my free hand down to my stomach, thinking he'll be a great big brother once the dust settles.

'Squirrel!' Milo pulls at my hand as he points to the brown animal streaking across the road. 'Catch it, catch it!'

Caught off balance by the sudden tugging, I try not to topple over. 'Milo, stop!' I say, tilting like the Leaning Tower of Pisa. A wave of nausea sweeps over me and I swallow hard. 'Milo, come on now—'

His fingers slip from my grip and he steps onto the road in hot pursuit of the squirrel. I reach out to scoop him up, but my fingers slide off the plastic of his raincoat and I can't get a grip. 'Milo!' I yell as I step out, too, my voice high-pitched and strained. 'Milo, come back here!'

From the corner of my eye, I see a grey car flying around the bend in the road. Before I can do anything, the car is just feet away, like a monster bearing down. I scream out Milo's name once more, but it's too late. He's cartwheeling through the air, landing silently on the soaking grass. I can't move for a second, frozen in shock and absolute horror. Then I race to his side, terrified he won't be breathing.

'Milo?' I grab his fingers, relief swamping me when I feel them twitch. *My baby's alive. Oh, thank god.* Blood is seeping from behind his head and there are deep gouges in his lips from where he must have bit them. One leg lies at a funny angle, divested of its welly, but other than that . . . well, I can't see anything.

'Don't move, Milo,' I say, not sure if he can hear me. His eyes are closed, the dark lashes looking even darker against the paleness of his cheeks. 'You've had an accident, but Mummy is here.' A sob tears at my throat but I force it down again. I can't let him see how upset I am. I need to be strong for him.

'Oh my God! Oh my God! Is he all right? I've called 999.' A woman's voice comes from behind me. 'I'm so sorry, I didn't even see him. Oh God, I'm so sorry.'

Her voice drones on as we wait for the ambulance, fading into the background. Rain starts to fall in heavy drops from the sky, and I take off my coat to make a makeshift tent for Milo. I can't feel the cold; I can't feel the damp. All I can focus on is my son and the rise and fall of his chest, praying it keeps moving.

Praying he stays alive.

60
EDWARD, SUNDAY, 10.30 A.M.

I pace up and down the concourse, waiting for Fiona's train. Of course it's delayed – I'd be surprised if it wasn't – and I can't help thinking of Zoe in the hotel room. At least I hope she's in the hotel room. I've tried ringing there several times and there's no answer, but I suppose she could be sleeping. After the ordeal she's been through, she deserves a good rest. How strange that the last time I was at this station, I was dreading being alone in the room with her. Now, I can't wait to get back and make sure she's all right. I don't know where we'll go from there, but I just need to see her. To exchange words, without the bitterness or resentment that's clouded the past few years.

First things first, though, I have to talk to Fiona. I'll grab her a coffee and try my best to explain how I messed things up. Fingers crossed she'll understand.

I wince as the pain in my head starts up again, even stronger now as the painkillers wear off. *Only two more minutes,* I think as I glance up at the arrivals board, and then her train will be here. I lean against a post and close my eyes for a second, then scan the stream of passengers swarming off the train.

There she is. Her blonde head bobs up, and I start towards her.

'Hello! You finally made it.' I smile in what I hope is a friends-only way, and she reels me in for a kiss on the cheek.

'Christ, what happened to you?' she asks when she pulls away. I give her full credit for not wrinkling her nose at my alcoholic aftershave.

I shake my head, taking her case. 'I know. Don't ask.'

'Well, don't worry, I'm here now. I'll sort you out.' She throws me a flirtatious grin, and my heart sinks.

'Let's go grab some coffee,' I say, then I lead her through the crowd and over to the nearest café. I buy us two cups and a croissant, then grab the last empty table.

As we settle into our chairs, Fiona reaches out to touch the wound on my head, then pulls me in for a hug. 'So what *did* happen?' she asks, moving back. 'Are you okay?'

I close my eyes for a second, the events of the past day running through my head. Where to start? I sigh and force my lids open, and that's when I see her.

'Zoe!' The word burst from me, and Fiona turns to follow my stare.

'Zoe? Did you see Zoe?' she asks, brow furrowed. There's nothing there but a sea of faces.

I shake my head, unsure for a second if I really did see her or if that knock on the head is causing hallucinations. But no, I'm certain it was her, although what she's doing at the station is a mystery. I spin frantically in all directions, trying to catch sight of her again, but the sea of travellers has swallowed her up.

Shit. I gulp air, trying to keep a grip on the emotions prickling my insides. If she saw me and Fiona together, what the hell must she be thinking right now? I can only imagine.

'I've got to get back to the hotel,' I say to Fiona, my voice tight with urgency, 'and see if that's where she's gone.' If I wanted to see Zoe before, now every bit of me is vibrating with desperation. I can't let her think I'm having an affair – although I came close to it, I know now that's not what I want. And I don't want her to think I didn't give a fuck about her being missing, and invited another woman out here to take her place. No one could take her place, even if things have changed, even if things can never be the same again. No one can, and right now, I don't even want to try.

Fiona's staring up at me, her face creased in confusion. 'What is Zoe doing here?'

I sigh and put a hand on her arm. Christ, what a mess. What an absolute *arse* I am. 'It's a long story. Look, I'm really sorry. I'll fill you in on everything, I promise. But right now, I need to find Zoe.'

'Do you want me to come with you?' Her voice is tight, and I can tell by the tense set of her shoulders she's not exactly happy with this turn of events. Not that I can blame her.

'No!' The word comes out a bit too forcefully, and I clear my throat. 'I mean, no, thanks. Look, Fiona . . .'

She puts a hand on my arm. 'It's all right, Edward. Well, sort of.' She stands, then grabs the handle of her case. 'I won't pretend I'm not disappointed. This weekend could have been a lot of fun. *We* could be a lot of fun. I always have a good time when I'm with you. But if that's not what you're looking for . . .' She shrugs. 'You're a great bloke, but it's obvious you and your wife still have some issues to sort out. I don't fancy getting caught in the middle of all that.'

Relief courses through me, and I let out my breath. 'Are you going to be okay? Do you want me to get you a ticket for the next train back?'

She lifts an eyebrow. 'After everything I've gone through to get here? I'm not going to turn around and head home now! Nope, I'm going to see Paris.' She waves a hand in the air. 'Don't worry about me. I'll hop on one of those naff city tour buses and I'll be fine.'

I nod, then kiss her quickly on the cheek. 'All right. I'm sorry, Fiona.' I am, too. She's a wonderful woman, but I realise now she's not what I've been looking for.

'It's okay, Edward,' she responds, swinging the case around in front of her as if she's ready to take off. 'Now, go.' She gives me a gentle shove. 'Go find your wife.'

61
ZOE, SUNDAY, 10.45 A.M.

I follow the tide of people down an endless escalator and through a smelly corridor, and then I bump up against a ticket barrier. This must be the metro; I'm in such a daze I didn't even see the signs. A man crashes into my back as I stop, and I step aside, watching person after person feed their ticket into the slot and the doors slide open and shut, open and shut.

'Madame?' I blink as a woman with kind eyes and a huge camera looped around her neck holds a ticket out towards me. 'I'm finished with this ticket and it has some extra journeys on it. Would you like it?' I struggle to make out the words with her heavy German accent, but I nod my thanks, take the ticket and slide it into the slot. The doors open with a clang and I push through them, trailing along another corridor until I come to a packed platform.

I stand in a trance as the trains whoosh by, feeling the grimy air smack my face just like those countless times in the days after Milo's death – like I still do, actually. But nothing, no matter how long I stand here and wish for an alternate reality, will change what happened.

There was a moment in the ambulance, right after the paramedics gently gathered up my boy and secured him to a rigid board, when it looked like he would pull through. One broken leg, the paramedics said, and a knock on the head, but all his vital signs seemed stable.

A lucky escape, I imagined Edward and I saying later, when Milo was tucked up home safely in bed, leg encased in plaster. I pictured one hand cradling my stomach and the baby nestling inside, the other entwined with my son's fingers. A reminder of how much we have, of how much we need to cherish. A reminder that we can't control life, but we can embrace all that we do have.

And then Milo crashed. By the time he got to the hospital, his heart had stopped beating. A massive internal bleed, the consultant said, after they'd tried and tried to resuscitate him. I stood beside my son, holding his hand, unable to let go . . . even when they said they needed to transfer him to the morgue. My phone rang and rang, and I knew I should answer, that Edward needed to know, but I couldn't. I was frozen, locked together with my son, unable to break the grip because I knew that once I did, he really would be gone.

The hot wind and clatter of another train passing by brings me back to where I am, and I shake my head. *Embrace all that we have.*

All I have right now is . . . nothing.

62
ZOE, SEPTEMBER 2013

It's almost three months since Milo's accident. Three months, and yet it feels like it was yesterday and also years ago. The only thing keeping me tethered to time, to the passing of minutes and days, is the baby inside me – the baby Edward still doesn't know about.

I know it's crazy that I haven't told him. I know I need to. It would give him hope, it would lift him up, even though he seems to be doing okay. He's functioning, and that's more than you can say about me. He gets up in the morning, he puts on his clothes . . . he even went back to work last week. I stay in bed for hours until hunger and the need to pee get the better of me. I wolf down whatever casserole or endless dish of lasagne is still piled up in the freezer, then crawl back into bed and sink into sleep. Sleep is my saviour right now, blotting out the world and everything in it. Everything except the life growing inside of me, cushioned inside my limp body.

This baby is my secret, the only part of me that's truly alive. I suppose that's why I want to keep her to myself – because for some reason, I know it's a girl. Once I tell Edward, the baby is out in the world, part of the fabric of our family. I can't bear that the fabric of our family no longer includes Milo. I don't want to give Edward another reason to move us on, either, away from the memory of the one we lost. He seems determined enough to do that already.

I wince at the thought of Milo's empty room, of my husband's blank face as he packed our son's belongings – moving back and forth, back and forth, robotically filling each box as if the objects meant nothing. I try to imagine placing those boxes on a shelf, then resuming daily life, daily *routine*, as if nothing has happened . . . like my husband has. God, just yesterday he asked what we needed at the supermarket. How the hell do I know? How the hell can I *care*? I can barely remember to breathe, let alone focus on loo-roll supplies.

A sharp pain goes through me and I roll onto my side in the bed, letting out a groan. The house is thankfully silent – Edward's at work, and my parents have given themselves the morning off from watching over me for once. I draw my knees up as the pain continues, gripping my abdomen and twisting it like someone wringing out a washcloth.

Ah, shit, that hurts!

I swing my legs over the side of the bed and pad down the hallway to the toilet for some paracetamol, and that's when I feel it: wetness between my legs, liquid trickling down the inside of my thigh. In a panic, I tear down my knickers, catching my breath at the blood staining the lining. I sink down on the toilet, feeling the *drip drip drip* of more blood leaving my womb, as my baby drains away and the very last piece of life inside of me dies.

63
EDWARD, SUNDAY, 11 A.M.

After leaving Fiona, I take yet another cab back to the hotel, my mind toying with thoughts of why Zoe was at the train station. Did she use the money I left to buy another ticket? Does that mean she's on a train home right now? God, I hope not. I can't bear to think I've hurt her like that . . . if she even cares any more. I suppose I can understand why she might not, given how cold I've been. I pop another painkiller, realising how selfish it was to try to force her back to me, force her to move on. You can't 'move on' from your son's death. I know. I've certainly tried.

I think back through the years and all the ways I've chivvied her forward. Marriage, the house, the second baby . . . I was the one to push all those things. Perhaps it hasn't just been her running the course of this relationship, like I'd believed. I may have resented her holding us hostage over the last couple of years, but we were in this thing together. *Are* in this thing together.

Finally, here I am, back at the hotel yet again. She has to be here; this must be the end of the road. After all that has happened, I need to tell her I understand. And that I love her, because I do. Buried underneath all that hurt and resentment – and under my own grief that I never really let myself feel – is a well of emotion for her, and for us.

'Oh, monsieur!' The receptionist's head snaps up as I enter, and my heart leaps. I'm sure she's going to say Zoe is waiting in the room. 'I am so very sorry, but it is now checkout time. Please pack your things and exit your room as quickly as possible, as we have other guests arriving.'

Shit. I manage to nod my head. 'Okay.' How the hell am I going to track down my wife if I'm booted from the one place she knows where to find me? I gather my things inside the minuscule space, noticing the note is just where I left it and the money beside it is untouched. Zoe obviously hasn't returned since this morning – the only thing I can think of is she's camped out at the station, waiting for our train. There's no reason for her to come back here, is there? Especially if she thinks I'm with another woman.

God.

I sink down on the bed and lower my aching head into my hands. Then I take the suitcase, head into the lift once more and give the receptionist the key. A few hours remain until the train home and right now, I need some fresh air before I pass out from either the lack of sleep or the pain.

I push open the doors and stand on the pavement once again, so very, very tired of moving. A strong urge for a bit of calm, of peace, of relaxation comes over me, and I know where I need to go.

It's not a long walk to the Seine, but each step feels like I'm trudging through sludge. Every bone in my body aches to sit down, to lie down, and close my eyes for just one second. The pounding in my head has subsided to a dull throb and my wound stings, but if I can make it to the river – to stare down into the water, like I used to so many times before – maybe the mess of my life will be bearable. Because no matter how I've tried in the past few years to make my world something I can cope with, I know now that what

I created was just on the surface, an alternate reality that dissolved in front of me.

I cross the bridge to a small island, then go down some stairs to a pathway by the river. I walk for a bit, breathing in the scent of trees and damp river water, a sense of calm slowly stealing over me. When my legs can't take me a step further, I sink onto a bench, close my eyes, and let the sound of water lapping concrete lull me to sleep.

64
ZOE, SUNDAY, 11.30 A.M.

I don't know how long I've been standing here as trains screech into the station, but I don't care. Even though I'm in a foreign city, years from when I lost the baby, this feels exactly like that day: the absolute emptiness, the despair, the finality. After the doctor told me what I already knew – then scraped whatever remained from inside me – I stood in the station for hours, thinking how I could get on one of those trains and disappear. Edward would adjust, like he already did after Milo, and he'd never know I lost another child too.

No, not lost – *killed.* Because that's what it is. I couldn't keep Milo safe, and I couldn't keep the baby safe, either, even though I tried to cocoon her from everything, from anything that harmed her. Of course the doctor said it was just one of those things, that miscarriages are common, and that there was nothing I could have done – a brutal echo of people's words after Milo's accident.

The death of that baby was the final nail in the coffin of my motherhood, and so when Edward started up again about having another child, I couldn't even listen to the words. I had to turn away, before he could see how they scalded me. Another baby my womb would discard? Another life to have taken away? No, not a chance. This baby was a gift, and I'd rejected it.

Perhaps if I told him about the miscarriage, he'd have understood. But I couldn't bear to face any more blame, to see it on his face even if he'd never say the words. Those accusations he'd flung at me after Milo had branded my heart, making it bloody and raw. There was no way I could open it up again.

And so I stood there, that bleak day, watching train after train, unable to move forward or step back. The sky darkened, the trains came less often, and the passengers became less numerous.

'Last train to London!' the stationmaster called, and the train glided into the station. My legs carried me forward and I sank into the plush seat, my womb still contracting. At Waterloo, I got off and walked across the concourse, then sat on a bench outside until morning – a bench away from the river, a bench on the street. I didn't call Edward; I didn't call anyone. I just sat there, numb, until some part of me urged me home. And ever since, every day, I follow that same route: home to Waterloo, Waterloo to home. Insert pub in the middle.

Someone jolts my arm, and I blink, momentarily surprised at the French babbling around my ears. *Home*. What is that? Why bother now, anyway? Milo's gone, Edward will go soon, but it's not the house I'm really thinking of. It's the people in my life who made me safe, who made me happy – what could have made me happy. That's what home is, but it's all over now, isn't it?

I think of the ring in my pocket and of Edward's promise of forever. I picture him leaning in to kiss Fiona, and resignation sweeps over me. I've lost him, lost *us*. I dig out the wedding band. Its solid band rests heavy on the palm of my hand, glinting in the harsh florescent light of the platform. I feel the vibrations of a train nearing, the hot air stirring as it approaches. I make my way to the edge of the platform and step forward.

'*Attention*!' A woman grabs my arm and levers me back from the edge as the train screams into the station.

'I'm okay, I'm all right.' I shake off her grip, forcing a smile. 'I was just going to throw this onto the track, that's all.' I open my palm to show her Edward's ring, and my hand is shaking. I *was* just going to throw the band on the track . . . right? I don't know. I don't know. I cover my eyes. The lights and the noise are all too much, as if they've been amped up.

The train doors slide open, and the woman helps me into a carriage, gently pushing me into a seat. 'You sit here for a second,' she commands, sitting down beside me.

'I'm fine,' I insist, although my voice sounds scratchy. My heart is racing, and my mouth is dry. I'm anything but fine.

'Where are you going?' she asks, her eyes holding mine as if she knows I've not a clue in the world where I'm headed.

I shake my head, not trusting myself to give a response that would halfway make sense. The metro rattles into a station, and together we watch the doors open and close as passengers get off and more get on. *The rhythm of life,* I think absently. One minute the people you love are there, they next they're gone. And the train relentlessly keeps moving.

'Life can be shit,' the woman says, and I raise my eyebrows in surprise. The harsh language seems at odds with her elegant appearance. 'But that's how it goes.' She shrugs, and then says something a thousand friends said, but never really sank in. 'You need to be good to yourself.' She pats my arm, then gets to her feet. 'This is my stop.'

'Thank you,' I say in a low voice as she nods and pushes out through the doors, then disappears amid the crowds of people.

The train rattles off, and I lean back in my seat. *Life can be shit* – that's putting it mildly. I shift, catching my reflection in the window. Life can be shit, but I'm still here, despite it all. I'm still alive after everything that's happened, after two years of pain that have lost me my husband.

Am I going to lose myself, too? I can't bear to think of what was happening back on that platform. What I almost did . . . or not.

Be good to yourself. The words echo in my ears, and I remember person after person uttering that phrase for months after Milo, so often I could predict the end of any conversation. They made me cringe; made my insides knot with guilt. How could I be good to myself when I'd done the worst thing a parent could: failed to protect their child – or, in my case, children?

Be good to yourself. As if.

The train pulls into another station, and the doors open. Before I know what I'm doing, my legs carry me onto the platform, where I follow the people up into the streaming sun.

I blink as my eyes meet the spires of Notre Dame Cathedral, then spin to take in a very familiar-looking façade: Hotel Dieu. Somehow, I've made it back to the same place I was this morning. I shake my head. How many times did I retrace my route over the past day, believing I'd finally intersected with Edward, only to see him with someone else?

I make my way to the river, gingerly stepping down old stone stairs to the edge. Couples mooch by, hand in hand, and I sink onto a bench, watching the sun glint off the water. I think of Edward's ring in my pocket and pull it out again, placing it on the bench beside me while I jimmy off my band, too. It slides from my finger easily, without resistance.

I flex my finger, thinking how strange it looks, how naked. It feels strange, too – like I'm uncovering a place that's been hidden away for years, a foreign patch of skin that hasn't seen the sun. *Who was I before Edward,* I ask myself? Even though we've barely spoken these past couple of years, we've still been bound together by everything that happened. It's hard for me to think back to the woman I was before we met.

But I don't think that matters. What matters now is finding a new way forward, a way to live despite the past. A way to let me be *me* again, whatever that means – and being good to myself, despite the guilt and mistakes of the past.

Why weren't you watching him? Why didn't you stop him? How could you let this happen?

I shake my head as the words ring in my ears. I'll always blame myself for what happened with Milo. I could have stopped that accident. As for the baby girl I lost, well . . . I don't know. Maybe it was because of Milo's death, the universe denying me another chance at motherhood. Or maybe it was just one of those things, like the doctor said. But whatever the reason, I need to find a way now not to forget – because who could ever do that? – but to forgive myself *enough* to carry on. To live, even if everything else has been taken away.

I place my wedding ring beside Edward's on the bench, then look at the river. Part of me is tempted to fling them both into the Seine, shoving forever back in the universe's face. But that would be like trying to erase our relationship, and I don't want to do that. We might be finished, but he's always going to be part of the fabric of my life, and trying to tear him out would only do huge damage. I think I've been damaged enough.

I slide the rings into my pocket and get to my feet. A final walk along the river, and then I'll head to the Gare du Nord. If Edward's not there with my ticket, I'll call my parents and ask them to send money. This time tomorrow – hopefully sooner – I'll be back in the UK and starting again. My gut clenches momentarily at the thought of leaving the house with so many memories, but I know the memories are inside me, not in a physical place. I don't want to bury them with guilt or drown them with drink. There's been a lot of good in my life, too, and I want to hang on to that.

I gaze up into the sun, its warmth soaking through my skin and into the heart of me.

65
EDWARD, SUNDAY, 12.45 P.M.

I jerk awake at the sound of two small girls scampering by on identical blue scooters. The sun is high in the sky, and I can tell by the stiffness of my body that I've been passed out here for a while. I raise my hand to check the time, every muscle protesting at even that small movement.

Shit!

I better get a move on if I don't want to be late for the train – and if I want to find Zoe at the station. I pray she's still there. Hopefully the journey home will give me a chance to explain exactly what Fiona was doing here, along with the fact that I never knew Zoe was missing.

I get to my feet, unable to believe I've only been here for a day. It feels more like a century. So much has happened: getting separated from Zoe, calling Fiona, going clubbing and ending up in hospital . . . then Zoe seeing me with Fiona. I don't know where things are with us or where they will be, but at the very least, my wife needs to know I never cheated. I shudder when I think how close I came.

I quicken my pace towards the bridge up ahead, the set of stairs leading up to street level. Just ahead of me is a woman walking quickly, too, her pace matching mine. Something about the way she moves is familiar, jogging a part of my brain. I narrow my eyes against the sun, tracing the outline of her body as my heart begins to beat fast. Could that be Zoe, or am I just imagining things? Her body isn't as familiar to me now as it used to be, her curves eroded away by the past few years, but as I walk even faster, her dark curls and the familiar baggy T-shirt come into focus.

'Zoe!' My voice is husky, and I clear my throat. '*Zoe!*' My call is swallowed up by the hum of a huge tourist boat gliding by, and I break into a run. I'm not letting her get away. Not now, not after everything we've been through.

My head pounds, my stomach churns, and I feel like I'm about to fall over, but finally I catch up with her.

'Zoe.' I touch her arm, and she wheels around, her eyebrows flying up with surprise. Close up, she doesn't look much better than I do. Her hair is flying everywhere, her T-shirt clings to her, and her face is sweaty with a streak of dust across her cheek. But right now, quite honestly, she's never looked better. There's something about her eyes that looks . . . different. Less pinched. More present somehow. A streak of emotion goes through me, so strong it almost powers me to the ground.

I found my wife, a voice inside my head says over the pounding. *I found her again.*

I reach out to take her hand. Then I notice she's not wearing her wedding band, and everything inside me goes cold.

66
ZOE, SUNDAY, 12.45 P.M.

I've been walking by the river for almost an hour now, I guess, and it's time for me to make my way back to the Gare du Nord. Just the thought of the long trek makes my feet throb painfully, but this is the last leg of the long journey I've been on this weekend. One more time, and then it's over. I've done more exercise today than in the past two years combined.

I spot a set of stairs leading up to a bridge and I quickly make my way towards them. I'm eager to traverse the Marais for the last time, to get on that train and head back . . . although I'm not sure the word 'back' is the right one. I'm going forward, finally, with the past inside me.

A touch on my arm makes me whirl around, and my mouth drops open. There, right in front of me, is Edward. I blink to make sure I'm not imagining things – I have been out in the sun all weekend, I haven't eaten and I've barely slept – but when I open my eyes, he's still there. I do a quick scan to see if Fiona is anywhere in sight. He goes to take my hand, but stops suddenly, letting his arm swing down by his side.

'What are you doing here?' I ask when I've recovered from the surprise. Christ, he looks absolutely dreadful – and he doesn't smell so great either. His shirt – one I don't recognise – is stained, and his eyes are bloodshot. My eyes widen as I notice the stitches on his forehead. 'Are you all right?'

He nods, grimacing at the movement of his head. 'I'm fine. It's a very long story. Well, not that long, actually. I went out to a club, I got drunk, I hit my head.'

Edward? *Clubbing*? I try to keep my face neutral, reminding myself that I really don't know this new Edward at all.

'Look, about Fiona . . .' He tries to take my hand again, but I move it firmly behind me.

'You don't need to tell me anything,' I say, stepping back in case he tries to touch me again. I don't think I could take it. 'I understand.'

'You do?' His eyebrows shoot up.

'Well, sort of.' I force a shrug. 'I mean, we're not together, are we? We haven't been for ages. I know you tried to get through to me after Milo's death, but I . . . I didn't *want* someone to get through to me.'

There's a silence, and we both stare out at the river. 'I don't think my way of coping was much better,' Edward says finally. 'I wanted to make a new start and forget everything. But I realised you can't forget everything; it just keeps coming back. It might have taken a knock on the head, but I finally got it.'

A half-laugh burbles out, and I reach up to touch his stitches. He sucks in his breath and I jerk back, realising what I'm doing.

'Sorry.' I glance down at the ground, thinking how weird this all is. I feel like we're really talking, finally, but it's too late.

'So what now?' Edward holds my gaze, his eyes boring into mine. I stare back, feeling that familiar connection spark between us for the first time in years.

I shrug. 'We head back to Cherishton. We put the house on the market, and we go our separate ways. I think that's the easiest thing.' It won't be easy at all, but I don't want him to see that. He's moved on to other women, and even if our relationship can barely be qualified as one, I can't say that doesn't hurt.

'The easiest?' Edward takes my hand, and this time, I let him. I don't have the energy to pull away. 'Since when have we ever done things the easy way?' He shakes his head. 'Nothing happened with me and Fiona. I thought you'd taken off, and I was angry. I'm not saying it was the right thing to do, but I called Fiona to come. Her train was delayed, so I went out and partied . . . and got so drunk, I fell into a wall.'

I can't help a small guffaw escaping, and Edward shakes his head. 'I know, I know. Pathetic, right? That's when I realised I was just running, trying to escape from everything.' He squeezes my hand. 'I don't want Fiona, or anyone else in my life, for that matter. I want *you*.' He takes a breath. 'Can we . . . maybe . . . try to be together again? I don't think we've done that since Milo.'

I look down at our hands, entwined together without our wedding bands, and I think how marriage doesn't have the power to bind – only the actions of two people can do that. 'Forever' and happy endings aren't a given, and life can be shit, just like the woman on the train said. But perhaps you do need to have faith, too. Faith in yourself, and faith in your relationship.

I take a deep breath.

'I have something I need to tell you,' I say. I don't know how he'll react that I've kept the pregnancy hidden from him for so long, but I know I need to tell him – for me, if not for us. I've enough guilt and blame inside of me, and right now I feel like he can help me carry it. I trust him to help me carry it.

'Okay.' He motions me over to a bench and we sink down, side by side, my mind flitting back to how we used to sit by the river for ages, back in London. Edward turns to face me and takes my hand. 'What is it?'

I meet his eyes, scanning the face I know so well. Without his beard, he looks naked somehow, and vulnerable. I fill my lungs, and push out the words.

'I found out I was pregnant the day before Milo died.' Even as I speak, a cloud inside of me releases a tempest of grief. I can't even look at Edward as I carry on. 'I lost the baby,' I say in a whisper. 'I lost her three months after Milo's accident.'

My words hang heavy in the air between us. I glue my eyes to his again, wondering what's going through his head. His face is frozen and he shifts his stare to look out at the river – away from me. He lets my fingers go and they slide limply from his grasp.

'Edward?' I say, when the silence has stretched too long and I can't take it any more.

He turns towards me, and I flinch at the shock mixed with hurt in his eyes – a look that says I betrayed him. Again.

'Three *months*? Three months you knew, and you didn't tell me?' His voice shakes, and my heart starts banging in my chest. 'How could you not tell me something like that?'

'I'm sorry,' I say, my mouth going dry. 'I should have, I know, but after Milo was gone, I couldn't cope. Couldn't *talk*. I was afraid – just so afraid. And then when I lost the baby, well . . . it was too much. Too much to even think of getting out the words.'

Edward jerks like I've slapped him in the face. '*Too much*? Too much to tell your husband you were pregnant? Too much to let me know you had a miscarriage?' His leg starts jiggling. 'I wanted to be there for you. I *tried* to be there for you – all those years we were together. But once again, it's about what you want, isn't it? What you can deal with. Never mind what it might mean to me. Never mind that not getting you pregnant was eating me up inside – *has* been eating me up inside. Never mind that just knowing I could would ease the pain a fraction.

'I guess I shouldn't be surprised,' Edward continues in a cold voice. 'You weren't even going to tell me you were pregnant the first time, either, were you?'

I struggle to breathe as his words hit me like bullets, trying to grasp the words clawing at my throat. But they slide away and more pop up faster than I can grip onto them, and all I can do is sit in silence.

'Let's go.' Edward stands, towering over me. 'The sooner we get back, the sooner we can put an end to all this.' He strides off towards the stairs and I've no choice but to follow. Bitterness and resentment cloud the air behind him, and I turn my head to gulp in oxygen. I should have told him, yes. I knew it was hard for him, that he took my not getting pregnant as a personal failure. Perhaps I didn't know how much, but still.

I trusted him. I took a leap of faith. I fell on cold, hard ice, and everything inside me rattled and jarred.

But I haven't cracked.

67
EDWARD, SUNDAY, 1 P.M.

As I cross the bridge, fury propels me forward. I'm not even tired any more – at least, I can't feel it. All I can feel is a blind, burning rage. How could Zoe not tell me she was pregnant? How, for three hideous months after Milo's death, could she keep that to herself? Sure, we were in a daze, barely managing to hold it together. I couldn't slow down to sit for a second, let alone talk to anyone. But news of another baby – of a glimmer of hope, in the darkest time of my life – would have helped, would have given me something to briefly hang onto, even if it came to an end.

And it's not just that. This whole time, these whole two years, I've been beating myself up for not being able to give us another child before Milo died, for my body failing us. Nothing would make Milo's death easier, of course. But knowing my body didn't cop out – that I *did* give us a chance at life – might have kept my heart from hardening. Because that's exactly how I feel right now: hardened. I picture Zoe going through a miscarriage alone, and my only emotion is anger. Anger that she didn't let me in; anger that she went through that alone, rather than leaning on her husband. Does she hate me that much?

So much for her promise never to lie. This is the worst kind of lie possible – again.

I spin to where she's trotting behind me, words forming then dying on my lips. There's so much more I want to say, but I don't have the energy to begin a conversation. There's no point, anyway. I must have been mad to think we could start over.

I flag down a taxi and wave Zoe in, then ask it to take us to the Gare du Nord. Everything feels like a strange déjà vu, except I know this won't be happening again. We've come full circle, right back to the place where we started the weekend, and I can't keep on cycling any more. Once we get home, I'm finished. We're finished.

Forever, happy endings . . .

Fuck that.

68
ZOE, ONE WEEK LATER

'Are you certain you want to do this? I'm sure your parents would be happy for you to stay with them as long as you need to.' Kate wipes a hand across her brow as she helps me pack the last box of clothes.

I nod, thinking how good it is to have her back in my life. I rang her up as soon as we returned from Paris, and even though she was surprised to hear from me and has a million things of her own going on, she was only too happy to help – the sign of a true friend. 'I'm sure. And yes, they did say I could bunk in with them. And Edward said I could stay here as long as I needed to.' I tape the box closed and sit back on my heels. 'But honestly, I need my own space, you know? Where I can try to build a life again.' I sigh, gazing around the room as memories hit me at every turn. 'It'll be hard to leave this house, but I have to.' I've rented a studio flat back in North London. It's tiny, but I can't wait to make it home. This place hasn't been home for years.

Kate nods and reaches out to touch my arm. 'I get it.' She shakes her head. 'But I still can't believe that after everything you both have gone through together, this is the end.'

'It's *because* of everything we've gone through,' I say. 'It's just too much for one relationship – well, for *our* relationship, anyway – to carry.' Edward's face when I told him of the pregnancy flashes into my mind, and I shudder. The anger and coldness reminds me of when he first saw Milo after the accident, as if I'd devastated him twice. The whole way home, in the taxi, then the train, then another train, we didn't exchange a word. He didn't even look at me, but this time was different. This time, there was no cold indifference. This time, I could feel the fury coming off of him in waves.

I was angry too. Angry that my faith in us had been misplaced. Angry that after that weekend, the weekend where I thought we might actually have a chance of making it again, we were broken – a clean snap, the pieces separated. But this time was different for me too. This time, I wasn't going to retreat into grief and sadness. This time, I was going to make a life. It wouldn't be how I thought my life would turn out, but I think I can still be happy, if I let myself.

'Where is Edward now?' Kate asks, helping me carry the box downstairs and placing it next to the other boxes by the front door. For someone who has lived here for almost four years, the pile is surprisingly small. There's not much I need to take, besides my meagre wardrobe. Everything else I'll leave for Edward to use until he sells the house. And, of course, Milo's room has been empty ever since Edward packed it up all those months ago.

'At work, I guess.' I shrug, wondering if he's with Fiona. A pang of hurt hits, but I push it away. We're not together any more, even in pretence, and he can do what he likes. I gaze down at my bare ring finger, wondering what I should do with my wedding band. I put Edward's in the top drawer of his bedside table, and . . . I swallow hard against the rising sadness. Perhaps I can take mine to a pawnbroker. I could certainly use the cash until I get my freelance business back up and running.

'Okay, I guess that's everything,' I say a few minutes later, when all the boxes are loaded in the car. 'I'll be out in a sec. Just want to take a quick look and make sure I've got everything.'

Kate nods and pats me on the back, and then she's gone. I stand in the doorway, gazing at the kitchen. Milo's laughter floats through my mind, and I picture the toys scattered around the floor; the thud of the door as Edward comes home and scoops up his son, then turns to me with a huge grin as we have a group hug. Then I blink, and all I can see is an empty space, the only sound the steady dripping of the tap.

'Goodbye,' I say, closing the door softly behind me. I don't know who I'm talking to – my vanished family, my son, my husband, or the mother who lived here – but I know that somehow, I'll be okay.

69
ZOE, TWO MONTHS LATER

Houses whizz by me, chimney after chimney blurring into one. I'm on the train back to Cherishton, back to the tiny, moss-covered graveyard where Milo is buried. Two years ago today, I lost my son. I lost *me*, in the haze of grief and blame. I'll never get Milo back, but accepting that he's gone has let me start to find my way to who I am. And after all this time, I can finally visit Milo, too. I haven't been able to do that until now.

I stare down at my hands clutching the bag with Milo's jumper. It's royal blue, with a huge pirate on the front. It took me ages to knit – I spent a good two hours every night – and it's full of holes and funky stitches, but I don't care. With every row, I felt like somehow, I was connected to Milo. He'd be four now, probably skinny, all elbows and knees like his father was. I hope he'd like pirates; Kate's kids are all mad about them. Strange how I used to think I'd fall apart if I thought of my son. It hurts like hell, but it's also comforting, like I'm keeping him with us. With me.

The train pulls into Cherishton and I get off. I walk through the station and the turnstiles, then hurry down the track to the church off the green. It's a beautiful June day, and the trees are bursting with fragrant blossoms and green. The church gate opens with a clang, and I make my way up the cobbled path. I haven't been here since Milo's burial. That day is a blur, but somehow my subconscious seems to know exactly where my son is.

I pick my way between several tombstones, and there he is.

Milo Morgan, 2011 – 2013. Beloved son of Zoe and Edward. The beginning of our own happy ending. Rest in peace.

I jerk back. *The beginning of our own happy ending?* I don't remember reading that before, but then, I could barely see straight at the funeral, let alone focus on the tombstone, and Edward took care of all those details. It's an echo of our rings, a nod to the fact that Milo brought us together, that he did set us on the path to our happy ending. We never got there, but he was part of us from the very start, even if there's no 'us' any more.

I reach into the bag and touch the jumper, then change my mind. Milo's not here in this damp earth. He's inside me, in my mind, and I can't bear to think otherwise. But there *is* something I want to leave. I slide my hand into my pocket and take out my wedding band. For the last time, I run my finger over the inscription, then place it on top of the stone. I don't know why, but it just feels right, as if it belongs here, along with all the other hopes and dreams I laid to rest. This ring is part of another life, a life that ended with my son.

I place a hand on the grave, whisper that I love him and that I'm sorry, then turn to go.

70
EDWARD, TWO MONTHS LATER

I've got to get out of this house. I cram jeans and T-shirts into my suitcase, barely even noticing what I'm packing. It's not like I'll see anybody I know in Majorca, where I've booked a week's getaway. The holiday will do me good, I think – give me a break from knocking around the place on my own. I don't know how Zoe could stand being here alone. I guess she couldn't. I still don't know where she went every day, I realise.

It doesn't matter now. What matters is getting the hell away from this building, where the emptiness is a constant reminder of what is gone. Even work, where I used to bury myself, has lost its hypnotic power. And Fiona, well . . . we don't talk. I don't have the energy; don't have the drive. All the anger I felt after Paris has burned out, leaving hollowness in its wake.

Now where the fuck is my passport? I pull open the drawer in my bedside table and root around inside, squinting as a flash of gold meets my eyes. What's that? I move aside some envelopes, and there it is: my wedding ring.

My mouth falls open as I pick it up, looking inside the band, tracing the script inside. *Our own happy ending.* My fingers close around it, and I sink onto the bed as my mind whirls. I lost this ring in Paris, I know I did. I can picture perfectly the moment I took it off, lying there as the man shaved away my beard. And I remember the moment I discovered it was gone. How has it ended up here?

My eyes close, and images fill my head. Zoe smiling as she slides the ring on my finger. Her eyes lighting up as she reads the identical inscription inside the next day – our first day as husband and wife. We may not have our own happy ending, but we did have a lot of great times, and I'll never forget those. Part of me will always love her, I guess, and nothing life throws at me will take that away. Not even her withholding a pregnancy, a pregnancy we were both desperate to have.

I sigh, thinking of that day in Paris. It's true I could have responded better, but my anger wiped everything out. In the weeks that followed, I wanted to sit down with Zoe and talk – to hear what happened, what the doctor said, and more about why she didn't tell me. But I couldn't. I just couldn't talk. My insides were locked up tightly, a corked bottle stopping anything from escaping. I guess that's what it was like for Zoe, too, once Milo died.

Funny how I understand that now.

I open my hand and stare at the ring on my palm, then slide it into my pocket. I'll decide what to do with it later. Now, before I take off to the airport, there's somewhere else I need to be. Two years ago today, Milo died, and I want to visit his grave. I tried to get Zoe to come with me last year, but I'm not even sure she heard my requests.

I cross the kitchen, my footsteps echoing in the silence, then open the door. Outside, it's a beautiful day, and the sound of birdsong meets my ears as I make my way down the narrow road, pausing where I think the accident happened. I've asked Zoe so many times to show me – I just need to know – but all she could do was shake her head and turn away from me.

I take a deep breath as I remember the night of the accident. Once Zoe finally passed out on the bed, I pulled on my jacket and boots, then walked down this road at a snail's pace, trying to find something, anything, that would give me a clue what happened – or rather, *why*. I never found any answers, but I did uncover something else. By the side of the road, Milo's orange welly lay wedged between the branches of a bush. I fished it out, ignoring the scratches on my arms, thinking Milo would need this tomorrow; it was supposed to rain . . . and then my legs gave way as reality sunk in.

I don't know how long I sat there, by the side of the road, that night. But I do remember getting up, carrying Milo's boot in my hand, then placing it with the other one in the bag of his personal effects they'd given us at the hospital. Staring at those small, glossy wellies, encased in crinkly plastic now, made me double over as every bit of air was squeezed from my body, replaced by something I can only feebly describe as *pain*. It was too much to bear, and I forced myself to straighten up and move. I made it through the rest of that night by making a start on funeral details, busying my mind with logistics and concrete items, as a way to keep the horror at bay.

And that's what I'd been doing ever since, until Paris. Until even now, I guess, remembering my reaction to Zoe's news and how I tried to stave off anger and grief by concentrating on selling the house and throwing myself into work – and escaping to another country.

I'm tired of running, I think, stopping in front of the gate to the churchyard. I'm so, so tired, and it's not working any more. Maybe it's time to finally stand still, to face what my life has become head-on. Once this trip is over and I have a chance to relax, I'll think about how to do just that.

The church gate squeals as I push it open, and I make my way to my son's grave. I reach out to stroke the top of Milo's tombstone, and my fingers touch a slender band. It's Zoe's wedding ring. I don't even need to look inside to see the inscription to know. Finally, after all this time, she's made it here. My eyes go from the script on the tombstone to the ring in my hand, and I understand instantly why she left it. What we had – our family, and the happy ending – is gone.

A great sadness comes over me and I sink to the ground, not even caring that the sodden wetness is seeping into my trousers. I can't bear to leave her ring here, along with my son, so I slide it into my pocket with my own.

I stay at the grave a few minutes longer, then head back to the house, grab my suitcase, and retrace my steps to the train station. A few minutes later, a train pulls into the station and I get on.

71
ZOE

As the train heads back towards Waterloo, a strange emotion steals over me . . . something like peace; something I haven't felt in years. Accepting Milo's death and how it happened feels like someone has brought my son back to me, as if I now have permission to remember him and his life. And permission to live my own, too.

I stand as the train nears its destination, threading through the busy corridor towards the doors.

'Ouf!' The train jolts and I crash into a solid form, my breath knocked from me. My eyebrows rise in surprise when I spot who it is. What on earth is he doing here?

'Sorry,' Edward says, reaching out to steady me.

'That's all right.' I straighten up and try to catch my breath. I start to move away, but Edward takes my elbow.

'Wait,' he says, then runs a hand through his hair. His eyes are red and his clothes hang off him, like he's lost weight. 'Look . . . I'm sorry for how I reacted when you told me about the pregnancy. Losing the baby, well, I can't even begin to imagine how awful it was to go through that by yourself. You took me by surprise, that's all – not that it's an excuse.' He shakes his head. 'You knew how much I wanted another baby, and I couldn't believe you didn't tell me. Not only because I needed to know I *could* get you pregnant again, but because I was desperate to be there for you too.'

I meet his eyes. 'I should have said something, and I'm sorry I didn't. I just . . . couldn't. I wanted to keep her safe, away from everything, away from the world. I wanted to keep her locked inside.'

Edward nods slowly, and I can see from the expression in his face that something I've said rings true for him. 'How are you doing, anyway?'

'I'm . . . I'm okay.' I've said that countless times, but now, I think I actually mean it. 'Business is picking up after a slow start. I like my new place, and I'm even knitting again.' I hold up the jumper. 'I made this for Milo. I know it's silly, but I'm going to make him one every year.'

Edward picks it up, a smile on his face. 'It's not silly at all. I think it's great that you're doing that. And knitting again, too. But no fluorescent socks?' That cheeky grin I remember flashes across his face, and I can't help smiling back.

'Maybe next year.' We stare at each other for a minute as memories tumble through my mind: that first night on the South Bank, losing each other, meeting up again and him wearing those hideous socks . . . and then everything after that. Sadness and pain stir inside, and I take a deep breath as the door hisses open. 'Oh, we're here. Well, it was nice seeing you.' My gut contracts as the words leave my mouth. *Nice* seeing *you?* It's like I'm saying goodbye to a stranger, not the man I've been with for years.

We are strangers, I remind myself, even though looking at him now, he resembles the man I knew: baggy clothes, shaggy hair, terrible beard. I have to stop myself from reaching out to tidy it.

I clamber onto the platform, forcing step after step, faster and faster, away from him. If I stop now, I know I won't be able to start walking again. I've just reached the main concourse when I feel someone touch my shoulder.

'Zoe, wait a second!' Edward sounds breathless and I spin around to face him. 'What are you doing right now?'

'Right now?' I repeat, wondering where he's going with this. 'I'm going back to my flat. Why?'

'Do you want to go for a drink?' He runs a hand through his hair in a gesture I remember so well. 'Okay, it might be a bit early for a drink. Maybe . . . a walk by the river?'

I meet his eyes, thinking it would be nice to chat. We may not be together any more, but he still has a piece of my heart – he always will, I guess. And it's just a walk, after all. 'Sure. But do you have somewhere you need to be?' I gesture to his suitcase. 'I mean, where were you off to?'

'It doesn't matter,' he says, waving a hand in the air. 'I'd rather be with you.' He smiles and his eyes crinkle up, then he takes my arm and leads me out of the station and onto the terrace of the South Bank. The sunny spring-like day has clouded over; a wind has come up and I shiver. Edward puts his arm around me to keep me warm, and I find myself relaxing into him.

'Want to have a seat?' he asks, pointing to our bench.

I stand for a second, staring down at the familiar wooden slats. This place is our starting point, the beginning of our journey, where we found each other. Now here we are again – but we're not back to where we started. We've been pulled apart and separated by grief, our marriage stretched to the breaking point.

But, as I meet my husband's warm eyes, I'm not sure it *has* broken. It was battered, a tender bruise we pressed on too many times without letting it heal. *We* needed to heal – separately – before we could come together again. Before we could finally find each other.

'Yes,' I say, settling onto the bench and pulling him down beside me. 'Yes, I do.'

ACKNOWLEDGEMENTS

A huge thanks, as always, to India Drummond, Mel Sherratt and Glynis Smy for their continued encouragement and advice over the years. I couldn't ask for three better people to cheer me on! Thank you to everyone at Amazon Publishing, especially Emilie Marneur for her support and enthusiasm for this book. Thanks, also, to my editor, Sophie Wilson, for her thoughtful suggestions and input. And, of course, a big thank you to my wonderful agent, Madeleine Milburn.

Finally, thank you to my husband and son for letting me wander around the house in a daze, figuring out plot lines while burning dinner. I love you both.

ABOUT THE AUTHOR

 Leah Mercer was born in Halifax, Nova Scotia, on the east coast of Canada. By the age of thirteen, she'd finished her first novel and received very encouraging rejections from publishers. Leah put writing on hold to focus on athletics, achieving provincial records and becoming a Canadian university champion in the 4 × 400-metre relay. After getting her BA, she turned to writing again, earning a masters in journalism. A few years later she left Canada and settled in London, where she now lives with her husband and their young son. Leah also writes under the name Talli Roland, and her books have been shortlisted at the UK's Festival of Romance.